Secrets of my
HOLLYWOOD LIFe

SECRETS OF MY HOLLYWOOD LIFE

a novel by

Jen Calonita

LITTLE, BROWN AND COMPANY
New York ❧ Boston ❧ London

Little, Brown and Company

Hachette Book Group USA
237 Park Avenue, New York, NY 10169
Visit our Web site at www.lb-teens.com

First Paperback Edition: May 2007
First published in hardcover in 2006 by Little, Brown and Company

Library of Congress Cataloging-in-Publication Data

Calonita, Jen.
  Secrets of my Hollywood life : a novel / by Jen Calonita. — 1st ed.
     p. cm.
  Summary: Longing to experience the life of a "normal" teenager, sixteen-year-old actress Kaitlin Burke assumes a false identity to attend a local high school.
    ISBN-13: 978-0-316-15442-0 (hardcover)
    ISBN-10: 0-316-15442-3 (hardcover)
    ISBN-13: 978-0-316-154437 (paperback)
    ISBN-10: 0-316-15443-1 (paperback)
  [1. Actors and actresses — Fiction. 2. Identity — Fiction. 3. High schools — Fiction. 4. Schools — Fiction. 5. Hollywood (Los Angeles, Calif.) — Fiction.]
  I. Title.
  PZ7.C1364Sec 2006
  [Fic] — dc22   2005026528

HC: 10 9 8 7 6 5 4 3 2 1
PB: 10 9 8 7 6 5 4 3 2 1

Q-FF

Printed in the United States of America

Book design by Tracy Shaw

The text was set in Golden Cockerel and the display was set in Filosofia and Castine.

To my boys, Mike and Tyler.
—J.C.

Many thanks to my eyes and ears, Cindy Eagan, Phoebe Spainer and Laura Dail, who worship Kaitlin as much as I do. I'd also like to thank Angela Burt-Murray for giving me a gentle push in the right direction, Gloria Wong, my "first" editor, and my mother, Lynn Calonita, and mother-in-law, Gail Smith, who keep Ty happily busy so I can write. Finally, I'd like to thank my grandfather, Nicholas Calonita, who has always wanted to see the family name in lights.

secrets of my
HOLLYWOOD LIFe

Foreword: *Scene One, Take One*

I'm going to let you in on a little HOLLYWOOD SECRET: Movie stars don't always get along. It's true. You can't believe everything you hear during interviews on *Access Hollywood*. When a star is asked about her costar, she'll gush about how the two are best buds who go to the Coffee Bean and Tea Leaf every Saturday morning after Ashtanga yoga for a fat-free vanilla Ice Blended. The truth is they probably haven't seen each other outside work in six months. Celebrities will say anything for good publicity.

How do I know? You've probably already guessed. I'm one of *them*. One of *Teen People*'s "25 Hottest Stars Under 25." Number six on *Entertainment Weekly*'s "It List." And, unfortunately, I'm as guilty as anyone of the secret I just shared. What can I say? My publicist, Laney Peters, says talking honestly about Sky Mackenzie would be bad for my image.

"You're America's newest sweetheart," she explains with a flip of her $300 honey-highlighted hair during one of our notoriously long lunch meetings at The Ivy. "You don't bash people — especially your costars. The Kaitlin Burke the public loves would never do such a thing."

Yeah, well, the real me is having a tough time sticking to that motto. Sky and I have *never* been friends and we've worked together since we were four, when we were cast to play fraternal twins on the nighttime soap *Family Affair*. I should have known we would have a volatile relationship from our first scene together. Seconds before the director yelled "action," Sky clocked me over the head with her pink Barbie Corvette. We delayed filming for a week — while we waited for the large bump on my head to go down.

Just like real life, our characters are polar opposites. Sky plays Sara, the scheming bad seed in our TV family. This season alone Sara has crashed our dad's Hummer, slept with his boss, and been in rehab for her rum and Coke addiction. My character, Samantha, is a bit of a goody two-shoes. In one episode, Sam skipped the winter formal to run a food drive for a local orphanage. Kind of makes you want to gag, doesn't it?

After twelve seasons, I've become a pro at ignoring Sky's comments. ("Nice zit, K," she said the other morning in makeup. "Ever hear of Clearasil?") I've even learned to tune out the tantrums she throws when she thinks I have more lines than her in an episode.

But this time Sky's gone too far. It all started when *TV Tome* voted me the most popular teen in prime time. Sky was so beside herself she trashed her dressing room and refused to work for days, saying she was suffering from "exhaustion." Personally, I think Sky was just mad that she ranked number eight.

It was right after those rumors about me began popping up in the tabloids. I'm not talking silly stuff like, "*Family Affair*'s Kaitlin Burke is an alien!" That I could deal with. These were cruel stories — ones that my mom feels compelled to read (she reads all my press) and show me. The stories said I threw a fit when *FA*'s new hottie, Trevor Wainright, asked Sky out instead of me. They said my parents were control freaks. They said I was thinking of leaving the show. This week, Mom showed me a cover story *Hollywood Nation* ran on my supposed downfall: "Is Kaitlin Burke No Longer TV's Good Girl?" the headline blared. I'm convinced Sky is behind the tabloid frenzy, which is why I marched into her dressing room yesterday to confront her.

"Skylar," I began, because I know she hates being called by her full name, "Did you see the new issue of *TV Tome*?"

"Hey, K," Sky cooed. She was lounging on her reupholstered zebra-print couch, which sits in front of her new leopard-skin rug. Her African safari–themed dressing room is very un-PC. "No, I haven't."

"I have it here." I shoved the worn magazine under her nose. "There's a story about *FA*."

"So?" She snapped the red Kabbalah rubber band she had on, acting all uninterested. "What does it say?"

"'Sky Mackenzie, *Family Affair*'s favorite bad girl, is heartbroken over rumors that her TV sis, played by Kaitlin Burke, might be killed off,'" I read calmly. "'Sources say Kaitlin's lovable character, Sam, may be stricken with a fatal disease, leaving her twin, Sara, an only child. "I don't know what I'll do without Katie around," Sky said sadly when asked about the rumors. "The two of us are really like sisters!"'"

"I was *devastated* when I heard that." Sky didn't look upset to me. Actually she stood up and yawned — keeping one hand on her Lucky jeans so they wouldn't fall off her bony hips — and walked over to her bamboo dressing mirror. "I had to take two Midol and lie down for a while," she added. "But not to worry, K — I asked the writers and they said it's not true."

"Of course it's not true! You made it up!" I was getting visibly upset despite my actor training telling me not to.

"I don't know what you're talking about," Sky replied as she examined her long raven hair and overtanned complexion in the mirror.

"So you don't know where *Celeb Insider* got that crazy story about me reshooting a kissing scene with Trevor to make you jealous either, huh?" I asked. "What did it say again? Oh, that's right. 'Kaitlin Burke made Sky Mackenzie fly off the set in tears.'"

"Someone must *really* not like you around here, K." She squinted her big brown eyes at me. "Come to think of it, I just read another story about you. Online. Something about your mom being a total Hollywood wannabe."

That was the last straw. I wanted to lunge at her. I pictured an insane catfight like Paige and Krystal always get into on our show (you know the type — someone always winds up

4

pushed into a pool wearing an evening gown), but then I remembered Laney's plea. So instead, I turned on my heels and slammed the dressing room door.

"Don't be a stranger, K!" Sky called out in a singsong voice. I CAN'T STAND HER!

I love my job, but between us, times like this make me want to buy a one-way ticket out of Los Angeles. I feel like everyone I know lives and breathes Hollywood 365 days a year. Whatever happened to a little downtime? You know, talking about something *other* than movies, curling up with a good book or going to the beach? Laney and my parents don't know it yet, but I've been thinking about making some serious changes when *Family Affair* wraps for the season. Like finding a remote island and clearing my head for a while. . . .

Who am I kidding? When your face is on TV every Sunday night at 9 PM, how do you disappear without people noticing?

one: *On the 101*

"Kates. Katie? KAITLIN! Get up!" Nadine's muffled voice calls as I lay motionless beneath my heavenly 600-thread-count comforter. "You're supposed to be at the shoot at eight-thirty, and it's already seven AM."

I hear Nadine frantically searching through piles of my unread magazines and clothes, looking for my cell phone. "You know how bad the traffic is on the 101. Get up!"

"Alright, alright," I groan as I throw back my *Star Wars* bed sheets. "It's just that we wrapped *so* late last night."

"At least you didn't have an hour drive home at one AM," she says with a yawn. I watch groggily as Nadine finds my cell lying on top of a still-packed suitcase I took to New York for a press junket last weekend.

I feel bad for Nadine, but the person I really feel sorry for is my makeup artist, Shelly. She's going to have a tough time covering my dark undereye circles for today's *Teen People* shoot.

"Throw these on." Nadine tosses me my favorite pair of worn boot-cut faded denim jeans. "Paul and Shelly are going to do your hair and makeup when you get there, so don't worry about that," she adds sharply. "Just wash your face."

I nod. I'm more concerned with finding my Sidekick, which has everything I need: my overbooked calendar, friends' digits, and e-mail to help me stay in touch even when I'm on location in remote Kauai. I scan the top of my cluttered dresser, then drop down on the cherry-wood floor and look under my custom-designed canopy bed. "Gee, you're in a great mood!" I yell. "Any chance it has something to do with my mom?" I spot my green bejeweled Sidekick peeking out from under my Dodgers cap and grab it. I pull myself out and stand up to face Nadine. Her pale white face turns as red as her pixie-length hair at the mention of Mom's name. She folds her lanky arms across her chest, which bears the words WILL WORK FOR FOOD across her army green Urban Outfitters t-shirt. "Forget I brought it up," I say quickly.

Last night Mom claimed she had a fever and bailed the *FA* set at seven, leaving Nadine to play chaperone. (Since I'm only sixteen, I need a guardian on set with me at all times. Not that I ever really think of Nadine as a guardian. She's only 23 herself.) I have a sneaking suspicion that Mom slipped out so she could go to that John Travolta dinner at the Beverly Hills Hilton, but if I tell Nadine that, she'll blow her top. She already thinks my mom is "vicariously living through her daughter's good fortune." She tells me this whenever we catch Mom flirting with my male costars in one of her PB&J Couture suits.

"Why are you up so early anyway? I thought Mom was taking me today," I ask as I race into my bathroom to brush my teeth with my Han Solo toothbrush.

"Your mom forgot about her tennis lesson," Nadine says wearily. "Rodney picked me up on the way. Thankfully I printed out your itinerary when I got home last night."

I spit out the toothpaste and dash over to my walk-in closet to find something to wear. I'm totally a jeans-and-t-shirt kind of girl when I'm not working, but since today is a business thing, I settle on my vintage tweed blazer and green suede size 9 Pumas. I think they make my feet look smaller. Which is a good thing since my younger brother Matt calls me "Bigfoot."

As I tie my shoes, I watch Nadine whip today's itinerary out of her brown leather binder. Nadine calls it her "bible." She keeps a list of my bra size, favorite designers, food likes (pork fried rice and veggie dumplings from Chow Mein's in Santa Monica) and dislikes (the smell of tuna makes me gag) and DVD must-haves for downtime on the set (*Star Wars* box set? Check. *Legally Blonde?* Check), plus a phone list of casting agents, talk show producers, and studio heads that I might need to call at any given moment. Basically Nadine likes any excuse to use a spreadsheet.

"Okay, so the shoot is supposed to end at two, and then you have that fitting at So Chic at two-thirty for the *Off-Key* premiere," Nadine tells me as she pins her thick red hair back with a Hello Kitty barrette. "On the car ride over you have two phone interviews. One with E! and one with *Weekly Entertainment*."

"Is that all?" I joke. I grab my Sidekick and shove it in my denim messenger bag. Several green jewels pop off the unit and fall to the floor. Next time I should just have my Sidekick bejeweled professionally, instead of attempting to Bedazzle it myself.

Nadine ushers me out the bedroom door and down the spiral staircase, into our family room. "Don't blame me," she mutters. "Your mom is your manager. She's the one who sets your schedule." Nadine opens her mouth to say something else, but stops. Mom's entered the room in her tennis whites and a pink PB&J Couture hoodie.

"Sweetie, you're up. I was just going to wake you," she says, giving me a quick peck on the cheek. My mom's birth certificate says she's forty, but looking at her, you wouldn't think she's a day over thirty-five. Platinum blond (kudos to Sergi, her colorist), bronzed (thanks to Fergie at Mystic Tanning), and in fantastic shape (daily training with Logan), she sometimes gets mistaken for my older sister. She *loves* when that happens.

"I was thinking," my mom begins, towering over me. (I inherited Mom's emerald green eyes, but not her statuesque height.) She grabs a clump of my naturally honey blond hair. "When Paul does your hair today, tell him not to pull it back," she says, eyeing the strands closely. "It should be down and curly, like Mina Burrows in this month's *Vogue*. I hate when your hair is pulled back. Your head looks too small."

Nadine mumbles something under her breath.

"I also want you to promise me you'll at least *try* on some couture stuff," Mom continues. "It makes you look more grown up and sophisticated. That's how you get the older roles, sweetie. Look older."

"I'm sixteen," I say as I untangle myself from her and make my way into our spacious kitchen. I open the Sub-zero fridge and toss Nadine a water, then grab a cinnamon raisin bagel for myself. "I like looking my age. I hate how Sky's always trying to be twenty-five instead of sixteen. She looks ridiculous."

"You may think so, honey, but Sky's going for an image. We've got to take yours to the next level too if you want bigger and better roles." Mom raises her eyebrow at me — never a good sign — and grabs the bagel out of my hand. She hands me a peach instead.

I know I could be grounded for life for saying this, but sometimes I wish my mom could be a lot more like my TV one. Paige Stevens always lets Sam cry on her shoulder. There was this one episode when Sam lost out on homecoming queen to the foreign exchange student from Bosnia. Paige canceled her business trip to Paris and consoled Sam by baking a double batch of brownies and renting *The Notebook* to watch together.

If I lost a movie role to Sky, I don't think my mom would

be baking me brownies. I don't think she even knows how to turn on the oven.

"We should go. Rodney is going to have a fit if we make him wait any longer," Nadine announces.

"Okay, have fun, Kaitie-Kat," Mom coos. I cringe. I don't really like it when she calls me that. "Sorry none of us could make it to the shoot today. I couldn't possibly cancel tennis with Paris's mom, and Dad is busy playing golf with Matt and that casting director from New Line. Those episodes of *ER* Matty did gave him a lot of buzz."

HOLLYWOOD SECRET NUMBER TWO: Everyone — and I mean everyone — in Los Angeles is in the biz. From the studious-looking Chateau Marmont bellhop who confides that he's writing a screenplay to the checkout girl at Bristol Farms supermarket with the two-inch-long fake nails who asks you how she might break into modeling, it's hard to find anyone who isn't obsessed with the glitz, glamour, and piles of cash Hollywood attracts, including my family. Ten years ago, my mom left her job as a receptionist at a cosmetic surgery office in Malibu to manage my career. ("No one will look out for you the way I could, Kate-Kate.") Three years later, Dad quit his salesman gig at Beverly Hills Auto to become a movie producer. So far, he's only worked on my films. ("If I help make decisions on all your movies, sweetums, we can rev up your earnings!" Dad exclaimed, using one of his terrible car expressions.) I guess it was only a matter of time then before my thirteen-year-old brother aspired to be the next Ashton Kutcher.

Nadine seems to be the exception. As she taps her frayed Birkenstocks impatiently, I notice she's carrying her GMAT prep book. Having graduated summa cum laude from Princeton, her goal is to stay in L.A. for a few years, make a ton of money, and then go to Harvard Business School. Nadine wants to be CEO of the world — or at least a *Fortune* 500 company. She'd be good at it too.

"Don't worry about it, Mom." I glance nervously at Nadine out of the corner of my eye. "I'll see you later." Nadine grabs my arm gently and we hurry out the front door. Lately it seems like all I do is run. We sprint down the long brick walkway and jump into the black sedan, where Rodney is waiting.

"Morning, Kates," Rodney mumbles, his mouth full of his usual breakfast, a bagel and veggie cream cheese. "Oversleep again?"

At six feet four inches and weighing in at almost three hundred pounds, Rodney looks like he could lay the smack down on any wrestler in the WWE, but the truth is, he's a big teddy bear. Rodney's been my bodyguard for the past two years. My parents hired him after I was mobbed at a Virgin Megastore in the Valley while buying a John Mayer CD. Rodney's real career goal is to be an action star — he's appeared as a bouncer in some club scenes on *Family Affair* — but the security gig, plus chauffeuring me around, must be good money in the meantime.

I settle into the comfy black seats and stare groggily out the window as the car winds down the long driveway and

Rodney punches the security code on our wrought-iron gates. We bought our house in the Los Angeles suburb of San Marino three years ago, when I re-signed my *FA* contract. I wish I could say I helped pick out the mammoth Spanish-style hacienda, but the truth is Mom and Dad went house hunting without me.

I close my eyes for what feels like a minute when the car comes to a sudden stop.

"Um, Nadine?" says Rodney calmly. I sit up and peek out the tinted windows. The freeway is totally backed up. "Unless you want to radio a chopper, we're going to be late for this shoot." Nadine frowns. "But think of it this way — they can't start without us." Rodney lets out a big, bellowing laugh.

Since we're not going anywhere for a while, I pull out my Sidekick to text-message my best friend, and only non-celeb pal, Liz Mendes. I know better than to call her house before 10 AM on the weekends. Mr. Mendes doesn't rise before noon. He's an entertainment lawyer who usually wines and dines his celebrity clients (like moi, which is how Liz and I met a few years ago) into the wee hours of the AM.

PRINCESSLEIA25: R U up?
POWERGIRL82: Yes. Got kickboxing.
PRINCESSLEIA25: Y??? U took class yesterday!!!
POWERGIRL82: I have 2 work on my roundabout kick for competition.
PRINCESSLEIA25: U R obsessed!

POWERGIRL82: Cute. U should take a class. Then U could kick Sky's butt.

PRINCESSLEIA25: Not a bad idea.

POWERGIRL82: Want to meet at A Slice of Heaven? 4?

PRINCESSLEIA25: K. I'll be done by then.

POWERGIRL82: C U then!

"Before we get there, Laney wanted me to go over a few things about the interview," Nadine announces when she notices the traffic letting up. "She won't be there."

"Okay." I put away my Sidekick.

"Number one, make sure you talk about the *Family Affair* finale," she reads off the printed e-mail from Laney.

"Piece of cake." I stifle a yawn.

"Number two, make sure you don't reveal too many details about what's going to happen at Krystal's wedding."

"No major plot leaks," I agree, shaking my head.

"And most importantly," she finishes, "downplay the animosity between you and Sky."

I pretend to be fascinated by the shiny Mercedes and Porsches whizzing by the window.

Nadine eyes me suspiciously. "Seriously, Kaitlin. Tell this Zara chick you don't want to talk about Sky or Trevor."

"That's *all* she's going to want to talk about," I protest.

"We went over this with Laney," she recites smoothly. "You and Trevor are friends. You're happy for him and Sky. Whatever you do, don't ramble on about the whole thing.

You think every reporter is your friend, Kaitlin, but they're not. They just want the story."

"I can't help it." I look over at Rodney. I can tell he's trying not to laugh. "They get me going about Sky, and I find myself coming up with excuses about why we don't hang together. I mean, I can't tell them she's positively evil, right? That would make me look bad. And the Trevor thing — I don't like him! Not that way. I feel bad he's been hypnotized by Sky, but . . ."

"You're doing it again." Nadine wags a finger at me. "You're rambling."

"Sky's a sore subject with me." I fold my tanned arms across my chest.

"When you're nervous, you ramble," Nadine says sternly. "I don't care if Zara claims to be president of the Kaitlin Burke fan club. *Don't* say anything negative. Let Sky bury herself."

"Okay," I agree wearily.

"Well, whatever you plan to say, figure it out quick," announces Rodney as we pull into the tiny parking lot at Fred Segal on Melrose. "We're here."

TWO: *Schmoozing at Fred Segal*

When *Teen People* told me they wanted to shoot my cover story at my favorite store, I immediately thought of this sci-fi shop on La Cienega where I buy *Star Wars* memorabilia. I know it borders on geekdom, but I'm obsessed with *Star Wars*. Not only is it the best good vs. evil story *ever*, with the cutest heroes (don't even get me started on my "it boy," the charmingly cocky Han Solo), but it also has a butt-kicking *heroine*. What I wouldn't give to play Princess Leia, with my hair in wacky bun braids....

But we won't be talking about my love of all things *Star Wars* today. Laney nixed the idea. "It's nerdy. Pick Fred Segal. That store is hip."

Even if you've never been to Fred Segal, you've probably heard of this celeb magnet. The two-story shopping mecca on Melrose (there's another larger location in Santa Monica) houses a maze of mini boutiques that are filled with trendy threads boasting high pricetags. I'm partial to their jean bar, where they shorten all my favorite brands (I'm only 5'3") free of charge.

Rodney, Nadine, and I grab our things and walk up to the vine-covered gray stone storefront at exactly 8:58 AM, where a security guard is waiting for us.

"We actually made it." Nadine breathes a sigh of relief.

The guard unlocks the doors to the closed building and ushers us inside. It's weird being here when music isn't pounding over the stereo speakers and the Fred Segal Beauty boutique isn't packed. As we pass the shoe department, I hear someone call my name. I turn and see a petite blonde with a tape recorder strutting towards me.

"It's so nice to meet you," she gushes. "I'm Zara Connors from *Teen People*."

"It's great to be here." I snap to attention and give her a big smile. "I love *Teen People*."

"We love to hear that. So you know why we're here then? We want to capture the *real you* on a shopping excursion. Laney said Fred Segal is your favorite."

"Yes, I shop here all the time," I tell her cheerily.

"You have an hour for hair and makeup before the store opens, then we'll shoot you pointing out your favorite things." Zara consults the schedule in her hand. "At the end, we'll go over some other questions. Sound good?" I nod.

Zara leads the way to the small crew. I quickly say hello to the photo editor, the assistants, and the photographer, Marc Bennet — making sure to compliment him on the last shoot we did together, a cover for *Lucky* — then I head over to my hair and makeup artists, Paul and Shelly. They've been my team on *FA* ever since I can remember, and I adore them. So does Mom. She makes sure they're hired for all my photo shoots.

"Doll, we've got to stop meeting like this," Paul wails dramatically as I approach the makeshift station of beauty supplies they've set up on a Fred Segal counter. "These nine AM call times after a heinous night on *Affair* are not good for my beauty rest. And let's just forget about Jacques's reaction. He was beyond bitter when I told him I couldn't meet him for breakfast at Joan's on Third this morning." Jacques, a fellow hair designer (Word of warning: Never call Paul a "hairdresser"), is Paul's latest crush. They've gone on two dates and already Paul is smitten.

"Oh please, you saw him yesterday!" Shelly punches him on the arm.

"Yeah, but that was more than twenty-four hours ago," he sniffs.

I swear Paul and Shelly would make a great reality show. He's a handsome California boy from Venice Beach and she's a loud-mouthed Southern broad with an imposing chest. They're complete opposites, and yet they fit great (unlike Sky and me). While Paul only wears designer duds, Shelly is a bargain shopper. She hits all the sales and only buys things if they're marked down sixty percent off or more. This horrifies Paul, who wouldn't be caught dead in last season's anything.

"Okay, Kates, what's it going to be today?" Shelly asks,

giving my face a once-over with toner, then dabbing concealer under my eyes. "How about some sparkly eye shadow to bring out those green eyes of yours? Or maybe some body glitter?"

"Do you think glitter is a bit much?" I wonder. "Real people go to the mall in sweats."

"Oh, not the real people thing again," Paul laments, spritzing my hair and pulling it into a low chignon, the way I like it. "Honey, let's get one thing straight. You're not real. You're Hollywood. You're supposed to look better than those people." Paul peers into my mirror, checks his curly brown hair for frizz, and gives me a wink.

I swat his face away. Everyone thinks I'm crazy to be so fascinated with "the real world" — a.k.a anything beyond the borders of greater Los Angeles. "People would kill to have enough money to fly their friends to Turks and Caicos for their sweet sixteen," Liz always reminds me. Yeah, but real people don't have to worry about someone like Sky talking trash about them on the nightly news either.

As soon as Paul gives me a final spritz of hairspray, Zara appears at my side, ready to start the interview. Our first stop is the perfume counter. ("I love anything with a hint of lavender," I repeat, just as Laney instructed. She said lavender traditionally evokes luck and trust or something, so Zara will be impressed.) Marc follows, snapping pictures of me posing with various products. Picking up the rear are Nadine and Rodney. Now that the store is officially open, Rodney's got his "Don't mess with us" face on. That plus his large frame, shiny bald head, and dark black sunglasses are enough to scare anyone away. Anyone but Fred Segal's PR woman.

"Kaitlin Burke! Not sure if you remember me; I'm Kathy Sutherland, public relations director for Fred Segal and Fred Segal Beauty." The tall, thin brunette in a killer tweed pantsuit holds her perfectly manicured hand out.

"Of course." I smile, shaking her hand. "Thanks for the spa day last month."

"No problem." She flashes her perfect pearly whites at me. "Fred Segal is all about taking care of their special customers. And this, by the way, is for you." She holds out several white Fred Segal shopping bags stuffed with products. "There's one for you and Nadine, of course, and I packed some of your mom's favorites as well."

"Thank you." I take the bags slowly. "That's so nice." If Kathy could only see my bathroom. It's exploding with free products. I could run a small spa out of my house.

HOLLYWOOD SECRET NUMBER THREE: Big stars get a lot of free stuff. Small stars get zippo. Okay, *maybe* they get a small discount or a free handbag now and then, but not often. This secret has no logic, I know. Once you can afford things, free stuff starts showing up at your publicist's office on a daily basis. Mention that you can't live without a certain moisturizer on *Live with Regis and Kelly* and they'll ship a box out the next day.

Kathy joins our posse as we hit the jeans bar. Marc has me pose with several pairs of denim while Zara fires off questions like, "What's your favorite thing to wear on your day off?" ("My Princess Leia t-shirt with cut-off green sweatpants. I find green soothing.") "What did you spend your first paycheck on?" ("When I was seven, I bought a massive trampoline for our backyard.") "How much is your current handbag?" ("I splurged on thousand-dollar cream canvas and green leather Prada bowler bags for my friend Liz and me — but I had to ask my mom's permission first.")

As we make our way to the shoe department, I notice our group has grown. A lot. Several girls are following us, even though they're trying not to make it obvious. "Isn't this cute?" one pipes up, holding up a pink sequined top and showing it to her giggling friend. Another tries to take a picture with her camera phone, but Rodney puts the kibosh on that. "Can Kaitlin take a picture?" she begs. Rodney takes another bite of his Almond Bar and says "after the shoot."

By eleven-thirty we've hit every department in the store. For the final shot, Marc gets the group of girls following us to pose for a picture of me "leaving" with dozens of Fred Segal bags. Most of the bags were actually mine since Kathy kept trying to give me anything I said was cute, including a pair of funky banana-yellow pumps.

Once I've signed autographs and posed for pictures, I finish my interview with Zara. After a few softballs (I told her my most embarrassing moment was when I accidentally spat food on Julia Roberts at a party), Zara wants to know the real dirt.

"Everyone in our office is obsessed with Trevor Wainright." She sighs. "We love his character, Ryan. What's it like to kiss him?"

"He's a great kisser. He has really soft lips," I giggle. Hey, it's true. Not that I have so many guys to compare him to.

"I'm sure it's awkward though," Zara comments, "since Sky has a thing for Trevor."

"You'd have to ask her about that." I calmly dodge the ticking time bomb.

"So there's no guy in your life right now?" Zara prods. I watch as she slides her tape recorder across the perfume counter where we're standing and closer to me.

I shake my head and smile. "Sadly, no. Between *FA* and my homework and charity obligations, I don't have a lot of free time."

"You seemed to make room last year, when you were spotted around town with Drew Thomas."

"We didn't date," I explain firmly. "We just had a few dinners. We were in talks to do a movie together." What I want to say is that Drew is an egotistical muscle head who is more concerned with how his famous dates can advance his career than having an actual relationship. I found that out the hard way, and I've had no desire to date anyone since. Of course, I truly haven't had the time to either.

"This week's *TV Tome* has a story about you and Sky fighting over Trevor," continues Zara. "Want to comment?" I look at Nadine, who motions for me to wrap things up.

"I think someone on set must be drinking too many lattes." I laugh. "They're hallucinating if they think we're fighting over Trevor. It couldn't be further from the truth. He's Sky's if she wants him. Trevor's a great guy, but he's a bit quiet for me. I like more assertive guys, you know? Trev's better suited for someone like Sky, who can walk . . ."

"TIME'S UP!" Nadine blurts out. Zara jumps. "Sorry," Nadine apologizes efficiently. "We've got to go." I look at my watch. It's 1:55. I had hoped to run into Mauro's Café & Ristorante, which is inside Fred Segal, to grab a strawberry smoothie, but there's no time. My stomach rumbles in protest. Sorry, buddy. Let's hope the So Chic store has a yummy Chinese takeout menu handy.

THREE: *A Slice of Heaven*

Liz is waiting in our usual rickety wooden booth in the back of A Slice of Heaven when Rodney and I arrive at 4:15. As we weave through the crowded tables, I pull my Dodgers cap down low so that no one recognizes me. Not that I don't stick out like a sore thumb with an intimidating dude trailing me everywhere I go. Liz sees us coming and taps her watch.

"Sorry." I cringe as I slide into the booth. "Rodney and I got stuck on Robertson."

"Autographs?" Liz asks knowingly.

"Camera guys," Rodney explains through a mouthful of pepperoni. Hey, how'd he get that already? "They were like a swarm of wasps."

"It's no wonder. You're big news this week, Kates," Liz offers, her long-lashed brown eyes sparkling. "You've been spotted all over town crying over losing Trevor Wainright to Sky." She grabs my worn hat and yanks it up to examine my annoyed expression. "I don't see any tears though." She laughs, her curly dark brown hair swinging.

"Cute," I comment sarcastically. "Real cute. Can we order? I'm *starving*."

"Sorry. I couldn't resist. Dad had the new *Hollywood Nation* in the bathroom."

"Did you use it as toilet paper?" Rodney takes another large bite oozing with cheese.

"I'll have to try that." Liz grins, then spies something behind us and whistles loudly. "Now that's what I call service!"

I turn to look. A Slice of Heaven's owner, Antonio, shuffles towards us, carrying our usual — a Sicilian pie with extra cheese, peppers, and broccoli and three Sprites. "Here you go," he announces gruffly. "Anything for my favorite girls — and Mr. Rodney, of course." He places the steaming pie down, and we scramble to get a slice.

There's no comparing other pizza to A Slice of Heaven's. It's the best pizza in Los Angeles, maybe the entire West Coast. (Antonio says the key is the water he uses to make the pie dough. He has tap water bottled and shipped from New York.)

There's another reason Liz and I are fond of this place: No one bothers me here. The restaurant is this totally no-frills pizza joint with almost vintage booths and unfashionable checkerboard tablecloths, in a strip mall in the Studio City section of L.A. Celebrities, and the paparazzi for that matter, would never think to come here. Most stars dine at other star-owned hot spots or hang at security-tight clubs like Star. I spend too much time in that circle as it is, which is why I favor A Slice of Heaven. When Liz and I sit in the back booth nursing our pie and Sprite refills, no one notices. It really is heaven.

I jump up and plant a kiss on Antonio's cheek. "Thanks, Tony. I've been dying for this all day. And today was pretty hectic — even for me."

He blushes. "You're lucky Liz told me you were coming. We were almost out of broccoli. I saved it for you."

"You're the best," I mumble, taking a big, juicy bite.

Antonio motions to Rodney. "Come on back. *Rambo: First Blood Part II* is on TV."

"You think you could whip up some meatballs while we're back there?" Rodney gets up quickly, knocking over the napkin holder. "Holler if you need me, Kates," he says before following Tony away.

"So how was the shoot?" Liz asks. I nod up and down, since my mouth is full. "And lunch the other day with Laney and your parents?" She grins slyly. I stop chewing and look down at my greasy plate.

"You've been dodging that question for days now! You haven't told me what happened when you brought up taking the hiatus off." I blink rapidly and stifle a sigh. Liz takes a monstrous bite of pizza, the oil dripping down her chin, and shakes her head.

"Let's just say I didn't make much progress," I answer slowly before filling her in on my ill-fated convo at the Ivy.

Between my parents' long-winded speech about my future

acting plans, Matty being signed by Laney, and Laney's signature name-dropping stories about her other clients ("I spent all morning with Reese and the kids," she'd drawled as my family listened intently. "She wanted my help picking out a dress for the Erase MS event this weekend"), I could barely get a word in. And when I did meekly suggest taking a vacation this hiatus, instead of doing the Kaitlin Goodwill press tour they were suggesting, my parents, Matt, and Laney acted as though I was certifiably insane.

"Take . . . the . . . hiatus . . . off?" Laney repeated slowly, tapping her long French-manicured nails nervously. "That's NOT a very good idea." She trained her almost-black heavily lined eyes on me. "The tabloids are devouring stories of you and Sky. If you disappear for a few months, she'll win."

"It's time to get in gear!" Dad gushed like a cheerleader. "Work, work, work, Kaitie-kins. It will pay off."

Matty was the only one on my side. Well, sort of.

"Laney, I could go on *Ellen* for Kaitlin." Matt flipped his blond mop top, green eyes glowing with excitement. "I don't need media training like Kaitlin does. I could be her cute younger brother who sticks up for her. And talk about my next project, of course . . . once I get one."

Matt's still never gotten over the fact that I could only get him a walk-on role on *FA*. He was so mad about it that he barged into the writers' room one afternoon and demanded a bigger part. I'm lucky the writers were good sports about my 13-year-old brother's outburst. They could have shipped Sam off to Cambodia to build schoolhouses out of mud.

"This is your career we're talking about, Kate-Kate." Mom smiled sweetly, sealing my fate to a hiatus full of TV appearances, interviews, and social events from the day *FA* shooting ends next week till I arrive back on set in August. "If we want your career to be a long one, we have to protect your image and squash these rumors pronto. You can take a *weekend* off, but then it's back to work. Understood?" She raised her right eyebrow at me scarily. Again, that's never a good sign.

"Understood," I had agreed quietly.

What I should have said is that *I'm exhausted.* Completely and utterly flattened from the gossip hounding, fights with Sky, and nonstop schedule. And if I don't take a break from all things Hollywood, I might wind up having a breakdown that prompts me to dye my hair a scary shade of platinum blond, stop consuming anything but Jamba Juice, and begin partying till four AM like some other young stars I know, but am too discreet to name.

"So I'm taking it you didn't bring up Cabo?" Liz jokes. The two of us were hoping to jet down to Cabo San Lucas for a little sun while I'm off from work, but I don't think that's part of Laney's schedule.

"Not even close," I say, eyeing another slice of pizza. Liz catches me.

"Go on." She grabs a second slice for herself. "It won't kill you."

I look around, almost thinking Mom will swoop in at any moment and have a fit, and pull another piece from the tray.

"Thatta girl," she encourages me. "First step is pizza, second is reminding your entourage who is actually in charge of your career."

Sometimes I envy Lizzie. Liz doesn't take garbage from anybody. She also eats what she wants when she wants. She says she burns up tons of calories in kickboxing, and what she doesn't goes straight to her "large and in charge Latina butt." "If it works for J.Lo, it can work for me," she says when we try on Lucky jeans at The Grove shopping plaza.

Liz is the type of person who has so much easy self-confidence that you feel good just being around her. She even gets to enjoy many of the same Hollywood perks I do, since her dad is in the business, without ever having to worry about the media concocting wacky stories about her.

HOLLYWOOD SECRET NUMBER FOUR: You don't have to be an actor, producer, or director to be treated like royalty in Tinseltown. Often it's enough just to be in the industry or a relative of someone famous. Publicists figure that by gifting celebrities' families free cell phones or passes to the hottest parties, the stars will eventually hear about what's being promoted anyway.

"I'm so frustrated," I complain wearily. "I just wanted a break from the Hollywood scene, you know? I'm not talking about giving up my job. Just a vacation from Sky, the tabloids, and my crazy schedule."

Liz stops chewing and looks at me curiously. "Unfortunately the baggage comes with the job," she reminds me gently. "Besides, it's not much easier sitting on my side of the booth. Sophomore year is rough. I just flunked my third bio exam — which means Mr. Harding is going to call my dad — I have a history term paper due next week that I haven't even started researching, and even though the Spring Fling is still two months away, I have absolutely zero date prospects."

"Okay, when you put it that way . . ." I roll my eyes. Liz throws an oil-soaked napkin at me. I toss it back at her. "I'd still gladly sit in class and let you deal with Sky and *Hollywood Nation* for a few weeks."

"You're a weirdo. You think school is fun." Liz makes a face. "Just say the word and I'll take your life. I could kick Sky's butt." She could too. In just a few months she's gotten pretty good at kickboxing.

I laugh, but I wouldn't mind switching places with Liz for a little while. It would be nice to slow down. And seriously, how cool would it be to go to school every day? The way she's always described Clark Hall, it seems so normal. That's probably because it is. Liz's dad hated the idea of sending his daughter to a stuffy boarding school just because they had money, so he enrolled her in Clark Hall. Tucked away on a sprawling campus in nearby Santa Rosita, the private school is famous for having a highly decorated curriculum (which basically means there's a ton of honors classes, which Liz is in), and prides itself on its large percentage of scholarship students from all over Los Angeles. Liz complains about

Clark a lot, but everything she mentions — the boring pep rallies, the school dances, cafeteria turf wars — sounds pretty enticing to me. "It would be nice to disappear for a while." I fantasize wistfully, and stare at a loud group of teens at a nearby table.

"You know what you need? To pull a total Houdini." Liz digs into the garlic knots Antonio also left us. "Hide out somewhere no one would ever recognize you. Let's think of fun places you could go. Um . . . Tahiti?"

I don't laugh. She's right. I *should* pull a Houdini.

"St. Bart's? We always wanted to go there." Liz is getting into the game. "Or Belize!"

"What about Clark Hall?" I offer half-jokingly.

"Yeah, right." She laughs, taking another bite of her garlic knot. "What — as my show-and-tell project? Be serious."

"You said I needed to pull a Houdini." A lightbulb goes off in my head. "Think about it. I *do* need to get away, and the truth is I can't go far. Rodney would have to come with me and he'd never leave Los Angeles during pilot season." (That's when the TV networks cast for upcoming shows, film an episode, and then pray their series will be picked up for the fall.)

"Kates, I was kidding," Liz interrupts, but I'm too excited to stop.

"I can't skip my schoolwork, right?" I exclaim. "Wherever I go I'd have to bring a tutor. Unless . . . Unless I didn't need one because I was at Clark!"

32

Liz's eyes widen nervously. "You can't be serious," she replies hoarsely.

"I *am* serious." I tuck my feet under me and lean into the table. This is exactly the change I've been looking for. The thoughts begin to fly furiously. "I have to finish my schoolwork for the year anyway, right? So instead of working with Monique, I'd enroll in classes with you every day. Think about it, Lizzie! I'd be getting away from the tabloid crap for a while, which would be a vacation, and I'd get to hang with you. And actually go to class, like I always wanted. I think the experience would totally clear my head. I'd do my press stuff for Laney after class so she wouldn't freak out, which would make Mom and Dad happy, and . . ."

"You're babbling, but I get the point." Liz's eyes look like they're bulging out of her head. She takes another garlic knot. "It's just not realistic, Kaitlin. The paparazzi would have a field day with you." She waves her hands wildly as if to drive home her point. "Do you really want your every grade printed in *US Weekly?*"

"Kaitlin Burke wouldn't exist if I hit Clark Hall. Laney would KILL me." I nervously bite my lower lip and think about tabloid pictures of me eating greasy french fries in the school cafeteria under the headline "Stars — They're Pigs Just Like Us!" Laney would have a coronary. "I guess I'd have to go in disguise."

"DISGUISE?" Liz's voice is so loud the teens at the next table look over. I pull my cap down lower. "I think you've watched one too many movies. This isn't like putting on a pair of glasses. Someone would *recognize you*. If that happens, you're finished. Sky would spin it that you're breaking your *FA* contract or something."

"You're right, she would, if she found out." I cut her off. "But she's not going to find out, Lizzie. I have a hair designer, a makeup artist, a bodyguard, and a crazed personal assistant who guards my privacy as if it were her own. I'm sure we can come up with a killer disguise." I look at her hopefully. "You could help me!"

"You're delusional." Liz shakes her head. "You're on a carb high from that extra slice of pizza. Tomorrow you'll come to your senses," she rationalizes. "This is a cool idea and all, but I was *kidding* about the Houdini thing. It would never work."

I slide the pizza pan out of the way and grab Liz by both arms, trying to shake the stubbornness out of her. "If you helped me, it would," I try to coax her firmly. "You could be my guide at Clark Hall. Help me fit in, show me around."

"I'm sure we wouldn't be in all of the same classes," she says wearily.

"You're missing my point."

"What? That you're committing career suicide?" Liz frowns. "Besides, your parents said you have to shoot a movie this summer."

"I don't want to act this summer," I remind her, trying not to whine. "I want some time to think. School would be that real break I need from Sky and Hollywood. I *need* this, Liz. The press tour won't bother me so much if I have school as a distraction. And then when school is over, and my press stuff is done, I would be refreshed for the new season of *FA*. Maybe Sky wouldn't get to me so much if I didn't have to deal with her for a while."

She rubs her temples. I think I'm giving her a migraine.

"Liz?" I say quietly. "*Say something.*"

"Ugh . . . FINE." She slams her hands down on the table, almost toppling my soda. "I think you're crazy, but I'll help you."

I jump up and give her a huge hug, practically knocking her over. We both start laughing wildly, causing the people at the booths around us to stare.

"Besides," I hear her muffled voice as I squeeze her tightly, "I'm the least of your problems. You've got to break the news to Laney and your parents first."

Oh yeah. I forgot about that part. I let go of my best friend and nervously start biting my lower lip again.

"You can do it." Liz changes her tune. "You've just got to find the right time and place to tell them."

"You mean somewhere public where they can't kill me," I comment wryly.

"You know where you have to tell them then." She grins. "At your premiere."

I look at her like she's crazy, but then I quickly realize she's right. The *Off-Key* premiere party will be loud, so reporters won't overhear us talking, and we'll be around people so Laney and my parents can't cause a big scene. I stare at Liz in awe. "You're brilliant, do you know that?"

"I can't believe it took you so long to realize that yourself." She slides over the garlic knot basket. "Now take a knot to celebrate your first step towards independence."

I grab the garlic-y dough out of the greasy basket and happily take a huge bite. For once, I don't worry about what Mom would think.

FOUR: *Sleepless in Hollywood*

After pizza, I call Mom and tell her I'm sleeping over at Liz's house. I am so excited that I want to get right to work on my "major downgrade," as Liz is referring to my makeunder. So far we've decided three things. I jot them down on my Sidekick:

Saturday 2/21
NOTES TO SELF ABOUT DISGUISE:
1. Rubber masks rock (Perfect example: Robin Williams in Mrs. Doubtfire). Sadly, they won't work 4 me. All that latex and glue would B horribly uncomfortable, not 2 mention 2 hard 2 rip off if I had 2 outrun the paparazzi.
2. New threads and a big hat R not a good disguise. What I really need is a good wig, colored contact lenses, and a cool accent.
3. The Rodney Issue. There is no way Mom and Dad will let me go 2 school solo, but if people catch sight of Rodney, I'm done 4.

Liz thinks the presence of a large guy with bulging muscles who has to squeeze into the classroom doors sideways screams "bodyguard." I'm going to have to bribe Rodney to park nearby. That way he'll still be close by if I run into trouble.

With *FA* wrapping this week, and the *Off-Key* premiere on Friday, I really have to get my plan in order if I want to get four months of school under my belt at Clark.

But first things first — I've got to get some more school supporters. I figure my best bets are Nadine and Rodney, so I'm telling them on the way to work this morning — even if I am *exhausted*. On Monday we pulled another sixteen-hour day on *FA*. After getting to sleep at two AM, I had to turn around and be back at work today at nine. I'm commuting in my pj's. (Why get dressed when I'm going to have my hair, makeup, and clothes picked out for me anyway?) Is it any surprise then that I just fell asleep eating Froot Loops? My face landed in the plastic bowl with a splash!

"It's no wonder you're a zombie," Nadine laughs lightly. She hands me a napkin to wipe my face. "I can't believe they had a sixteen-year-old shooting at midnight!" She shakes her head. "It's terrible. They couldn't have shot the car crash scene when the sun went down?"

"They had to shut down the roads." I pull a stray Froot Loop out of my hair.

"I told your mom we should check the child labor laws to make sure you can work that late, but she didn't want me to cause any trouble," Nadine comments dryly. "You know your mom, always looking out for your best interests."

I'm just glad Mom wasn't there to see the Froot Loops incident. She would die if she knew I was eating a high-sugar cereal.

"Speaking of my best interests, I've got something to run by you guys," I begin gingerly. I tell them both my plan and then nervously wait for their reaction.

"So?" I finish up. "Will you help me?" I think this is the first time I've actually seen Nadine at a loss for words.

"Why would you want to take on another persona?" she questions me, tapping her pen across her mammoth Kaitlin folder, aka her bible, with this seemingly very concerned expression on her face. "I just don't get you. Don't you think your brain is clogged enough with both Kaitlin and Sam in there?"

"I'm an actress," I remind her. "That's what we're good at — pretending to be someone else."

"Yeah, well, you better be prepared to play the role of your life then, because if the press gets wind of this one, you're going to have to exit stage left immediately." Nadine's ears redden with worry. "I'm sure Laney already told you that dropping everything and going to school isn't the smartest move. Your fans will think you're tired of Hollywood and not interested in working. *Not* that you're just taking a vacation!"

"I thought you, of all people, would be happy I was doing this," I reply innocently. "You're always saying I need a break."

"Yeah, but I never thought you would take me seriously. Your mother is going to *kill* me when she hears about this." Nadine begins biting her already chewed-up nails. "Rodney, help me out here."

Rodney hasn't said anything, come to think of it, but he is a man of few words. "I think it could be good for Kates to have a normal life," he finally responds.

"Rodney, I love you!" I throw my arms over the front seat and around his large neck.

"Careful, I'm driving!" He's holding on to the steering wheel with one hand and has an Egg McMuffin sandwich in the other. "I didn't say you could pull it off."

"I will if you guys help me." I gaze at Nadine imploringly. She starts biting her nails again.

"If I'm going to be in on this plan, it's going to require some serious prep work," Rodney muses thoughtfully. "I need to check out the school grounds, flag all the exits, survey the paparazzi situation."

"There won't be any paparazzi. It's a regular school with *no* Hollywood drama. Doesn't it sound amazing?" I imagine my locker decorated with pictures of Chad Michael Murray.

"You've lost your mind," Nadine states solemnly, "but at least you're finally standing up to your parents and making your own decisions."

"I haven't told them yet," I mumble. "Or Laney." Nadine looks at me blankly.

"Ohhhhh boy." Rodney whistles. "I want to be there when she tells her mom!" He turns around and looks at Nadine, and they both suddenly burst out laughing.

"Come on, you guys. It won't be that bad." Their laughter only gets louder. Nadine actually leans back in her seat and grasps her chest.

"I ... can't ... breathe ..." she spurts out. Rodney howls more.

"Look, I was hoping you guys would help me. That's why I told you first. I was hoping we could role play the conversation."

Nadine stops laughing and looks at me, baffled. "You mean you want me and Rodney to play your parents?" She and Rodney burst out laughing again. Nadine is heaving so hard, tears are rolling down her cheeks.

"Guys, be serious!" I beg. I swear, sometimes I feel like I'm the parent here.

"Okay, okay." Nadine calms down. "Let's try it." She straightens up in the seat and purses her lips. "Kaitlin, dear, I wish you'd wear your hair down more. It's so *in*."

I give her a look. "Actually, *Mom*, there was something important I wanted to talk to you and Dad about."

"Yes, Kates? What is it?" Rodney says in a higher voice that I guess is supposed to sound like my dad. He chuckles to himself, then takes another bite of his breakfast sandwich.

"I'm on hiatus now, and my schedule is already jammed," I recite awkwardly. "I don't want to back out on my press commitments, but I ..."

"Good, honey, because that's what we expect you to do!" Nadine cuts me off. "Work, work, work! That's what Reese and Renée did at your age! You can't become a megastar if you don't work your butt off." Nadine is clearly enjoying her role.

"Yeah, um, okay, *Mom*. But I really need a breather too. A break from the scene, you know? I was talking to Liz, and she was saying how great school is, and I thought to myself,

'What a cool idea!' I could try something different and study at the same time."

"Study? STUDY?" Rodney bellows. "Now why on earth would you want to do that? Actors don't need school!"

Nadine is wide-eyed. "Studying is for . . . studying is for . . . well, *regular* people. We're *famous*, Kaitlin. We don't need to work hard."

Rodney laughs at that. So does Nadine. I throw up my hands.

"Forget it," I say, almost mad that I am laughing myself. "You two are enjoying this too much. I'll just wing it."

An hour later (accident on the 101 again between a Porsche and a Lamborghini), we arrive at the studio. Nadine and I race to the hair and makeup room and find Sky sitting in the chair next to mine.

"There you are, K," she sings when she sees me in the mirror. "I thought you were going to blow our call time and hold everything up. I've been here a half hour already." Raphael looks at me guiltily as he curls Sky's hair.

"You know me, Skylar," I reply coolly. I take a seat in Paul's chair. "I'm always causing problems." I give Sky a wink and she purses her lips.

"Now girls," Raphael interjects nervously (He's Sky's latest hair designer. She practically fires a new one every other week.). "It's too early to argue."

"I don't recall asking your opinion, Raphael," Sky snaps.

Paul whistles under his breath, and I suppress a giggle. Sky wouldn't admit this, but I think even she is too tired to have a full-blown argument this morning. For the next half hour the only sound I hear is Paul's and Raphael's styling tools. Paul's washed my hair in the sink and is now blow-drying it straight before putting it in rollers. He has to give me an updo for today's scene, which is Krystal's scandalous wedding. Sky and I are bridesmaids.

There's a loud knock on our door and our executive producer, Tom Pullman, comes sweeping in. "Morning, love-lies!" Tom's always cheerful, even on three hours' sleep. He looks kind of like a well-fed hobbit with his five-foot frame and shiny bald head. "We're setting up the wedding chapel scene as we speak." Tom's walkie talkie is blaring orders from his waist. "STEVE, I'll be there in two!" he shouts at his Diesel jeans. "Girls, we're going to start off in the atrium today. Krystal will give you your bridesmaids' gifts. From there, Sam will get Krystal to spill the beans about the baby. . . ."

"Sam, Sam, it's always Sam who gets the great lines," I hear Sky mutter quietly.

Tom must have overheard too because he stops talking and pulls his tortoise-shell frames off his nose to look at us both with fresh eyes. "Now girls, I want to remind you that we have visitors on set today," he orders sternly, ignoring Sky's comment. "Brian Bennett from *Celeb Insider* is coming to do a segment on the season finale."

"I don't remember an interview with that twit being cleared with my publicist, Tom," Sky warns flippantly.

"Sky, you did the pre-interview yesterday, remember?" he responds wearily. Sky doesn't answer. "Let's all try to get along today, okay, ladies? No talk of set discord or any of that nonsense." Tom's walkie talkie starts yelling again. "I'll see you in a few," he calls as he dashes out.

Today's interview with Brian Bennett is an easy one. He'll come to the set and talk to us about the finale, our characters', and what we like to do when we're in-between scenes. It's basically the same interview Sky and I have had to give to about a dozen entertainment shows, morning programs, and newspapers the past few weeks to promote the season finale. There are always the same questions ("So Kaitlin, can you give us any clue as to who the father of your Aunt Krystal's baby is?") so it's easy to memorize the answers ("I can't tell you that," I reply cheerfully. "It's a surprise the viewers will want to see for themselves.")

When you appear on a talk show though, the rules are different. Since the interview is longer, you usually talk about things other than the project you're promoting. That's HOLLYWOOD SECRET NUMBER FIVE: When stars go on a talk show, they usually know the questions ahead of time. Why do you think Jay Leno and Ellen Degeneres know a star's just swum with sharks or returned from a trip to the Baltic Sea? Or how they have their baby picture ready to show the audience? It's because the star, or her publicist, will have a pre-interview with the show's producers to discuss possible show topics. I like to do my own pre-interviews, but Sky gets her publicist to do hers.

After Sky and I finish in wardrobe, we emerge onto the set wearing our custom Violet Wade bridesmaids' dresses

(Violet is a big fan of *Family Affair*). They're strapless tea-length dresses in a pretty shade of periwinkle with a coordinating brown sash. I'd totally wear this to my prom. Well, if I actually got to go to a prom.

Sky and I take our marks next to Maggie, who plays Aunt Krystal, on the hot, brightly lit soundstage. We're on the portion made to resemble the lush gardens and atrium on Blake and Paige Stevens' estate. This setting is a permanent fixture on the *FA* soundstage (along with the family's state-of-the-art kitchen, Sam's and Sara's cluttered bedrooms, and the Stevens' tricked-out living room) since so much goes down at the atrium — torrid love affairs, breakups, and secret rendezvous. Outside the shot's perimeter, the large camera crew is stationed at various angles to catch the action. Paul, Shelly, and Raphael, along with Maggie's makeup artist, wait patiently behind them to see if any of us need a touchup. I see Brian Bennett and his crew standing nearby too, taking "behind the scenes" footage of the shot. After a quick line run-through, Tom calls action.

"Aunt Krystal, are you okay? You look kind of pale," I declare aloud as my too-innocent, always-sweet alter ego.

"Sam, give her a break. She's probably just nervous about the wedding," Sky recites on cue, twirling the piece of green gum she's pulled out of her mouth. "Right, Aunt Krystal?"

Maggie turns away from us and faces the camera behind her. She's wearing a lace-covered ivory Violet Wade wedding dress that is so tight she looks like a mummy. Maggie's bleached blond hair is swept back into a low bun, and a long cathedral-length veil covers her head. Maggie looks at Sky and me tearfully and covers her face with her white-gloved hands. She starts to sob uncontrollably. Sky and I look at each other, then walk to our marks on either side of Maggie and put our arms around her shoulders. We hold for thirty seconds, pretending to be unsure of what to do. Then I say . . .

"I saw you in the bathroom, Aunt Krystal. You were throwing up."

"Girls, I can't lie to you," she announces after a long dramatic pause. She dabs her eyes with a pink handkerchief I've handed her. "I'm pregnant."

Sky and I squeal with delight and hug her tightly.

Maggie pulls away and sits down on the nearby white wicker bench with tacky turquoise cushions. She places her veiled head in her lap and whispers, "You can't tell Andrew."

"Why not?" I ask, concerned. I join her on the bench and place my hand gingerly on my aunt's shoulder. Maggie tears up again and sobs loudly. She looks up at us with shiny wet eyes and proclaims, "Because I don't know if the baby is his."

God, is this stuff fun to act out or what?

"AND, CUT!" Tom calls out. He sprints onto the stage. "Okay, girls, that was very good, but I feel like you can do it with more emotion. Kaitlin, Sky, I want more concern coming from both of you. Your Aunt Krystal is getting married and she seems miserable. Why? Reflect on that." Tom pulls his glasses off his face and wipes his sweat-lined brow. "Maggie, the tears are great, but don't overdo it, okay? Use body language to convey your distress. We've got to save the hystericalness for things like Mark's funeral. Okay? Let's try this again!"

When we finally nail the scene an hour later — after Sky complains that the camera guy on the right isn't taping her best angle, and Maggie suggests tweaking the dialogue a bit so that she has more "emotional drama" moments, we get an hour break to chat with Brian Bennett and eat lunch. Sky and I put on our best poker faces and plop down in the director's chairs to take his questions.

"Okay, even I know that you two are wearing bridesmaids' dresses," Brian points out in that overly friendly newscaster voice of his. "The rumors must be true, then: Krystal's getting married."

Sky and I glance at each other, giving our best impersonation of co-conspirators. "Should we tell him, K?" Sky asks sweetly.

"Oh alright," I giggle. "You caught us. It's actually Sam and Sara who are getting married. It's a double wedding!"

"We can't lie, Brian," Sky explains with a smile. "It is Krystal, but if we tell you any more than that, we might not live to see next season ourselves!"

Hmm . . . how great would it be if they shipped Sara off to some exotic island for reform school?

"You two really seem to get along," Brian's voice booms in awe. "I guess rumors of you fighting aren't true then."

"Definitely not." Sky pretends to be shocked. "I could never believe that K was jealous of my relationship with Trevor. I mean, you're not jealous, are you, K?" she says, and flips her black hair over her tiny shoulders. "I know it's been a while since you dated anybody so it must be a little hard to see us together." Brian quickly motions to his camera guy to move in closer.

I blink rapidly. "Definitely not, Skylar," I respond calmly. "You two make a *great* couple. Trev needs someone cunning who can show him how to survive the sharks in this town." I look innocently at Billy. "It's a shame the rumors have gotten so out of control, though. I just wonder who would plant such terrible lies about me and my family in the press."

Sky pounces, cutting me off. "I hate what the press is doing to my K. I just can't believe the awful, awful things they're saying about her. They couldn't possibly be true! K and I are like sisters. It's going to be tough not seeing her every day this summer, but we'll talk on the phone all the time." Sky bats her brown saucer eyes at me lovingly.

Brian seems moved. I think I may throw up.

"Ladies, as always, it's been a pleasure," he wraps up, and kisses Sky's hand.

"The pleasure is all mine, Brian," she calls out as I stride ahead of her towards my dressing room. Even that's a competition as we race each other down the hall. I reach my room first and slam the door. HA! I pull my Sidekick out of my new Gucci clutch and type a "to do" list.

2/24

NOTES TO SELF:

Ask Nadine 2 pick up chai tea. Calming effect should help soothe premiere jitters.

Book Air Brush Tanning appointment 4 premiere morning! (Make them swear not 2 turn U orange, like Sky)

Spill school plan 2 Mom, Dad, Matt and Laney — in that order.

FIVE: *Off-Key Premiere*

Off-Key is my first grown-up movie role and I'm really proud of it, especially since it's the first film I've done where I get above the title billing. (My name is above the title of the film on the poster, which is a spot reserved for the star. Totally exciting, right?) I play Mac Murdock's daughter and I get chills just thinking about my A-list costar. Even though he's much older, slightly weather-beaten and has, like, eight kids, Liz and I find him completely sexy — as does the rest of the world! Anyway, in the movie, my character, Katherine, is kidnapped by Russian mobsters who are after Mac's (or should I say his character, Bo's) fat inheritance. Of course, Bo gets me back. The mob guys don't know that he's more than a famed piano prodigy; he's also highly trained in the art of Jitsu.

So with the *Off-Key* premiere being such a big deal, you'd think I'd have a really cute date to walk the red carpet with, right?

Not! When would I find the time to get one? I'm taking

my usual escort tonight — Lizzie. She's always on time, makes me laugh, and isn't obsessed with being interviewed by the media. That makes her more appealing than any boy I know (as of today, of course). And besides, I need Liz's support one-hundred percent when I spill my hiatus plans to my parents and Laney at the after-party.

Telling them is all I can think about as I sit across from Mom and Dad in the black Escalade limo that's driving us to the premiere at Grauman's Chinese Theatre in West Hollywood.

"Let's go over tonight's itinerary," Nadine happily suggests to our group, which includes Matt, Liz, and Rodney. "Rodney and Kaitlin will step out of the limo first. Laney will be waiting at the edge of the red carpet to take Kaitlin through the press line. We've already cleared *Access Hollywood* and *Celeb Insider* for interviews."

I nod and play with the pleats on the bottom of my '50s-style silver halter dress. The gown is beautiful, but a tad itchy. As I squirm, the sound echoes through the quiet, tinted-glass cabin.

"Don't crease your dress, Kate-Kate!" Mom warns, sitting perfectly still in her low-cut fuchsia Monique slip dress. "Wrinkles look bad in pictures."

"Nadine?" Matt interrupts, his long, lean body practically scraping the roof of the cabin. "What about the rest of us? Aren't we walking the line too?" Matt was really anxious about the red carpet. He went through three outfits before settling on a three-button navy blue Dolce and Gabbana suit with a silver-collared shirt he swears Orlando Bloom just wore to the Golden Globes.

Nadine sighs. "Can I finish?" We all nod. She opens her bible and efficiently begins rattling off important details for the evening:

1. We're seated in Row E, seats 1, 3, 7, 9, 11, 13, and 15. Laney has our tickets.
2. Fellow attendees: Brad Pitt, Ali Kensington, Adam Brody (yum!), and Mac Murdock are all expected to be there.
3. The rockin' after-party is being held in an empty airplane hangar at Los Angeles Airport that they've decked out to look like a scene in the movie — the one where Mac finds me in the cargo hold of a plane ready to take off for the Greek Isles.

As we pull up to Grauman's famed entrance with its Asian architecture and colorful dragon statues, the overflowing crowd lined up behind the velvet ropes starts cheering. When a limo cruises up, they know there is a 95 percent chance a celebrity is inside.

Rodney jumps out first and comes around to my side to open the door. I grab his extended hand and teeter out on my silver three-inch spiked heels. Flashbulbs start popping immediately, practically blinding me. God, if you're listening, please don't let me trip over my big feet.

As I strain to see in front of me, Laney approaches and grabs my free hand. She's wearing a black pinstripe pantsuit accessorized with a headset. "SHE'S HERE. Tell everyone," I hear her bark. Laney leads me onto the red carpet. The first stop is the photographer corral, lined up several feet deep with paparazzi. I take a deep breath, open my green eyes wide (they tell me they're my best feature), and then start to pose.

"Kaitlin, look over here," one cameraman yells.

"Give us a big smile, Kaitlin," another calls out.

"Hey, Kaitlin, where's Trevor?" someone hollers, trying to drown out the dozen other paparazzo screaming for me to turn one way, then the other.

HOLLYWOOD SECRET NUMBER SIX: How to Pose for Photographers. You want a flattering pose to wind up in *US Weekly*, right? So you swivel your torso sideways so that you're standing at an angle. This will make you look svelte. Then, place one foot in front of the other. Tilt your head back slightly and plaster a semi-toothy grin on your face. It's hard to hold a smile for more than ten seconds, but if you practice enough, it will definitely get easier.

"Okay, guys, thanks!" Laney waves finally, tossing her hair and pulling me away happily. Laney loves premiere nights. She gets a rush from gossip columnists and photographers begging her for a minute with her clients.

"Kaitlin, this is Mark from *Access*." Laney stops at the first of several reporters waiting on the next leg of the red carpet.

"You look beautiful tonight, Kaitlin," the guy in the tux with a graying soul patch says as he holds out his microphone. His cameraman trains a light on me. "Who are you wearing?"

"Thanks, Mark. This is So Chic. They designed it especially for me, so I feel pretty special," I reply cheerily, turning on the 100-watt smile I've perfected over the years.

"What was it like working with Mac?" he asks, geniunely interested.

"Mac is amazing," I answer automatically (Laney's been going over these types of questions and answers with me all week). "I learned so much from watching him. It was a great experience."

"*Family Affair*'s ratings are hotter than ever, with your help, of course," Mark segues. "People can't seem to get enough of Samantha."

"Why, thank you. It's a team effort, though. We all work really well together, but that comes from years of being a family."

"Thirty seconds," Laney whispers gruffly to Mark's cameraman.

"Speaking of family, how are you and Sky getting along these days?"

Laney grimaces. She grabs my arm to lead me away, but as she does, I tilt my head and say with a toothy grin, "As fabulous as ever, Mark."

Next stop is a short freckle-faced twenty-something girl who is sweating down the sides of her green silk slip dress. She looks pretty nervous and drops her note cards when I walk over. Laney whispers her name in my ear.

"Hi, Frances." I extend my hand graciously. Frances is a new gossip writer at *Hollywood Online.*

"You're . . . you're . . . um, welcome, Kaitlin," Frances stutters. She's staring at me as she fumbles for her tape recorder in her pocket. "I'm a huge fan of *Family Affair.*"

"That's nice to hear. Thanks for watching." Poor Frances. I want to tell her not to be nervous. I'm just a person doing a job, like she is. But I don't want to embarrass her. Besides, plenty of people react this way. It happens so often, I barely notice anymore.

"Um, I was wondering if things on set have been as fun as last year." I see Frances awkwardly glance at Laney out of the corner of her eye. "There's been a lot of press about you and Sky feuding on set. Care to comment?"

"Tonight is about *Off-Key,* remember?" Laney replies hotly. Frances looks like she might pass out. "I told you on the phone today that if you were going to ask about Sky, we weren't going to do an interview."

Laney can be scary when she wants to, even if she does look like a teenager. (I couldn't tell you how old Laney is; she won't even tell me that.) With her girlish figure, Laney wears the same brands I do, accessorized with the hottest handbag draped on her tiny arm. ("Kaitlin, you don't want that Birkin bag they just sent over, do you? Because the color would look unbelievably *great* against my Audi.")

"I, um, told my editors I'd ask her that question," Frances stutters mechanically. The color drains from her face as Laney continues to glare menacingly.

"Sky and I play sisters so like all sisters we disagree some-times, but it's nothing as dramatic as you've read," I reply, hoping it doesn't sound too rehearsed. Laney starts pulling me away. "Enjoy the movie, Frances!"

Why fight it? This is what people want to know — not what I think of Mac Murdock. It's just a shame that Sky's and my personal relationship is so different from our onscreen one. On *FA*, our characters always stick up for each other. We shot an episode a few weeks ago where Sara charged a pair of $1,000 Manolo Blahnik butter-suede boots on Dad's credit card and he wigged out. Sam claimed the boots were hers, sacrificing her weekend plans so that her sister could go out on a date with this James Dean-like hottie she was crushing.

In real life, Sky would have charged the shoes to my ac-count, called the tabloids, and told them I stole from her (even though I never could squeeze my hoofs into her size five boots).

After a few more pictures, Rodney, Laney, and I head in-side the theater to take our seats. *Star Wars* premiered here. Maybe I'll be sitting in the same seat that Harrison Ford once sat in. Just the thought gives me goose bumps.

As Laney, Rodney, and I make our way past the Asian wall murals decorating the red- and gold-columned lobby, I spot my *FA* costar Trevor Wainright. He's shoveling butter pop-corn in his mouth.

"Hey, beautiful," he beckons when he sees me, then gives me a big hug.

Right about now you're thinking the tabloids are right, I do like Trevor. Well, the answer is yes, but seriously, just as a friend. Trevor is a little too quiet for my taste. I prefer someone funnier and more dynamic, like . . . um . . . Han Solo.

FA is Trevor's first role. When he arrived in Hollywood a year ago, fresh off a bus from Idaho, having left his whole family back on the potato farm, he was immediately snatched up by an agent. Trevor still needs help in the wardrobe department (tonight he's wearing a seersucker shirt and beat-up jeans), but looks-wise he's totally a California boy — tall, blond, and blue-eyed with mega muscles. Must be all that hay he hauled.

"I'm glad you could make it, Trev." I smile genuinely, squeezing him back.

"Gosh, are you kidding, Kaitlin?" He takes another handful of popcorn. "Did you know they're giving away free food?"

"You don't say." I deadpan. Laney rolls her eyes and walks away. She's not too fond of Trevor, having tried to sign him as a client once, but he told her he didn't see the point of a publicist. I don't think he knows yet what a publicist does. Seeing Trevor's popcorn prompts Rodney to head over to the snack line to grab something himself.

"Seriously," Trevor continues his routine when Rodney walks away, "they're even giving out bonbons and gummy bears. Gummy bears are, like, four dollars a pack." I'm still laughing when I notice a blood red–manicured hand slip itself around Trevor's waist.

"I was wondering where you scooted off to, sweetie," Sky coos after planting a long wet kiss on Trevor's surprised face. Sky's wearing a black satin strapless dress with a corseted waist. "I told you to *wait* for me outside the ladies room."

What is *she* doing here?

Before I can say anything, Liz runs over and grabs my shoulders.

"Adam Brody is sitting two rows behind us!" she screeches, then looks at my blank face and turns around to see why I'm so pale. "Oh, hi, Sky," Liz coolly greets her, smoothing out a crease in her white linen dress. Liz accessorized it with a purple-and-yellow Pucci scarf that only she could pull off. "Who invited you?"

"Trev, of course," Sky answers flatly, turning her bony bare back to us to plant another kiss on Trev's beet red face. Poor guy. Give Sky two weeks and she'll have moved on to someone else, like she always does.

"When Trev told me he was coming to K's premiere, I asked who his date was." She flashes her trademark smirk. "When he said he didn't have one, I told him there was no way I was letting him do the red carpet alone. Everyone knows that's premiere suicide!" She looks from Liz to me. "Speaking of dates, who are you with, K?"

"ME," Liz states, taking a confident step forward.

I'm speechless. Suddenly I have comeback-itis. I can't form a single zinger. I can't believe Sky is crashing my movie premiere! Well, it's actually Mac's movie premiere, but I'm in the film too.

"Figures you would be here, Liz," Sky purrs. She takes Trevor's buttery popcorn from his hands and takes a step towards Liz and me. "You're always Kaitlin's date. I'm surprised the *Star* hasn't done a story on that yet. People are probably wondering why you two are always together." Sky grabs a fistful of the greasy popcorn. "Want some, K?" She holds the dripping kernels in front of my face. I move to swat her hand away, but they drop right down the front of my dress. "Oops!" she exclaims in mock horror.

I want to throw something, or yell that Sky is pulling yet another childish antic, but before I can freak out, Trevor swoops in with a packet of pre-moistened wipes. "Here." He offers them quickly. "I always carry these in my pocket in case of an emergency."

I pull the kernels out and dab the dress gingerly. Thankfully, there doesn't seem to be a stain. "Trev, you're a lifesaver." I breathe a sigh of relief and shoot daggers at Sky. Where is Rodney when I need him?

"Funny how that happened though, isn't it, Kates," Liz comments, moving closer to Sky. Her face is wrinkled up in disgust. "When Sky is around, there's always a problem."

"It was just an accident," Trev protests, stepping between them.

"That's right, sweetie," Sky agrees innocently, looking up at him wide-eyed. "Maybe we should find our seats though before there's another one." Sky turns Trev around, slips one bejeweled hand into his back pocket, and steers him away.

"Can you believe her?" I whisper incredulously to Liz. I check my dress again. I have to remember to tell Nadine to buy thoses wipes.

"Kaitlin, the movie is going to start," Laney informs me, reappearing suddenly. She looks at my shell-shocked face. "What happened?"

"You missed the fireworks," Liz responds dryly. She quickly fills Laney in on the popcorn debacle as Rodney, carrying an assortment of snacks, helps us find our seats in the large auditorium.

"The nerve," Laney seethes as we walk past the beautiful Asian vases and statues that decorate the 2,000-seat theater. Even though the lights are dimmed, I recognize many industry folks seated nearby. Behind me I hear a fan call out, "HI, KAITLIN!" "Looking, good Samantha!" someone else screams.

". . . showing up at your movie premiere," Laney is fuming in an undertone, spitting out her words in disgust. "She's unbelievable."

"I gave Trevor two tickets," I explain sheepishly, wiping my arm from Laney's wet rant, and take a seat next to Liz. Mom, Dad, and Matt are already seated and busy greeting everyone around us.

"Is Trevor a moron?" Laney asks, and then shakes her head. "Never mind, you just enjoy yourself. I'm going to find Barry Weinberg and tell him that we don't expect to see Sky at the after-party."

"I don't want to cause a scene," I protest. "I'll stay clear of her."

"I'll make sure she does," Liz promises. Liz hates Sky. Their dads are partners at the same entertainment law firm and Liz says Sky's father is always trying to steal Mr. Mendes's clients.

The theater lights start flickering to signal the movie starting. Laney mouths "stay put" and walks away to find her seat.

"We're so proud of you, honey," my dad leans over and whispers as the credits roll. Mac's name appears on the screen, and the audience cheers loudly. My name follows, and our whole row hollers along with the auditorium. It's an amazing feeling.

"Kates, did you see who's sitting in front of us?" Mom looks like she's going to have a conniption. "Hamilton Weinberg." He's the head honcho at the hot new indie company, Famous Films. Everyone wants to work with him — including me. "Make sure you go over and introduce yourself after this."

I smile weakly in the dark. It's going to be a long night.

SIX: *The After-Party*

I'm not sure if I should laugh right now or cry.

When the *Off-Key* closing credits begin to roll 136 minutes after the opening credits, and Mac Murdock's and my entourages are escorted out a side exit of the theater to thunderous applause, I start to hyperventilate. It's not because I could hear Sky's high-pitched cackle during the whole movie (she was a few rows behind me), or because I had just spent over two hours watching myself onscreen. The real reason for my freak-out is that I can't stop thinking about what's next on tonight's agenda — the big talk about hiatus.

"Take deep breaths." Liz puts a firm hand on my shoulder as we're ushered inside the after-party. I exhale slowly. Okay, I *think* I'm ready to do this. . . .

I lied. I want to throw up.

Well, at least I'll be sick somewhere fabulous. The LAX hangar where the *Off-Key* party is being held is lit almost entirely with tall white beeswax candles, and the fake-palm-tree-bedecked dance floor is packed with people swaying to a Kanye West tune mixed by DJ-AM. Waiters are milling about the room dressed in Russian military uniforms, just like the one Mac steals to sneak onto the base where Katherine is being held captive. In a separate area is a piano bar where musicians are playing the same tunes Bo and Katherine practice during a scene in their Brooklyn loft.

Smack dab in the middle of the hangar, Liz and I are escorted to a reserved booth and given virgin "Macho Mac Margaritas." (Party planners think it's cute to come up with custom drinks named after the movie's stars. Tonight there's even a "Kaitlin Kola," which is vanilla-, raspberry-, and cherry-flavored Coke. It's actually pretty good.)

Nadine slides in the booth next to me. "Okay, I just saw your parents and Matt talking to Sandra Bullock," she murmurs, glancing around the room. "They should be making their way over here shortly. That is, unless Matt begs her to make *Miss Congeniality 3* with him as her costar."

I take another deep breath. "I can do this," I reassure Nadine and Liz. "What's the worst thing that can happen anyway?" An annoying laugh pierces my eardrum. The three of us turn to see where the noise is coming from and spot Sky and Trevor holding court with a reporter and camera crew from *Celeb Insider*.

"Um, that Sky overhears you and sets out to singlehandedly destroy your career?" Nadine offers brightly.

Liz nudges her. "That's *not* going to happen," she instructs us both.

"Of course not." I pluck the lime from my Macho Mac Margarita. "Sky's already got her tabloid story for the night." Liz and Nadine look confused. "Guys, how could you forget so quickly? Didn't you see me spill my popcorn all over her in the lobby? It's a good thing Trev was there to save her from my evil greasy clutches."

Liz giggles.

"I'm glad you two think this is funny." Nadine shakes her head. She stops suddenly and sits straight up in her seat. "Parental units, twelve o'clock," she whispers sharply. I look up and see my parents and Matt headed straight towards us.

"We just had the loveliest talk with Sandy Bullock," Mom announces as she slides into the booth. "She's a huge fan of *FA*. She said she hates summer Sunday nights because *FA* is in reruns. Sandy thinks you should have new episodes year-round."

"Maybe *then* Kaitlin could get me a part," Matt grumbles under his breath.

"Year-round?" Nadine repeats. "When would Kates have time to rest?" She steps on my foot a little too hard, considering she's wearing white Nine West stilettos. There's my segue.

"Time off is for people who don't have a hot career," Laney admonishes as she appears from behind a plastic palm tree. "Guess who I was just talking to?" We look at her dumbfounded. "Hutch Adams's agent," she shrills.

Hutch Adams. He's my absolute favorite director (not counting George Lucas, of course). All the big stars want to work with him. He does everything from smart dramas known for their witty dialogue to action-packed sci-fi fare with cyborgs and aliens — done the right way. I especially like *Seeing Is Believing* and *Rock On*. (I've forgiven him for doing *High Stakes Part Deux*.)

Mom squeals. "What did he say?"

"We were talking about Nobu," Laney starts off. "I said I had been there the other day with Sarah Jessica. We had her son James Wilkie with us, so we wanted something quiet for lunch. Asiade Cuba is just *too* loud. Anyway, Keith says he was just there with Hutchie and he's officially signed on to direct a sci-fi film for Wagman Brothers Studio. Are you ready for the best part?" Laney's French manicured fingernails tap the table dramatically. "The movie is shooting during hiatus and the lead is going to be a teenage girl! Kaitlin will *definitely* get an audition!"

"Oh my God," I whisper. My head spins. I've wanted to work with Hutch forever, but this hiatus? No, I can't audition . . . I *need* a break . . . Oh God I'm confused. This wasn't how my conversation was supposed to go at all. . . .

"What's the movie about?" Dad asks eagerly. "Do they need a producer?" He scratches the shiny bald spot on his head.

"The movie takes place in the distant future," Laney explains breathlessly, ignoring Dad's second question, "and it's about a young man and a woman who suddenly realize they're part of a government experiment. They're being bred to form a super-human race!"

"Have they cast the man, Laney?" Matt interjects. "I *love* sci-fi." Everyone starts talking at once.

"When does it start filming?" I ask quietly.

"June," Laney exclaims. "*Perfect timing.* Your press commitments will be done by then."

"A Hutch Adams project would be perfect for us, Kaitie-Kat," Dad says. "We need a strong vehicle this summer."

Hmm . . . I could still go to Clark all of March and April and be free to do pre-production work in May. My schedule would be clear if Hutch wants me. . . . Who am I kidding? I don't even have an audition! Hutch Adams probably doesn't know who I am. "Speaking of my press commitments" — I clear my throat, gripping my chair under the table — "I wanted to talk about the hectic schedule."

"What about it, Kate-kins?" Dad bites into a juicy crab cake. "Laney makes it and you do it. She's a machine, this girl." Dad pats me on the back. "The more work, the better!"

"Actually, Kaitlin was just telling me how tired she is," Liz says, nudging me.

"Did you?" Mom asks me impatiently. "Now's not the time to be tired. We're talking about Hutch Adams here. What *we've* wanted for a long time."

"Liz, that's crazy!" Laney chuckles. "It's not like Kaitlin's working twenty-four-seven. She's on a soap series, for God's sake."

Everyone laughs. Even Matt, who has no clue what he's laughing about.

"I *do* work hard," I try to speak up, but not so loudly that people in nearby booths will hear me. "And I'll keep working hard. But I need some time off." I sit up straight. "And I'm going to take some this hiatus."

It's so quiet I can hear the 50 Cent tune that's being mixed in the background.

"We shouldn't be talking about this in public," Dad grunts. He loosens the blue-checkered Armani tie around his neck. "The competition could be listening."

"No one can hear us over 50 Cent, Dad," I remind him. "Now's the perfect time to talk."

"Sweetie, you're just tired," Mom says. "You don't need to change your hiatus plans. We gave you a week off before your press starts. That's plenty of time!"

"It's not, Mom." I look her in the eye. I pause and glance at Laney and Dad. "I need some time to do what *I* want to do this hiatus; otherwise I'll get burnt out —"

"You're not getting burnt out." Laney cuts me off. "Are you?" Did a shadow of doubt just cross her sun-kissed face?

"I will be if you keep pushing me like this." I'm surprised at the confident sound of my own voice. I glance at Nadine. She nods her red head for me to keep going. "You guys can't decide everything for me. This is my career and I think the best thing for it right now, with all this tabloid garbage and the stuff with Sky, is to take a breather."

"A breather is code for retirement!" Mom gasps, clutching her chest. "You're not thinking of retiring, are you?

Because you have a three-year contract with *Family Affair*. You can't break that, Kaitlin, you just can't!" Matty rolls his eyes and fans her with his white linen napkin.

I want to remind Mom about Hollywood Secret Number Seven, but I think better of it. The word "retirement" doesn't exist in this town. Stars can be washed up, or overworked, or claim they want to spend the rest of their life sipping margaritas on St. Vincent — but they always have a shot at returning to the bright lights if they want it enough. Look at John Travolta. After a string of movies about talking babies, the guy did *Pulp Fiction* for peanuts and totally revived his career. I'm not worried about mine though. Two months off is not going to kill it.

"I'm not retiring," I say firmly. "I'm just taking two months off to . . ." Laney chokes on her Scotch (neat) and coughs explosively. "Go to school," I finish.

Everyone is quiet. Glasses clink as a waiter brings over a tray with Kaitlin Kolas. Mom grabs the Russian military officer's arm. "I'll have a sour apple martini. Make that two."

Dad blinks. "School? But . . . you study already. You have a tutor."

"No, Dad, I mean a *real* school," I correct him. "With classrooms and other kids. Not Monique and me perched in my dressing room summarizing evolution. I want a chance to be an ordinary teenager. I want to see what it's like to have homeroom, school dances, and gym class."

"And what are you going to do?" Matt snorts. "Just walk into the school and say, 'Hi, I'm Kaitlin Burke, I'd like to enroll here for a few months?' E! would be staking out the school in no time." My mother moans.

"That's right," Dad bellows. "You'd be too much of a distraction to the other students, Kaitie-kins."

"Shh!" Laney hisses, glancing around suspiciously.

"I already thought about that." I squeeze Liz's hand for support. "That's why I'm not enrolling as myself."

"Kaitlin, don't be silly," Mom shakes her platinum-blond head dismissively. "Just because you change your name doesn't mean people won't recognize you."

I open my mouth to speak and Laney cuts me off.

"Don't even say it! Don't even think it!" Laney shouts crazily. She seems to have forgotten where we are. And Laney *never* forgets that she's at an exclusive Hollywood party. "If you're thinking what I *think* you're thinking, it's suicide!"

I ignore her — for the first time ever. "Everyone: I'm going to go to school in disguise."

"What? What's she talking about?" my Dad asks Matt.

"Beats me," Matt mutters, and reaches for a mini filet mignon on crispy bread.

My mom narrows her green eyes at Nadine and Liz. "Did you two put her up to this?"

"Kaitlin, listen to me." Laney looks around the room again nervously. She grabs my hands in hers and holds my gaze fiercely. "I can't believe we're discussing this here. . . . Okay, look, I understand you're a teenager and you want to do normal teen stuff once in a while." I nod. "But now is not the time to disappear. You've got tabloid rumors plaguing your every move and a costar out for blood. Now is not the time for games! If someone catches wind that you're disguising yourself to go to school, they'll think you're doing it because you're unhappy with your work. If people start believing that, Kaitlin, you'll never get another role!"

"Laney, no one is going to find out." I stare into her eyes, which are wide with horror. "I'm not dropping off the face of the earth. I just want to do what I want for a change this hiatus. I promise I'm going to do my press as well, and be seen, and do everything."

Laney raises one razor-thin eyebrow doubtfully. "Well, how do you expect to do that?"

I look at Liz again, and then launch into my foolproof plan. My words tumble out so quickly that they don't even interrupt me, almost. How I'll only be going to class in March and April, all the while keeping my press commitments, which would be scheduled around classes. How I'll be enrolling as a sophomore at Liz's school, so I won't be going alone. How I plan on staying in the public eye and going to select events. Dad gets a little crazy about the security issue, but I reassure him by promising that Rodney will chaperone my trips to and from school. Laney's big concern is the disguise itself, so I tell her that she can have approval over it. That seems to calm her down. A little.

"I want Paul and Shelly to come on board and supervise your look," she demands. She runs her long fingers through her hair. "I can't believe I'm even entertaining this."

"You have to." Liz slurps her kola. "You work for *her*." I kick her under the table.

Laney purses her plump lips. The table is silent for a minute. "I'm going to be watching you like a hawk, Kaitlin," Laney finally mutters. "Remember that. But I'll support you as long as you promise you won't tell *anyone* who you really are."

"Why would I do that?" I ask. "Liz is the only one who will know."

"Who can guess why?" Laney says, narrowing her black eyes at Liz. "You could meet some guy and want to spill your life story, but I'm warning you, don't do it."

"I won't. I'll be too busy for guys anyway." I try to suppress a grin. Once Laney caves, Dad and Matt aren't far behind. I can't believe it. *They're all actually listening to me!* Everyone looks somewhat placated, except for Mom. "Mom?" I reach for her hand. "Say something."

She sighs and pulls her arm away. "I don't understand this, Kaitlin. I just don't. We do everything for this career and now you're . . . I don't know what you're doing."

"We'll keep up my social calendar," I reassure her. "You can talk to everyone in town about what parties I need to attend while I'm off, okay?"

She takes a big gulp of her martini. "I guess I do know about all the best events," she murmurs almost to herself. She says, playing with the olive in the bottom of her glass, "Okay. I'll say yes to this school diversion on one condition only — that you audition for the Hutch Adams movie."

I bite down hard on my lower lip. "I don't even know I'll *get* an audition," I start to protest.

"We'll worry about that." Mom looks at Laney and Dad. "But if you get the audition and the movie, you leave school. Got it?"

I would never turn down Hutch Adams. But the likelihood I'd get a part is slim. He'll probably cast some hot twentysomething actress who *looks* sixteen instead of hiring an actual teen. "Got it." I lean over and plant a kiss on her cheek. "Thank you!"

"At least she hasn't totally lost her mind," Laney growls. Mom slides her remaining martini over to Laney, and she drains the whole thing down in one gulp.

I can't believe it. *It's really happening!* I turn to Liz.

"What are you doing tomorrow?" I whisper.

"Nothing, it's Saturday," she whispers back. "Why?"

"We're going shopping." I can't stop smiling. "I need a whole new wardrobe for Clark Hall."

seven: *Makeover Central*

"Hello?" I mumble into my sparkly green cordless phone that was buried under my comforter.

"KAITLIN? ARE YOU AWAKE YET?" Laney shouts in my ear.

I turn over and look at my *Revenge of the Sith* alarm clock. It's 9:15 AM the morning after the *Off-Key* premiere.

"Um, yeah, I am now."

"GOOD, BECAUSE I JUST SPOKE TO YOUR NEW SCHOOL."

"Laney, why are you yelling?"

"I'M GOING THROUGH COLD WATER CANYON. THE PHONE IS BREAKING UP."

"Oh." I yawn. "Did you just say you spoke to Clark Hall?"

"YES. MRS. PEARSON, THE PRINCIPAL. YOUR MOM WANTED ME TO CALL AND EXPLAIN THE SITUA-TION. YOU START NEXT MONDAY AND ... HEY!" I hear Laney's car horn beep like mad. "THIS ISN'T SENIOR CITIZEN DAY! SPEED IT UP!"

"LANEY!" I shout into the phone, trying to get her attention. "Did you just say I start next week?" I can feel my stomach start to ache immediately. I don't have anything ready yet. No disguise, no clothes. No fake life story. "Next week?"

"YES. NEXT WEEK. NO TIME TO WASTE, KAITLIN. HUTCHIE'S MOVIE STARTS JUNE FIFTEENTH. DID YOU GET THE SCRIPT FROM YOUR AGENT YET?"

"You just told me about it last night."

"OH RIGHT. GET IT. I HEAR IT'S BRILLIANT."

"Okay." Now my heart is racing too. "But Laney, what did you tell this woman. Mrs. Who?"

"PEARSON. STRANGE WOMAN. WANTED YOUR TRANSCRIPTS AND TO TALK TO YOUR TUTOR, BUT OTHERWISE YOU'RE ALL SET. SHE SAID YOU CAN REGISTER UNDER ANOTHER NAME, GIVEN THE CIRCUMSTANCES, AND SHE'LL SIGN A CONFIDENTIALITY AGREEMENT. BELIEVE ME; SHE'LL BE SORRY IF SHE BREAKS IT."

I'll bet. "Okay."

"GO STRAIGHT TO HER OFFICE NEXT MONDAY MORNING. GET THERE BY EIGHT. SCHOOL'S OUT THIS WEEK FOR SPRING RECESS, BUT I TOLD HER WE'D CALL AND LET HER KNOW YOUR NEW ALIAS AND . . ." I hear tires screeching in the background. "WATCH WHERE YOU'RE GOING! DON'T YOU KNOW YOU SHOULD SIGNAL WHEN YOU CHANGE LANES?"

"Thanks, Laney."

"YEAH, WELL, I DON'T LIKE THIS, AND YOU'RE *STILL*

DOING PRESS. *THE TONIGHT SHOW* TAPES NEXT WEDNESDAY, BY THE WAY. NADINE IS PREPARING THE REST OF YOUR SCHEDULE AS WE SPEAK BECAUSE IT'S GOING TO BE REALLY BUSY AND YOU'RE GOING TO HAVE TO JUGGLE BOTH KAITLIN, NO . . ."

"Laney?" I hear a dial tone.

I lie down again and pull the soft down comforter over my head. Just as I close my eyes, the door creaks open.

"Kaitlin, get up."

It's Liz. She pulls my warm down blanket off me.

"Hey," I say, yawning. "What are you doing here?"

"What am I doing here? What are *you* doing in bed? We have a ton of work to do!" Liz sits down next to me, bouncing on the mattress. "You said you wanted to go shopping."

"Yeah, but Fred Segal doesn't open till ten," I gripe.

"Fred Segal? You aren't wearing anything from Fred Segal," Liz corrects me, jumping up. "Nadine is out at Discount World right now picking some clothes up."

"Discount World?" I bite my lip. "I didn't know Discount World sells . . . clothes."

"Yep, apparently so." Liz rummages for my robe in my still-packed luggage. She finds it and pulls it out. "Here, throw this on. Everyone is waiting downstairs. We're going to create the new you."

Wow, for people who wanted no part of my idea, they sure got on board quickly. I throw on the green robe and slide into my fuzzy slippers. I can't help smiling.

"What are you grinning at?" Liz asks.

"You. Laney. Mom. You're . . . all . . . so . . ."

"So . . . ?"

"Supportive," I say. "I guess I'm just surprised."

"We just don't want you to fall on your face," Liz explains bluntly.

"Well, thanks, I think," I say wryly.

As we walk downstairs, I can hear the commotion already. Paul's loud voice can be heard over everyone.

"NO . . . NO GOOD . . . NOPE. UGH . . . TOO PAMELA ANDERSON."

Liz and I walk into the kitchen and see Shelly holding up several wigs. Paul and my mom are standing on the other side of the glass table nixing them one by one. Wigs, clothes, makeup, and hair supplies clutter the tile floor and marble kitchen island. The group sees me standing there and looks up.

"Hi, sweetie," Mom chirps. She looks at her watch. "Wow, you really slept late this morning."

"It's nine-thirty," I protest.

"We've been down here an hour already."

I look at Liz. She rolls her eyes and yawns without covering her mouth. That's when I notice Liz is still in her comfy white drawstring karate pants. She only wears those to class or bed.

"Your mom called us all last night," Shelly explains. She looks amused, her round gray eyes twinkling. "She told us about your *emergency*."

"Well, it certainly is an emergency, isn't it, sweetie?" Mom grabs my arm and leads me towards the stool by Paul. She's wearing a pink PB&J Couture sweat suit and looks a little flushed. "We don't want you to make a fool of yourself next week," she adds.

"Mom, everything is going to be fine, I promise."

"Right, right. Did you talk to Laney?" she asks, still clutching my arm.

"Yes."

"She told you about the principal?"

"Yes."

"And the Hutch Adams script?"

"Yes," I sigh.

"What about . . ."

"Um, Mrs. Burke, why don't we show Kaitlin what we have for her to try on?" Liz suggests gently.

"Oh, right. Paul? Shelly?" Mom says distractedly. "Want to get Kaitlin started?"

Paul slides the wrought-iron stool over and I take a seat.

"Let me just say that despite the fact that I'm up early on my first day off in two weeks, I think this is a fabulous idea," Paul coos, as he brushes out my frizzy hair.

"You do?" I question.

"Yes, because now we *finally* get to have fun with you." Paul twirls my stool around. "No more dullsville. Shell, grab the wigs."

Shelly brings an overflowing box of rainbow-colored wigs over.

"We already started to go through them, sweetie," Shelly

tells me. "We need something that won't stick out like a sore thumb." Shelly holds up a pile of blond wigs perfect for a drag queen. "These, for example, won't do."

"What length do you want, Kates?" Liz asks.

"I don't know." I twirl a strand of my waist-length honey-colored hair around my finger. "Same as now? What do you think, Mom? Redhead or brunette?"

"Brunette, sweetie. Redheads are a passing phase." Mom grabs a long brown wig with huge curls. "Look how pretty this is."

"Very Julia Roberts." Paul nods approvingly.

"Too adult," I argue.

"What about this one?" Shelly holds up a shoulder-length brown wig with blond highlights. The hair is pin-straight and smooth.

"Who would have time to iron their hair like that in the morning?" I ask. I mean, I would for *FA*, but normal people don't see their hairstylist every morning, right?

"Girls at our school do," says Liz. "Some get their hair blown out before class in the morning."

I shake my head. "No, no. I want something plain. I don't want to stand out."

"Yeah, because it so stinks to look like movie star royalty," Liz comments dryly.

I ignore the dig and start rummaging through the box. On the bottom, I find a short, straight brown wig. It's set in a bob. "What about this one?"

Paul frowns, then takes it from my hands, holding the

wig out in front of him as if it's a piece of trash. He helps me put the wig on and shows me how to pin my own hair back so that it fits under the skull cap I'll have to wear. The wig fits pretty snugly, which is good. I turn around and look at everyone.

"Well?"

No one looks happy.

"It's mousy," Mom pouts.

I look in the mirror that Shelly holds up for me. My face framed with short brown hair stares back.

"It's perfect." I smile at my unfamiliar mirror image.

"I kind of like it," Liz pronounces. "Very Natalie Portman in *Closer*."

Shelly eyes me carefully. She walks over and plays with some strands of the wig. "It's so *not* you. This could work, Meg," she tells my mom.

"I guess." Mom looks at me glumly. So does Paul.

"Paul, I'm not supposed to be glamorous. We don't want anyone to know who I am," I remind him.

"Whatev." He's not looking at me.

"I'll tell you what," I offer. "You can style me however you want for *The Tonight Show* next week."

"Anything I want?" he asks. "Even hair extensions?"

"Yes, anything," I laugh. "Now what's next?"

"Well, as dull as your hair looks, I can still tell it's you," says Shelly. She scrutinizes me. "Hmm . . . let's try some contacts. If we're going for wallflower, then we've got to cover those beautiful green eyes of yours." She pulls out a box of contacts and hands me a lens. It takes me a few minutes, but I finally get one in. I look in the mirror. One brown and one green eye stare back at me. I pop the other lens in and turn around.

"Well?"

Everyone crowds around to get a better look.

"You look boooring," Paul moans.

Liz tilts her head to the side. "It's pretty convincing."

"You really can't tell it's me?" I ask excitedly. "Maybe we should try this disguise out." I head towards the door.

Shelly blocks my path. "We're not done yet. Try these." She puts a pair of thick oval tortoise-shell glasses on my face. Everyone *oohs*.

"Now you definitely can't tell it's you!" Shelly exclaims incredulously.

"You kind of look like Jen Garner did on *Alias* — when she was having an ugly disguise day," Paul utters slowly. I hope that's a compliment.

I look at Mom and Liz.

"You look . . . ," Mom starts.

". . . like a nerd," Liz finishes flatly.

I grab Shelly's mirror. With the short straight hair, brown eyes, and glasses, I do look geeky. Nothing like myself.

"I like this look," I say defensively.

"Yeah, but you do want people to like you, right?" Liz twirls a strand of her shiny curly hair. "I have to be your friend! What are people going to think of me?" Paul snorts.

The front door slams shut. "I'm back," Nadine yells, striding into the kitchen with several thin Pepto Bismol pink plastic bags that have DISCOUNT WORLD stamped on them. She sets them down on the table. "I did *amazing*. I got, like, eight outfits for a hundred dollars."

"Child, the shirt I'm wearing costs more than that," Paul cries, thumbing his button-down gray silk Dolce and Gabbana shirt. "What did you buy her? Polyester?"

"Yep." Nadine smiles and holds up a long-sleeved plain white V-neck top and a cheap-looking purple pleated mini-skirt with a vinyl belt. Yikes.

"Does Kaitlin have to look ... well ... poor?" Mom demands, wrinkling her forehead with worry.

I take the shiny black belt gingerly and try to buckle it around my waist. The plastic doesn't have a lot of give. I won't say it out loud, but I have to agree with Mom. Does anyone *really* dress like this? "Does this look okay?" I look down at my waist skeptically.

Nadine's eyes narrow darkly. "You look fine." She walks over and adjusts the belt so that it sits higher on my waist. "Plenty of people shop at Discount World. You can get some pretty good things there if you look hard enough."

"I guess you didn't look hard enough," Paul mumbles.

Nadine ignores him. "Clark Hall is a melting pot for kids from all over L.A.," she explains firmly. "Some people are going to dress really well because they have money and others are going to be dressed in outfits ten times worse than this one. Right, Liz?"

Liz frowns. "Yeah," she replies slowly, "but I don't hang

out with anyone dressed like this. I have a reputation to keep up."

"And what type of reputation is that?" Shelly asks.

Liz takes the question seriously and considers for a minute. "My friends aren't as rich as Kaitlin and I, because even though I have dough, I hate when people think they're better than everyone else because of it. But my friends do have taste in clothing."

"I think you should hang out with the rich kids, sweetie," Mom advises. "You wouldn't have to buy a thing —"

"The Discount World clothes are perfect for Kaitlin," Nadine interrupts. "We want her to fly below the radar. If she's too rich and wears her own high-end clothes, she stands out. Too trashy and she won't have any friends. The middle is the same clothes most of America wears. Like me." Nadine smiles pointedly at Mom.

That sounds reasonable to me. "Can I wear some stuff from the Gap too?" I suggest. "Gap ads are in all the magazines. They're like a symbol of normalcy."

"She could have a rich grandmother who sends her nice clothes," Mom offers.

"Express, Limited, New York and Company," Shelly rattles off the clothing stores. "That's where the new you would shop."

"Aren't those places in the mall?" Mom shrieks. If she ever shopped in malls, she's forgotten about it. She looks like she might faint.

"Mom, think of it as costumes for my greatest role," I suggest gently.

"Okay." Her face crumples.

"There's one thing we won't be able to change." I point at my fuzzy green slippers. "My freakishly big feet."

"That's for sure," Paul says with a smirk. "I hope Discount World carries size nine shoes." I punch him in the arm.

"Well, I'll tell you one thing," Liz mutters. "No one will mistake you for vintage queen Kaitlin Burke with this wardrobe."

I love that no one will care what designer I'm wearing. It takes a lot of pressure off.

HOLLYWOOD SECRET NUMBER EIGHT: No matter how many squillions you make on a movie, you can't afford to buy a new outfit for every event under the sun. The majority of your wardrobe is borrowed. The only problem is that sometimes you'll go searching through your closet for that Marc Jacobs black tweed pencil skirt only to realize you don't actually own it.

"What about a name?" Liz points out. "Did you think of one?"

"Yes," I say. "Rachel Rogers from that Disney Channel movie *Mission Aborted*. I liked that character. Plus, I played a British spy so I can do an accent."

Liz looks at me smartly. "Okay, the film was cheesy, but the experience is about to pay off."

"Can you do a convincing British accent?" Paul questions skeptically.

"'Cuse me. Do you know where Mr. Hammond's flat might be?" I pronounce in my best British prose. "I'm new here."

"Not bad." Shelly nods. "Not bad at all."

"Well, now that we've got your disguise worked out, I'll come up with where you lived, went to school, parents' names, and all that jazz, and print you up a report tomorrow. You can memorize it before school next week." Nadine grabs her bible and begins furiously scribbling notes.

"Aww, look how happy our princess is." Paul smiles broadly as I grin ear to ear.

"I *am* happy," I admit giddily. "This is going to be fun." I pull out my Sidekick.

Saturday 2/28
NOTES TO SELF:
Call Seth about Hutch Adams script.
Buy jeans at the Gap.
Have Nadine go 2 B&N. Buy books on London 2 brush up on Britain (i.e. Tony Blair is the Prime Minister. The Osbournes R so over. Guy and Madonna R still hot.)
Practice accent ("Jolly" means good. "Bugger" is bad.)
BUY NEW NOTEBOOKS! GET PENS!

eIGHT: *Clark Hall*

"Principal Pearson will see you now, Rachel." Clark Hall's school secretary points to the principal's office.

I take a deep breath and step forward. I don't think I was this nervous the day I met Brad Pitt!

I've only been at Clark Hall for fifteen minutes and already I need another swab of Bliss Underarmy antiperspirant. Rodney dropped me off at school early so that I would have a few minutes to poke around, but even with the map Liz drew me I got completely lost.

This place is *huge*. On *FA*, the local school we shoot at is a quaint old schoolhouse from the '20s. Clark Hall, on the other hand, is a sprawling campus, with five vine-covered brick buildings and outdoor walkways brimming with daffodils and roses. There are connecting archways that cover rows of shiny silver lockers, and what looks like a large outdoor patio full of shaded teak wood tables and chairs. After walking around aimlessly, since Liz wasn't answering my texts, I bumped into a gardener pruning roses. He steered me to the main office. I forgot to thank him before running off.

Today I've got my wig firmly glued to my scalp, my contacts in, and my glasses on. I think I look almost cute in my boot-cut dark denim Gap jeans, simple white button-down shirt, and slightly itchy polyester red sweater vest. But I feel like I stick out like a sore thumb.

"I don't know what you're worried about," Nadine had reassured me last night. I was trying my "first day of school outfit" on for the fifteenth time. "You *really* can't tell it's you. And you know I would tell you if I thought you could."

I know she would. All week long Mom, Dad, Nadine, Laney, and Liz grilled me on my knowledge of Great Britain, my family history, and why my parents moved to the States. (We're saying my dad is a visiting professor at UCLA. So I'm strapped for cash.) Everyone was supportive except Matt, who still thought I was insane. "Maybe they'll want to keep a Burke on *FA* after your career tanks," he said one night as I was practicing my accent. "Then they can just hire me instead."

"Come in, Rachel," a cheery voice calls as I open Principal Pearson's door. "I've been expecting you." A short, heavy-set woman with graying black hair lumbers towards me. She's wearing a red polka-dot dress that is too snug around the waist, reminding me of Mrs. Claus.

"Come in! Come in!" She pushes a weathered brown leather chair out so I can sit. "Mara, hold my calls," she yells to her secretary. She slams the door, rattling the framed merits hanging on the wall behind her, and takes a seat behind a cluttered mahogany desk. For a minute, all she does is stare.

"Kaitlin? Is that really you?" Principal Pearson finally asks.

"Actually, it's Rachel," I reply in a perfect British accent. "Cheerio."

Principal Pearson laughs and claps her hands wildly. "Wow! I never would have guessed." *Thank goodness.* One person down. Nine hundred and sixty-four to go.

"Sam! In the principal's office!" Principal Pearson continues. "That would *never* happen on *Family Affair.*" She chuckles loudly.

"No, I guess not," I agree. "Listen, thanks so much for letting me enroll, Principal Pearson."

Principal Pearson doesn't answer. She's staring again.

"Wait a minute! Sam did go to the principal's office once," she exclaims, her gray eyes open wide. "She went with Paige and Dennis to talk about Sara breaking into the guy's locker room." She claps her hands again and laughs.

Wow, this woman is a *Family* Fanatic. (That's what we call our über fans.)

"Um, is there anything I should know before I start classes today?" I try to steer us back on course.

"You need your class schedule," she remembers. She rummages through the papers on her desk and then holds one out to me. "Here it is. Your first class is beginner French with Mrs. Desmond." I take the schedule from her as a bell rings in the hallway.

"That's the warning bell for first period," Principal Pearson tells me. "We should get you out of here." She stands.

I smile weakly and grab my black messenger bag. I don't want to be late for my first class. "Thank you, Principal Pearson —," I begin, but she cuts me off.

"But before you go, I just want to say, I'm so glad you chose Clark Hall for this experience. I can't tell you what it means to me to have Sam walking our hallowed hallways, even if you don't look anything like her. And of course, I hope you will feel comfortable coming to me if you have any problems." I nod. Another bell rings, but Principal Pearson ignores it. "I told Laney that my lips are sealed, of course. I'm such a big fan of the show."

I smile and try to squeeze past her to the door. I assume that was the final bell and I don't even know where I'm going yet. "Well, I'm glad you're a fan." I try to smile sweetly. "Was that the final bell? I don't want to be late."

She nods, but doesn't move out of the doorway. I'm not used to walking away from a fan without Rodney here to guide me, so I'm unsure how to excuse myself.

"Do you think — Rachel — from time to time I could ask you about the show?" Principal Pearson suggests, blinking nervously. "I'm such a big fan and I'm so excited about the finale. I can't wait for Krystal's wedding! I could swear she's pregnant and I just need to know."

"Um, yeah, I'll be happy to fill you in, Principal Pearson, but maybe later?" I try to sound gentle. "After class?"

"Oh, no one will mind that you're late on the first day," she assures me. "I just have to ask you about last week's episode." She stares at me expectantly.

I lower my heavy messenger bag onto the hardwood floor. This could take a while.

"What is the deal with Penelope?" Principal Pearson asks breathlessly. "Is she really Paige's long-lost twin? In season three, Penelope died in a helicopter crash. There was no body, but I assumed it had been incinerated."

I quickly spill HOLLYWOOD SECRET NUMBER NINE: In the soap world, anything that happens can be reversed. Characters can come back from the dead, find out they have long-lost children or meet an evil twin. No plot twist is too far-fetched if it will help boost ratings. Since the actress playing Penelope decided to come back to the show, *FA* resurrected her character. After another ten minutes of intense discussion about Paige's birth mother, I look at my watch. It's 8:45. I'm already a half hour late.

"I should really be going, Principal Pearson," I murmur.

"Oh right. Okay, yes, dear, move along." She sounds disappointed. I get the feeling she could chat about *FA* all day if I let her. "Mrs. Desmond's room is in South Hall."

I grab the weathered brass doorknob and race out of the office. It's not until I reach the outdoor corridor, which is pretty much deserted, that I remember: I have no clue how to get to South Hall. I quickly scan the lush green lawn and spot that gardener again.

"Sorry to bother you, but where is South Hall?" I ask breathlessly with my British accent. He points. "Thanks, sir!" I yell, and run through two stone archways. Room 114 is at the opposite end of the building.

I throw open the door and dash inside, knocking into the teacher. Yikes.

Two dozen students take their eyes off the projector screen they're watching and look at me curiously. They're seated at rows of long puke-green-plastic-topped tables taking notes, some students using laptops. The scene is quite different from *FA*, where Sam and Sara sit on plush suede couches for class and have lively discussions with their jeans-clad teachers. Come to think of it, I don't think we even take notes.

"You must be Rachel," Mrs. Desmond says, arranging her disheveled red curls.

I pause. Think, Kaitlin. "Um, yeah." I look around the room nervously and adjust my glasses. Please don't let anyone realize it's me.

"Charming entrance," she remarks sharply, fixing her crisp white linen shirt and denim skirt. "Let's start over. Principal Pearson said you're a first-year French student, oui?" She blocks my path to the nearest table as she towers over me in her black pumps. I can't help but notice this young teacher is wearing too much of my favorite Chanel perfume.

"Yes. I mean, oui," I stutter. "Sorry. I'm just out of breath. This place is *mammoth*. How do you get around without a map?" A guy laughs in the back.

"Well, Rachel, I don't stand for tardiness in my class." She ignores my question and walks towards the far side of the room, which is decorated with a poster of the Eiffel Tower and French word charts. "*Especially* on someone's first day. So before you take a seat, why don't you tell us a little about yourself? In French, of course."

Oh God. I try to stare at the picture of the Notre Dame Cathedral on the back wall to calm my nerves, but I notice some students in the back row instead. A matchstick-thin brunette smirks at me and whispers something to the tall platinum blonde next to her. They both giggle. The cute sandy-haired guy next to her, who's wearing a Clark Hall lacrosse jersey, rolls his eyes.

"Jolly good." I try not to be discouraged. I quickly smooth out my itchy vest, then begin. "Uh, *Je m'appelle Rachel.*"

"*Bonjour, Rachel,*" Mrs. Desmond says encouragingly. "*Ça va?*"

That means "How are you?" Uh . . . "*Ça va bien,*" I answer. I can feel the sweat beginning to form on my forehead. The longer I stand here, the greater the chance someone will figure out who I am.

"*Bien,*" Mrs. Desmond continues. "*D'où venez-vous?*"

I think she just asked where I'm from. Mrs. Desmond taps her high-heeled foot impatiently.

"Oh, sorry." I blush. "I'm a little out of it. I'm still on London time," I explain nervously. "Um, *Je viens de Grande-Bretagne.*"

"*Grande-Bretagne!*" Mrs. Desmond exclaims. "Class, that means 'Great Britain.'"

"As if we couldn't have figured that out by her accent," the lacrosse guy calls out. Everyone around him laughs, including that leggy blonde, who lets out a fake-sounding shrill. "Austin, you're *so* funny," I hear her say.

Mrs. Desmond frowns at him. *"Rachel, avec qui êtes-vous?"*

Geez, Monique and I are still doing vocabulary words and verb conjugation! I haven't had to really hold a conversation yet. I'm good at accents, not languages. I look at Mrs. Desmond helplessly.

"Rachel?" she repeats. *"Avec qui êtes-vous?"*

Hmm . . . Monique always asks me about the weather after I tell her where I'm from. This must be a weather question. I'll just say it's a nice day. I know how to say that. *"Il fait beau,"* I respond.

The class laughs. Are all these kids geniuses? What did Mrs. Desmond ask me?

"Rachel, I asked whom you were visiting the U.S. with," Mrs. Desmond explains patiently.

"Oh, my parents," I say quickly.

"In French!" Mrs. Desmond scolds.

"Wait. Can I start over? Ask me how to get the library," I blurt in a panic. "I know the answer to that question really well!" The lacrosse guy laughs again. He's getting on my nerves.

Mrs. Desmond glances at the clock. "Oh, never mind. We don't have the time. You may take a seat."

I can feel my face burning as I walk towards the nearest desk. I plop down wearily. Auditioning for Steven Spielberg would have been easier than that.

"Did you see her vest?" I hear someone whisper. I wish Liz and I had all the same classes. I need some backup here.

"I guess the British aren't known for their taste in clothes," Someone else hisses. Ouch. How rude.

"Cut it out, Lori," a guy's voice says.

"Austin? Is there something you want to share with the rest of us?" Mrs. Desmond demands, turning around from her blackboard.

"No, Mrs. D," he answers. I don't turn around.

The rest of the class blurs by. My Sidekick vibrates several times, but I ignore it. Mrs. Desmond talks so fast I can barely keep up writing notes. When the bell finally rings at the end of class, I'm the first one out of my seat. I've got to find Principal P. Maybe she'll let "Sam" drop French. . . .

"Hey, you dropped your la book," a deep voice calls after me.

I turn around. A pair of gorgeous wide turquoise eyes meet mine. I jump back. Oh. It's that rude lacrosse guy.

"You mean 'mon livre,'" I say grumpily, and snatch it from his hand. It's a dumb joke that could be kind of cute if it weren't coming from him.

"Whatever you say." He grins. "So you're from London, huh?"

"Hey, Austin," someone in the hallway calls. Another guy punches his shoulder as he passes by. "Great game yesterday, man."

"Listen; don't sweat Mrs. D, okay?" Austin tells me. "She's

harmless. I was the new kid last year and she put me on la stage my first day too." I just nod and try to shoot daggers at him with my green — oops, brown — eyes. Why's he pretending to be nice? He just made fun of me in class!

"I have to go," I grunt. I attempt to maneuver around him, trying not to touch his muscular arm, and I bump into someone else.

"There you are, A. I've been *waiting*," the girl whines in a nasal voice. I recognize her as the blond sitting next to Austin in French class. The girl's platinum hair is blown out pin straight and she's wearing a brown-and-pink-tweed Chanel jumper, which I *know* is from last season's collection because I have the very same one.

"We're going to be late to the next class," she says, looming over me and tapping the toe of her knee-high black leather boot. I notice she's practically the same height as Austin in those stiletto heels. Is this school populated by giants or something?

"This is my girlfriend, Lori," Austin says. "Lori, did you meet, um . . ." His face goes blank. He runs his fingers through his sandy blond mop top. I notice his arm hair is bleached blond, probably from the sun. Not that I care or anything. "Sorry, what was your name again?"

"A, did you hear me?" Lori whines, not even acknowledging me. "We're late. Swing by my Beamer and grab my cheerleading uniform. I need it for practice."

Eww. I so don't like either of them. "Nice meeting you guys," I state flatly, and walk away.

"Catch you later," Austin yells. I ignore him and rush down the hall. Great, now I'm late for second period. Why didn't Liz tell me to steer clear of the jocks at this school?

Thankfully Mr. Hanson doesn't give me a hard time in trigonometry: I'm a whiz at math. I make it to third period on time, but cause a scene when I leave my desk during class. Who knew you had to ask for permission to go to the bathroom? My history teacher, Mr. Klein, seems to think this is a universal law and I get a lecture on how the hall pass works.

Liz never told me how many notes you have to take. My tutor, Monique, usually just hands me printouts in my dressing room. She doesn't stand in front of a blackboard and make me write down inverse trigonometric functions, the evolution of apes, or French verb conjugations. I hear my Sidekick go off yet again and pull it out when Mr. Klein isn't looking.

POWERGRL82: Where have U been? Meet me @ the caf in 10.
PRINCESSLEIA25: Where is the caf????

Liz doesn't answer. When the bell rings, I wander into the hall and look around. The greasy smell of french fries hits me so I move in that direction.

The cafeteria is in North Hall. Right away I notice it re-sembles a mall food court we shot at once for *FA*. There are stir fry, pasta, deli, and tossed salad stations. Large refrigera-tors house drinks. There's a frozen yogurt bar, too. It's huge.

"Hey." Liz grabs me by the arm as I stand there in disbe-lief. She's wearing an acid green-and-yellow head scarf, a cute black tank that says DIVA in crystals, and a beige peasant skirt. On someone else it might look like a ridiculous hodgepodge, but on Liz it's perfect. "Rachel, right?" Liz grins mischievously. We've had our "first" meeting planned all week.

"I'm sorry, I forgot your name . . . Rebecca?" I ask.

"Liz." She turns to a short African American girl and a lanky brunette wearing jeans and a CABO RULES tee. "Guys, this is the girl from London I told you about," Liz says. "I ran into her at the main office this morning." They both smile at me. It's a relief to finally see some friendly faces. "This is Beth." Liz points to the short girl. "And Allison." She motions to the brunette.

"London, huh?" Allison chimes in. "Have you ever met Prince William?"

"Um, no," I answer, clearing my throat, "but he is a cute bloke."

"Bloke," Allison repeats, elbowing Beth so hard that she drops the black wire-rim glasses she's cleaning. "I love it!"

"You should sit with us for lunch," Beth suggests, picking up her tortoise-shell frames. She cleans the glasses with the edge of the simple cream-colored V-neck sweater she's wearing with wine-colored corduroy pants. I think Nadine bought me the same pair at the Limited. "Allison and I will grab a table on the patio and Liz can show you around the caf," she adds. "Lizzie, grab us some roast beef sandwiches and two Cokes." Liz nods.

As soon as Beth and Allison walk away, I spill the details about my morning to Liz. "Mrs. Pearson is like this freaky *FA* fan, and you didn't warn me that I need a hall pass to go to the bathroom," I whisper as Liz hands me a lunch tray and we get in line at the deli counter. "I messed up my French verbs in Mrs. Desmond's class, and she made me get up and introduce myself in French. In French! People laughed at me."

"Don't worry about it," Liz whispers back as the line moves forward. "Tuna salad, chicken, roast beef, or peanut butter and jelly?"

"You don't have cracked peppermill Boar's Head turkey?" I ask, surveying the deli meats. "Cal always stocked that for me."

"Sorry, your highness. We don't have a craft services guy here. Why don't I order you a chicken sandwich and you can grab me a sparkling water from the refrigerator."

I take my empty tray and walk over to the drinks. There's tons of soda, but no Fiji water. I reach for the lone Poland Spring sparkling water with lime, but someone else grabs it first.

"Sorry," a girl in a short red-and-white cheerleading uniform spits before walking away. I'm tempted to snatch it right out of her hand, but I resist.

"Got everything?" Liz comes over to me.

I reach inside my black mesh messenger bag for my wallet and then remember: I didn't bring one. Rodney or Nadine always grabs lunch for me, so I'm not used to carrying my own cash. "I forgot my wallet," I admit sheepishly.

Liz shakes her head. "I'll pay," she tells me. "Let's move. We only have forty-five minutes." We grab our trays and head out to the sun-soaked deck. Liz maneuvers past several tables, saying hi to people along the way.

"You know everybody, huh?" I comment as we set our trays down next to Beth and Allison. They've found us a shady table near the edge of the concrete patio.

"On the patio she does," Beth answers. "Not everyone sits outside."

I'm confused. "What do you mean? You have assigned seating?" The whole Clark cafeteria scene is foreign to me. On *FA*, Sam and Sara always lunch off-campus at Becca's Bistro.

"No," Allison clarifies before taking a bite of her roast beef sandwich. "But it's hard to come by a table out here unless you have some pull."

"Ah, you mean popular people." A light bulb goes on in my head.

"Usually the athletes hang out here," Liz explains. "Espe-

cially the lacrosse and football players. They get priority seating because Clark wins so many state championships . . ."

". . . which makes the alumni eager to keep giving Clark
money . . ." adds Allison.

". . . and allows more of us to come here on full scholar-
ships," Beth finishes, nodding towards Allison and herself.

"So who sits inside then?" I ask, thinking of how things
work at *FA*'s Summerville High, "blokes who want to study
and club kids who hate the sun?"

"Pretty much," Liz agrees. "You forgot the Anime Club.
We have one of those too."

Beth motions to a table behind us crowded with kids
who are all wearing way too much cheap makeup and greasy
hair products. "That's the drama students," she explains.
"They're guaranteed a table because everyone loved their
version of *Hairspray*. Then there's the class reps." She motions to a group of people bent over books in the corner.
"They run the student government, belong to the debate
team, write for the school newspaper . . ."

"Sounds like they'll be running the country one day," I
joke. "What about you guys?"

"We go with the flow," Liz replies.

Beth laughs. "Liz means, *she* goes with the flow," Beth says.
"Everyone loves Liz because she chairs the dance commit-
tees. I don't have time for that stuff. I'm a mother's helper
in Brentwood three days a week. I love kids, even the
spoiled ones!"

"And I can't be bothered with school activities," Allison says, rolling her light brown eyes. "I'm in the Santa Rosita Dance Academy. I dance hip-hop and I also study ballet, so I have practice five days a week."

"But Liz ropes us into decorating for school dances," Beth laughs. "Watch out, Rachel. She'll be signing you up for the Spring Fling committee before you know it."

Dance committee, school paper — those are things I could see myself doing — if I had the time. So I lie, "I was part of the dance committee at my old school."

"Well, you're welcome to hang with us then." Beth smiles. "We wouldn't want to see you get recruited into the Brainstormers Club or anything. Sometimes the math folk try to brainwash new students into thinking *they're* the hip quotient, instead of the other way around."

I laugh. "I'm glad you warned me." I look at the tables around us, since we're seated in the middle of the patio. "So do you usually get this prime of a location?"

"We're not *that* popular," Liz quips. "Usually Lori's gang snags the shady table. Where are they today?"

"Cheerleading tryouts at lunch," Allison says. "So the table was empty."

"Wait, did you say Lori?" I ask. "Is she a whiny tall blond cheerleader?"

"Yeah," Beth chuckles. "That's the one."

I shudder and quickly explain what happened this morning in French class. "She and Austin were so rude." I shake my head sadly.

"Austin? Austin Meyers?" Liz echoes. "He was rude to you?"

"Chad Michael Murray clone?" Allison questions. I nod, taking a salt-and-vinegar chip from the bag Allison holds out to me.

"He's, like, the nicest guy in school!" Beth sounds surprised too. "What did he do?"

"He laughed at me," I offer meekly. "Then he . . ." I replay what happened in my mind, "handed me my book when I dropped it rushing out of class."

"Yeah, sounds really rude," Liz retorts. The three of them explain that Austin moved from New York to Los Angeles last year. He's the captain of the lacrosse team, on the honors list, coaches Little League baseball, and tutors elementary school kids from the inner city. He sounds too perfect, if you ask me.

"Are you sure he was laughing at you?" Beth adds. "Maybe it was just Lori. Her I could believe."

"I don't know what he sees in her," Allison remarks, checking her face in the compact she just pulled from her olive green messenger bag. She pulls out some Mark concealer and dabs it on her freckles.

"I heard they were fighting at Stacy Weinberger's party last weekend," Beth confides, leaning in close to the table so that no one around us can hear.

"He really picked up your book and handed it to you?" Allison repeats. "And tried to talk to you?" I nod again. She sighs. "I wish he'd talk to me."

I laugh.

"You didn't think he was cute?" Liz asks incredulously.

"I didn't really notice," I lie. The three of them groan. "Besides" — I grin, looking directly at Liz — "I'm not in the States for the guys. I'm here to learn."

"Aren't we all," Liz says dryly.

nine: *School Daze*

Monday 3/8
NOTES TO SELF:
Reread Hutch script 1 last time. Could it really B that amazing???
Work on Civil War paper. Due in 2 wks!

Monday 3/15
NOTES TO SELF:
Leno pre-interview w/ Kat Simcock. Tues. 10:15. Ask Principal P 2 use her phone. Bring autographed FA shirt as bribe.
MUST WORK ON CW PAPER (DUE IN 1 WEEK!)
Call back Seth Meyers. He called 2 x.

Friday 3/19
NOTES TO SELF:
Call Seth Meyers. Again.
Ask Nadine 2 research British hot spots (Where does Wills hang?)

Buy Hello! and OK

CW PAPER DUE ON MONDAY!! (Beg Nadine 4 help.)

I'd like to kiss the person who invented the Sidekick. My poor little machine is working overtime trying to contain the pieces of my "double life," as Nadine calls it. I've written more "Notes to Self" the three weeks I've been at Clark Hall than I have in the year since I got the thing. But what choice do I have? I'm not used to running my life without an assistant's help and there isn't much Nadine can do for me when I'm sitting in a classroom. ("This is what you always wanted," she chided when I whined about my Civil War paper. "You're a *real* girl now with homework and deadlines. Isn't it fun?")

HOLLYWOOD SECRET NUMBER TEN: Schoolwork is infinitely easier when you're being tutored on set. I'm not saying you don't have quizzes and term papers, but a tutor is a lot more understanding about deadlines. "Monique, I have my big kidnapping scene on Friday. Can I have till Monday to write an essay on *To Kill a Mockingbird?*" And just like that, I have an extension. That would never happen at Clark Hall. Even Sara's creative homework excuses on *FA* — mother overdosed on sleeping pills, grandfather having an affair, family mansion in Majorca on fire — would not fly here.

That's why I owe Mr. Klein an extra credit essay for turning in my Civil War paper a day late. It was either do the *Hollywood Nation* interview Laney set up or finish my paper on time. Laney is scarier than Mr. Klein any day.

I reread Mr. Klein's note:

Rachel, since your paper was tardy, I suggest you bring up your overall grade by completing another assignment. It's outlined below. – Mr. K

HISTORY EXTRA-CREDIT: In a 1,000-word essay, describe an unforgettable moment in American history.

Do you think *Family Affair*'s highly anticipated season finale counts?

After turning my paper in late this week, you'd think I would suck up to Mr. Klein a bit. Sit up straight in class and smile or offer to clean the projector, like Sam would do. But noooo ... I'm spending fourth period hiding in the back row signing a stack of Kaitlin Burke glossies Laney wants me to finish for a charity auction this weekend. This is what happens when you overextend yourself, I guess. I haven't had a single free minute to get them done. I've almost finished when I hear Mr. Klein's deep voice boom, "Rachel, is there something more interesting in that folder than my discussion on the plight of the buffalo?" I'm so startled, my purple Sharpie shoots out of my hand and flies into the air.

"No, Mr. Klein," I murmur nervously. I try to hide the glossy I've just signed in my C-3Po folder.

Mr. Klein isn't buying it. He thunders to the back of the classroom in two long-legged strides. He pulls his glasses from the ink-stained pocket of his white oxford and puts them on so that he can glare at me clearly.

I am so busted. I am SO busted.

Maybe I should make a run for it. . . .

Out of the corner of my eye, I see Liz's face frozen in panic. I notice Austin is sitting behind her, watching me curiously. I look away as my cheeks burn. I've avoided talking to Austin since our awkward first meeting.

"What's this?" Mr. Klein asks, pulling on his salt-and-pepper goatee. I jump as he whips the glossy out from C-3PO. He waves a Kaitlin Burke autograph in the air. "Who's this Kaitlin . . . uh . . . Burke?" he reads slowly. The class giggles.

"She's, like, this total babe on *Family Affair*, Mr. Klein," Rob Murray from Austin's lacrosse team shouts.

"I love that show!" Fran Pluto gushes. "Did you see it Sunday night?" She asks a pale girl sitting next to her wearing black lip gloss. The girl shakes her head no. "Paige's sister is actually ALIVE." Suddenly the class is buzzing with talk of the show. Over their chatter, I distinctly hear Lori say, "Kaitlin's not *that* hot."

"Okay, settle down, everyone." Mr. Klein sighs. He turns back to me. I can feel the sweat beading on my forehead.

"Rachel, what are you doing with a Kaitlin Bubble —"

"Burke!" Rob yells.

"Thank you Rob," Mr. Klein says firmly. "What are you doing with a Kaitlin Burke autograph?" Everyone stares at me expectedly. Lori whispers something to her friend Jessie, who laughs.

"It's for my cousin," I explain quickly, looking at Liz for support. "The show just began airing in England, and er, she loves it. A friend of mine got this for her."

"Why were you scribbling on it then?" Mr. Klein asks.

Oh boy. Oh boy. Think, Kaitlin. *Think!* Liz looks at me pleadingly. "I, uh, it only had her signature on it so I decided to try to personalize it," I take a deep breath and continue. "My cousin's little, you know, and she is such a big fan so I couldn't let her down. It's hard enough for her to handle me living so far away. If I can make her feel just a little bit better by getting her this autograph and personalizing it so that it says 'Dear Claire' then I'm going to do it because . . ."

"That will do, Rachel." Mr. Klein looks tired. "But class is no place for making presents for your cousin, however nice that might be. I'll hold on to this till next period." He waves the glossy.

"Her cousin, give me a break," I hear Lori snort. Jessie and a few of the other cheerleaders nearby snicker.

When the bell finally rings, I grovel to Mr. Klein to get my own autograph back (he gives it to me, thankfully), then duck into the hallway to look for Liz. I spot her shiny brown hair and walk towards the row of lockers she's standing by. That's when I realize she's chatting with Austin. After what Beth and Allison said the other day at lunch, I'm more embarrassed than ever about our first encounter. Maybe I misread him.

"Hey, Rachel," Liz calls me over. "Are you okay?"

"I'm fine." I peek at Austin out of the corner of my eye. He's a foot taller than Liz and me.

"Whenever I see you, you're causing a spectacle." Austin

grins, showing his white teeth. "I think you like being the center of attention."

"I do *not* like being the center of attention," I huff. Okay, I was right. He is obnoxious. Liz raises an eyebrow at me, just like Mom does when she's disappointed with my behavior.

"I meant it as a compliment," Austin explains, oblivious to my tone. He leans a tanned arm on the nearest locker. His Polo shirt swings open to reveal a taut tee that says LAX — JUST DO IT. "That autograph thing was pretty funny," he says as he waves to someone walking by. "You saved us. I was going to doze off if I had to hear Mr. Klein describe one more thing the Native Americans used buffalo skin for."

Liz laughs.

"Good luck, Austin!" someone passing by shouts out. Clark Hall's number-one-ranked lacrosse team is playing their biggest rival, Santa Clara, today.

I'm still surprised when groups of people walk past me without paying any attention. Being Rachel is like wearing an invisibility cloak. In my usual life, someone would be sure to turn around and stare, or run over and ask for an autograph. I'm half relieved and half miffed at being ignored.

"Well, that wasn't my intention," I say sourly. One minute he's insulting me, the next he's trying to butter me up. This guy is smooth. "Some of us are here to learn."

"Is that why you were busy doing something else yourself?" Austin asks wickedly.

I'm too flustered to answer.

"Don't get crazy," Austin laughs, seeing my angry expression. "I'm just joking with you. My brain is fried today. I was up late last night with one of the kids I tutor. He needed help with a science project."

I look at him skeptically. He really tutors? I thought only Sam does things like that.

"And then I had to proofread my Civil War paper. I did mine on the effect the Civil War had on the Native Americans," he adds.

"Huh, didn't think of that angle," Liz rejoins.

"Yeah, actually a lot of them fought in the war on both sides and . . ." Austin trails off when he sees me looking at him curiously. He leans over and whispers in my ear, "Okay, don't tell anyone I'm a nerd." His hair smells like cut grass and shampoo. I can't help breathing it in deeply. I laugh nervously.

"Laughing at me, Rachel Rogers?" Austin teases. Liz looks at me with an amused and knowing expression on her perfect oval face.

"You remembered my name, huh?" I retort, composing myself.

"Not that you'd tell me yourself." Austin runs a hand through his spiky blond hair. "I had to ask around after you ran off that day."

"I wasn't going to stand there and be made fun of," I snap, remembering my anger again over our first ill-fated meeting. Liz's jaw drops.

"Make fun of you?" Austin looks confused. "What are you talking about?"

"I saw you. In class. With Lori," I stutter. "You were both laughing at me."

He kicks his Jansport backpack between his feet. "I was laughing *at* Lori," he says finally, looking up.

"At *Lori*?" I question, ignoring Liz's fingernails in my back.

"Yeah, she always feels threatened when Clark gets a new girl." He shakes his head. "So she starts in on them." He sighs. "It's getting old."

Liz looks at me smugly.

"But . . . you laughed every time I got an answer wrong!" I persist.

"It was funny!" Austin explains. "You were cute."

"Oh." I feel my cheeks burning. Now I feel stupid. But it's hard to imagine how Rachel could seem cute with her mousy brown hair and dowdy clothing. Quaint maybe. Clueless definitely. But cute? Before I can say anything my Sidekick begins to vibrate. I pull it out of my pocket and look at the message.

FUTUREPREZ: Urgent. Call me immediately!!!!!!!

"I have to go," I tell both of them.

"Um. What are you guys doing Friday night?" Austin blurts.

Liz looks at me. "Not sure yet, why?"

"Are you coming to Lori's party?" he asks, looking directly at me with his wide turquoise eyes. I look away. "I was going to mention it to Beth and Allison in bio."

"We hadn't heard about it yet," Liz comments coolly.

Even if it is at Lori's, I've been dying to go to one of these high school parties Liz always tells me about. I try to picture my Sidekick calendar. Shoot! Friday is the *FA* wrap party at Sky's. Well, I'm sure I could go to Lori's for a little while, then dash over to Sky's. Her parties never start on time anyway. "We'll be there," I say quickly.

"Great." Austin slides his backpack over one shoulder. "Four-twenty-nine Harvard Street." He saunters away down the hallway. "Don't forget," he calls back.

As soon as he's turned the corner, Liz slugs me in the arm.

"Ouch! What was that for?" I ask, rubbing my scratchy green polyester sweater. I have to remember to tell Nadine to buy me only cotton from now on.

"Lori Peters? I hate her parties," Liz groans.

I look at her pleadingly. "I haven't been to a party yet," I protest.

Liz rubs her temples. "Okay, I guess I could go for a short while," she concedes. "I have kickboxing early Saturday morning." I squeal. My Sidekick vibrates again. I look at the screen.

FUTUREPREZ: CALL ME NOW! I MEAN IT!

I wonder what's wrong. I pull my cell out of my black mesh bag and dial Nadine's number.

"Besides, it will be fun to watch you pretend you don't like Austin," Liz snorts.

"What are you talking about?" I demand before hitting Send.

"Austin likes you," Liz groans. "Or should I say, Rachel Rogers. Why, I have no idea." Now it's my turn to punch her. She laughs. "It's only a matter of time before he dumps Lori. They've been on the verge of a breakup for weeks." I keep looking straight ahead. I'm trained at dodging questions. Liz is not going to corner me on this one.

"I know you think he's hot," she points out. "He looks like Chad Michael Murray and you think he's hot."

"I never said that. Besides, Austin's too cocky for me."

"You *like* cocky guys," Liz counters. "Whenever you make me sit through *The Empire Strikes Back* you say how sarcastic and cute Han Solo is."

"That's different," I say, and hit Send on the phone. Nadine answers on the first ring.

"If you say so," Liz responds in a singsong voice. She can't stop grinning.

"WHAT TOOK YOU SO LONG?" Nadine shrieks. I hear Laney and Mom yelling in the background.

"What's wrong?" I ask, clutching my chest. Liz looks at me worriedly.

"You've got to meet Rodney at the quad right now," Nadine shouts over the racket. "Seth just called. Hutch Adams wants to meet with you about his movie."

"Oh my God. Oh my God," I say, trying to catch my breath.

"Rodney is going to rush you over there," Nadine instructs. "Your Mom gave him your favorite Chloe jeans and a Stella McCartney cami for you to wear. It's in the car."

"What? What is it?" Liz pumps my limp arm.

I put my hand over the phone and whisper. "It's Hutch Adams! He wants to meet with me about his movie." I'm so nervous my voice cracks. I never thought that would happen. Now what do I do if I get the movie? Leave school? Yes, a voice in my head replies. You've always wanted to work with him. No, another voice says. You've only been at school a few weeks! I block out both voices. "I'm on my way," I murmur calmly to Nadine. I flip my cell phone shut, then race to the quad, where Rodney is parked. Liz jogs over with me. As soon as we get to the grassy knoll I see the black sedan idling in the circular drive.

"Wish me luck," I say distractedly.

"You're changing, right?" Liz frowns, looking at my cords and Pumas. I nod. "Call me right after!" she yells. Unable to speak, I nod and open the car door.

"Hey, Rach." Rodney grins. For a second, I think I'm in the wrong car. Then I remember.

"Call me Kates, Rodney." I laugh nervously. "Otherwise I may forget my own name when I meet Hutch Adams!"

I change in the back of the car as Rodney cruises over to Wagman Brothers Studio, where Hutch has an office. I finish getting dressed, then slip on my silver Jimmy Choo strappy sandals. Aaah . . . I feel better already!

I've never met Hutch Adams before. I've only seen

him from afar at his recent AFI Life Achievement Award show (I begged Laney to snag me tickets). Maybe that's why I feel like throwing up right now. I exhale slowly, then step confidently out of the car as Rodney holds the door.

Hutch's office is in a low brick building with large windows. We step reverently into the narrow hallway lined with framed posters from Hutch's movies. There's *High Stakes Part Deux* (his one bomb), *Amnesty Amy,* and *A Call to Action.* Just looking at those posters and imagining my name on one in the future makes me hyperventilate.

I try to calm down by reminding myself that I don't want a movie role anyway. I want to stay at Clark Hall. Clark . . . GEEZ! I just remembered that I have a math quiz tomorrow and I forgot my notebook in my locker!

Okay, one problem at a time. First, I have to tackle this Hutch meeting. I'll just walk in there and smile and tell him that I'm flattered that he called me in to audition, but I'm busy right now. I'll thank him for his time and say that I'm sure there'll be other opportunities to work together in the future when both of our schedules are clear. . . .

AARGH, fine! I'm lying to myself. This is the role of a lifetime! This is my idol! My dream job!

This *is* Hutch Adams we're talking about. Who am I kidding? I'm going to beg for the role if I have to.

ten: *Lori's Turf*

"... So then he says that he's a fan of *Family Affair*! His nieces make him watch it all the time!" I recount to Nadine and Liz for the hundredth time. They're both camped out in my room, going through my closet to find something for Rachel to wear to Lori's party tonight.

I twirl around the room and then land with a *thud* on my bed. "Can you believe Hutch Adams is considering me for a role in his next project? ME! He doesn't even need to see me audition. He just watches tapes of your other performances and then if he likes what he sees, he calls you in for a meeting to study your aura," I explain breathlessly. "He wants to make sure our auras match up."

"How many other girls' auras is he studying?" Nadine asks wryly.

"Several," I admit. "But I'm not going to worry yet. That bonsai tree I sent as a thank-you should remind him of my aura whenever he passes his desk."

HOLLYWOOD SECRET NUMBER ELEVEN: Actors don't always

have to audition for a part. When you're a big, bankable movie star (like the Toms — Cruise and Hanks), you can pretty much have your pick of projects without ever memorizing an audition scene. Casting agents, directors, and producers come to you with promises of lucrative paychecks, royalties, and chances at Oscar gold. But when you're like me, a young star trying to prove you've got the chops to handle something other than teen comedies and soapy melodrama, you have to work at it.

"For someone not interested in working this hiatus, you're pretty jazzed up about this meeting." Nadine pushes her glasses up her nose and looks at me thoughtfully.

I sit up and smooth my wrinkled comforter. "Yeah, well, it *is* Hutch Adams. I couldn't turn down the meeting." Nadine and Liz exchange glances. "Okay, I want this," I admit, bouncing on my mattress. "Satisfied?"

"Yes," says Nadine smugly. "I just wanted you to admit it."

"I just feel torn," I add. "I like going to school and having friends my own age and teachers who ask me questions that have nothing to do with lighting and makeup. It makes me feel real." I frown. "But I want this Hutch movie too. The character I'd be playing is running for her life for half the movie so I'd get to hang glide, do karate, and have a big fight scene." I bite my lip. "What's wrong with me?"

"Nothing," Liz yells from my walk-in closet, where she's searching for a skirt for me to wear. "You just want it all. Doesn't everybody?" I shrug. "So what's the movie called?" she asks.

"The Untitled Hutch Adams Project," Nadine pronounces. "Quintessential Hollywood. Greenlight a movie with no title."

"The Untitled Hutch Adams Project sounds great," Liz cheers. "So when will you know if you have the part?"

"A few weeks." I pull a strand of my hair out. "Hutch told me he has to wait for the decision to come to him."

"Well, until then, let's concentrate on the now," Liz orders. "First things first — what are you wearing tonight? We have to pick up Beth and Allison in a half hour."

Nadine holds up an army green polyester sequin sweater with Discount World tags on it and a denim mini-skirt with a frayed hem. "What about this?" she asks.

I groan and keep sorting through Rachel's clothes. Something here's got to be party-worthy. Maybe I could just borrow one piece from my own closet. . . . "No more polyester! Can't I wear my Blue Cults?" I beg. "Maybe Rachel babysat a lot and bought a pair."

"Out of character." Liz shakes her head.

"But they look good on me!" I protest. "I can't look my best without my own stuff!" I don't want to admit it, but I'm imagining how "Rachel" will look to Austin.

"Save the Blue Cults for Sky's," Nadine instructs. "You can change in the car on the way over there."

"Fine," I agree grudgingly.

"And don't forget, Cinderella," Nadine teases. "You turn back into a pumpkin at ten when Rodney picks you up to go to the *FA* party."

I tap the cheap black plastic Timex Nadine got me. "Got it," I say.

An hour and a half later, with Beth and Allison in tow, Liz's dad pulls up in front of Lori's house. I have to admit, the place is pretty nice, even from the outside. The turn-of-the-century mock Tudor sits on an acre of perfectly green lawn. Behind the house, I can vaguely make out a maid's cottage and a pool.

"Blimey, what do Lori's parents do for a living?" I pretend to be as impressed as I imagine Rachel would be, even though just about everyone I know lives in mansions at least this big.

"They're both doctors," Beth explains as we walk up the limestone path. Beth pulls her curly black hair back into a low ponytail and smoothes the front of her pink V-neck sweater, which she's paired with jeans that were ruined by her marker-wielding babysitting charges earlier in the day. The red and green splotches across the knees actually give the denim a cool look. "Lori's dad is a plastic surgeon and her mom is a dermatologist," Beth adds. "They have these big Hollywood clients. Lori's mom is the one who removed Sly Stevens's mole."

We make our way to the front door, Liz leading the charge. I'm glad I wore my black sequined Dr. Scholl's sandals. They make my feet look smaller, and look almost cute with the straight knee-length Levi's denim skirt and army green sequined top I settled on.

The door to the house is unlocked and Liz pushes it

open. The four of us walk inside as Maroon 5 blasts from the stereo. To my right, people in the den are dancing. Straight ahead I can see Lori holding court with a group of male and female admirers in the kitchen.

"I told my mom that Easter break wouldn't be Easter break if we weren't spending it in Tahiti," I hear Lori tell the crowd as we walk by unnoticed. I see she's wearing a turquoise beaded sundress by Velma that is *so* last season. "She wanted to have this family dinner thing here at home, but who does that?"

Liz pushes through the sea of people in the crowded main hallway, looking for a spot for us to stand. We lose Beth somewhere near the bathroom when Rob Murray steals her away to show her how he can balance sterling silver spoons on his nose.

"She so has a thing for him," Allison declares when we finally find a space to squeeze in on the back veranda. She's wearing a khaki mini-skirt that shows off her long lean dancer legs. "I think he's just a bonehead. Rachel, stay away from American guys. They're such losers."

"England has some fit blokes," I comment, but I'm not really paying attention. Secretly, I'm scanning the crowd for Austin.

"You guys have such cuties over there," Allison is saying. "Orlando Bloom is gorgeous. Then there's Prince William, Jonathan Rhys Meyers . . ."

"Hot," Liz seconds. "So cute in *Bend It Like Beckham*."

"Exactly," Allison says. "And Hugh Grant."

"Old but cute," Liz affirms. "I love when he dances down the stairs in *Love, Actually*."

"Don't forget Ewan McGregor," I add. "He's an awesome Obi-Wan Kenobi."

"O-bee what?" Allison asks.

"You're joking me, right?" I exclaim. "Haven't you seen the new *Star Wars* movies?"

"I don't like sci-fi," Allison sniffs. Liz laughs. She knows I'm going to lose it.

"But they're not *just* sci-fi!" I protest. "They're romance and drama and all about good versus evil. . . ."

"And they've got stormtroopers and Darth Maul," I hear someone say. I turn around. It's Austin. He's wearing a white polo shirt with his lacrosse number stitched on the pocket. He looks cute. I bite hard on my lip. I feel so stupid after freaking out on him the two times we've spoken.

"You seriously like *Star Wars*?" he asks me as Allison and Liz stare in silence.

"*Live* for them. I have good taste," I say coolly. "Not all girls just like romantic comedies." I decide to leave out that I sometimes watch those too.

"I'm going to get a drink," Liz says with a sly grin. "Ali, want to come?"

"Yeah, sure," she agrees. "Let's leave these geeks alone."

"Why do sci-fi fans always get called geeks?" Austin asks once they walk away.

I laugh. "Why aren't we just called forward-thinking?"

Austin and I talk about *Star Wars* for the length of the

Maroon 5 album. He's brave enough to tell me he bawled the first time he watched Darth Vader die at age seven. And it's sweet that he takes the time to watch the movies with his kid sister, Hayley. I'm having fun talking to a guy who is actually interested in what I have to say, rather than what I do for a living. And I have to admit, Austin smells really good (Is that Eternity he's wearing?) and looks even better (Who knew guys cared about using hair care products? Austin made me promise never to reveal that he swears by Aveda's Control Stick.).

"We should get together and have a *Star Wars* marathon one weekend," Austin suggests. "I've always wanted to watch all six in a row, from start to finish."

I blush. The idea of a weekend alone with Austin sounds kind of appealing. But what about Lori? He looks at me searchingly. "Sounds like fun, but I won't have a weekend free for a while," I say, trying not to look him in the eye. "I turned in my history paper late and now Mr. Klein wants me to do bloody extra-credit."

"I'll make you a deal," Austin tells me. "I've seen you rattle off equations in math. If you help me with my geometry, I'll help you with your paper." He flashes me that gorgeous smile. "I'm not surprised you're having trouble in history. The only thing you Brits know about American history is the story of the Boston Tea Party."

"Very funny." I roll my eyes. What do I have to lose? "You've got a deal." I extend my hand.

"Great, because I have to bring up that C I have in geometry or I'm going to be toast." Austin shakes my hand tightly. His fingers feel rough from hours of cradling a lacrosse stick. "I have to keep a B average to stay on the lacrosse team." He stops shaking my hand, but doesn't let go. "Want to meet on Monday after school?"

"Works for me." I pull my hand away. I have to keep reminding myself he has a girlfriend.

I'm about to ask Austin what he thinks of Jar Jar Binks, when I feel something cold and wet on my neck. Ew! I strain to look and see that the back of my shirt and part of my skirt are soaked. Behind me, Lori is standing there with an empty cup.

"Oops, I must have slipped!" She doesn't even try to sound sincere. This girl is classic Sky Mackenzie. I can't believe I didn't see this coming.

Austin looks annoyed. "Stay right here," he instructs me as I shake out my shirt. "I'll go grab some napkins."

"I think that's going to stain," Lori coos when Austin is out of earshot. "I don't think Dr. Pepper comes out of Discount World material." She tosses her platinum blond hair.

I'm tempted to throw my Coke at her. I don't think that will come out of the dated sundress she's wearing either. I take a step towards her, and she looks at me smugly.

"Lori, come inside. We're watching last week's *Family Affair*," I hear her friend Jessie whine. "Sam's Prius just got carjacked."

"Don't bother waiting for Austin," Lori spits at me, ignoring Jessie. "I'm sure he's forgotten about you by now, just like everyone else at this party. With a face like that, there's nothing to remember."

I glare at Lori, tempted to tell her exactly what I think of her.

"I guess that means you can leave now," Lori adds.

"LORI, did you hear me? Sam's being held at knifepoint by a carjacker!" Jessie calls. "Bring that British girl with you, okay?"

"This Brit has better things to do than hang out here," I retort hotly. I glance at my watch. It's 9:30. I have to start wrapping up anyway, and there's no point waiting for Austin. He's probably not coming back. "If you'll excuse me, I've got to find my friends."

"You don't want to lose those," I hear Lori yell out as I push through the people standing on the veranda. "You don't have that many!"

Maybe I was wrong about this school thing. In Hollywood, people give me some respect. To my face at least.

Friday 3/26
NOTES TO SELF:
Send Hutch a gushing thx note. (Keep him thinking about your aura!)
Buy Rodney b-day gift!
Think of fave U.S. history moment (The Boston Tea Party?).

eleven: *The Sky's the Limit*

HOLLYWOOD SECRET NUMBER TWELVE: A star's home is never as fabulous as it appears in the pages of a magazine. The truth is, magazines are so desperate for the intimate details of celebrity life that they'll do almost anything to get a star to unlock her front door. Haven't had a chance to finish decorating your Malibu weekend pad? No problem. The magazine will hire an interior designer to add the finishing touches — everything from flesh flowers on the kitchen table to satin throw pillows on the couch. Sometimes they even bring in new furniture. One magazine was so desperate to profile my friend Gina's apartment that they offered to have Home Du Jour outfit the entire place for *free* if she'd agree to let them photograph it. (She let them, of course. Who wouldn't?)

I have a pretty good idea that Sky's home got the same treatment. Sky's stodgy old maid takes the Burberry trench I changed into, revealing the cream-colored Chloe tank and jeans that I threw on in the car. When she walks me through the living room, I recognize at least a dozen items from that swanky furniture store, Destination Home. Cut crystal lamps, Persian rugs, leather couches, even monochrome art all scream the store's name. I know because Mom drags me through Destination Home every time she redecorates a room — which is about once a month.

Sky would never admit it because it would make her look phony, but I think the place hooked her up when she agreed to let *Life and Style* profile her parents' house for the cover a few months back.

Oh wait. Maybe what you're *really* wondering is: Why would I ever set foot at Sky's? I'm doing my official *FA* cast-member duty, that's why. Tom wanted us all to watch a taping of the season finale together (something about boosting cast morale) and Sky offered — or should I say insisted — the viewing be at her place.

"It's been such a trying season for all of us," Sky's hand-delivered shiny fuschia invitation read, "that I'd like us, at Tom's request, to bask in the glow of our successful efforts with an intimate dinner at my parents' estate."

Intimate includes a five-person crew from *Access Hollywood*, whom she invited to tape the festivities.

Sky's maid leads me down a long corridor lined with framed photos of Sky. As the Mackenzie's only child, Sky's parents devote their lives to her career (Sky's mom is her manager too). Sort of like mine, actually.

I examine each photo on the hallway wall out of the corner of my eye. There's a picture of Sky with the *FA* cast at last year's Emmy's.... There's Sky's "Best Villain" MTV Movie Award.... There's a picture of Sky hugging Tom Cruise at the Carnival of Hope benefit.... There's Sky as a toddler on *FA*.... Wait, that picture looks cut in half. I look at it closely and see pudgy little fingers and blond hair. Hey, that's me they cut out!

"Kaitlin, there you are," cheers Melissa, who plays my "mom," Paige. She gives me a tight squeeze. Her long black hair puddles around the white fitted blazer she's wearing with tight Lucky jeans and coral heeled sandals.

"Sorry I'm late." I kiss her cheek. Rodney hit traffic going to Sky's so it took twice the time to get here.

"As long as you're okay. I got worried." She smiles. Even off-screen, Melli totally mothers me, and I have to admit, I love it.

"We're all in the den waiting for the show to start," she says, linking her arm with mine. "Sky's mother has been entertaining us with stories about Sky's *FA* audition." Melli winks at me.

I giggle. As we walk down the steps into the modern great room, decorated with paint-splashed couches and abstract sculptures, I can see most of the cast and crew milling about. Everyone is laughing and having a good time, like they haven't seen each other in years. It feels good to be together, I realize. This group is like my second family. Suddenly, someone grabs my waist from behind and swings me into the air.

"Kates, you're here!" Trevor exclaims. "Sky said she wasn't sure if you were coming. You didn't RSVP."

"Funny, I know I left a message on her voicemail." I give Trevor a bear hug when he puts me down. "I guess she missed that one."

"K, you made it," Sky announces dramatically. She's wearing a corseted floor-length red satin gown. Were we supposed to dress up for this thing? I look at Melli and Trevor. They're both in jeans, just like me. "It's 10:30. I told everyone you weren't coming," she adds. "You didn't RSVP."

"I *did* RSVP, Sky." She ignores me.

"Missing the season finale." Sky lowers her dark eyes sadly. "I told Tom that maybe you just didn't want to be in the same room as me." She sniffs, wiping an imaginary tear from the corner of her eye. When she wants to, Sky can really act.

"I think it's time we put the past season behind us," Melli suggests briskly, and pulls the two of us in tightly. "I'm going to need both of you girls' strength if I'm to survive that car crash!" At the end of the season finale, Paige's limo is hanging off the edge of a cliff.

Sky and I smile faintly. Neither of us likes to fight in front of Melli. She feels too much like, well, our mom.

"Kaitlin, there you are," Tom says, walking over with a plate of fried shrimp. "Want one? These are delicious!" He munches on a shrimp and hands the tray to Trevor. "Where did you order these from?" he asks Sky.

"We use the same caterer that Demi uses for all her affairs," Sky answers coolly. "Demi and Ashton are old family friends. We've known them forever."

"Old?" Trevor repeats, with a confused look on his face. "I thought Ashton was in his twenties."

"It's a figure of speech, sweetie," Sky explains through gritted teeth. Trevor takes another shrimp and shoves it whole in his mouth. "Why don't we get you a seat on the couch next to me?" She leads Trevor away like a puppy, still carrying the shrimp plate.

"Five minutes to showtime!" Sky yells as she tucks Trevor into a white leather couch next to her. "Everyone find a seat." I roll my eyes, and Melli catches me.

"She just wants to be liked, Kates," Melli says, putting a hand on my arm. Now I feel guilty.

Someone dims the lights in the den and Melli, Tom, and I quickly grab seats. Sky's fifty-inch flat-screen plasma TV is large enough that you can see clearly from anywhere in the room. The first half hour of the show moves quickly — Sara and Sam meet Krystal at the church for the confrontation about Krystal being pregnant. Elsewhere, Penelope shows up at Paige and Dennis's house and tries to seduce her brother-in-law. Flash to Paige, alone, stepping into the limo idling outside to take her to the church. But wait — that's not the regular limo driver, that's Penelope's boyfriend! Why would he be driving the limo?

When lights come up during a commercial break, I make my way to the makeshift bar that's been set up in the adjacent dining room to get Tom, Melli, and me some sodas. Sky apparently has the same idea.

"How have you been, K?" she chirps when I walk up beside her. "Hon, pour me a Red Bull," she orders to the bartender.

"Great, Sky," I answer and flash her a huge grin. I so don't want any problems with her tonight. I'll make it through the next hour, and then I don't have to see Sky again for a while.

"You weren't at the Motorola party last week," she points out accusingly. "Or the Havanas Fiesta at L'Ermitage."

"Yeah, I had to miss those," I explain, thinking quickly, "I had a meeting about a possible summer project."

"Yeah, I heard," Sky says coolly. "*The Untitled Hutch Adams Project*. My agent is getting me a meeting with Hutchie too." My stomach takes a sudden lurch.

"You're . . . auditioning?" I stutter. I can feel the blood pumping through my veins. Uh-uh. There is *no way* I'm losing this role to Sky Mackenzie. "I thought you already picked a project to shoot this summer."

"I did." Sky adjusts the "S" diamond pendant dangling around her bony neck. "It's an NBC miniseries that's shooting in Mexico for a month. I play a teen runaway who uncovers this plot to assassinate the president and has to stop it. Shiva Snow is playing the FBI agent on my tail. I'll have plenty of time afterwards to shoot Hutchie's movie." She scans my face for a reaction.

"That's cool." I grab the sodas from the bartender and try to push the idea of Sky getting the Hutch Adams flick out of my mind. "Good luck with the miniseries."

"Yeah, it's going to be pretty intense," she adds. "We're filming in all these remote areas of Mexico and we have to, like, totally rough it and wear Discount World clothes." She shudders.

For once, I sort of understand. "Well, I better go take my seat before the lights dim again," I say, balancing the drinks in my hands.

I've barely made it back to Tom and Melli when my Sidekick begins vibrating.

> FUTUREPREZ: Call Beth @ 868-4321.
> PRINCESSLEIA25: Y?
> FUTUREPREZ: She called the phone. Emergency.

Nadine set up a separate cell phone number that we're using for my school calls.

> PRINCESSLEIA25: What did U say?
> FUTUREPREZ: I'm ur mom.
> PRINCESSLEIA25: LOL
> FUTUREPREZ: Just call!
> PRINCESSLEIA25: Do me a favor — call Laney. Sky said she's auditioning 4 Hutch 2.
> FUTUREPREZ: No way. RU serious?
> PRINCESSLEIA25: Sadly yes.
> FUTUREPREZ: OK, I'm dialing now . . .

I hear Tom clear his throat. "Sorry," I whisper to him. "My mom. I've got to call her. I'll be right back." I tiptoe out of the room, hoping no one but Melli and Tom notices I'm gone. When I swing through the double door to the kitchen, I can see this is the right place to make a call. The chef is busy barking orders at assistants readying fruit tarts and freshly stuffed éclairs while the waitstaff keep running in and out with trays of fried shrimp, mini filet mignons on toast, and crab cakes.

No one will hear me make a phone call in here. I look around once more, making sure Sky is nowhere to be seen, and dial.

"HELLO?" Someone yells. Loud music is pumping in the background.

"Hey, it's, uh, Rachel," I say, almost forgetting who I am at the moment. "I was in the loo."

"Can you hear me?" Beth yells. "I'm with Liz and Allison." Liz. Why is she letting Beth call me when she knows where I am?

"Yeah, I can hear you." I glance at the door. So far so good. "Is something wrong? My mum said it was an emergency."

"You missed it," Beth screeches. "Austin and Lori had a HUGE fight and they broke up!"

"What?" I'm shell-shocked. I just saw him an hour ago, though it seems like it was on a different planet. "Why?"

"Because of YOU," she bellows. I hear Liz hoot in the background, "Go Rach!" "He was yelling at her about throwing her drink on you or something and he said he'd had enough with her games and jealousy and that it was OVER. Lori threw a plate of nachos at him and said the party was officially finished. She's kicking everybody out right now. Can you believe it? Austin broke up with Lori over you!"

I can't actually. This is crazy! There's going to be no dealing with Lori now. But wait, does that mean Austin's single? *What am I thinking?* I should be concentrating on getting the Hutch Adams part.

A waiter behind me drops a platter and it crashes to the floor. The chef closest to me starts cursing at him in French. Hmm, maybe he can help me with my French homework. I have a quiz tomorrow morning.

"What was that?" Beth asks.

"I dropped the bloody phone," I blurt nervously. "It's late. I should probably go. . . ."

"Yeah, terrible curfew you have," Beth says, reminding me of the excuse I used to leave the party early. "Don't worry. Call me tomorrow. I'll fill you in on the rest."

I hang up the phone. A waiter drops another plate of chocolate eclairs and strawberries, and I don't even flinch. I've got to call Liz when I get out of here and find out more about Austin and Lori and tell her about Sky and Hutch Adams.

I walk towards the kitchen doors and they swing forward, almost smacking me in the face. When they swing back again, I see her immediately. It's Sky, and she's quickly walking away from the kitchen.

Oh God. Did she hear me?

TWELVE: *A Study Date*

At school on Monday morning, I'm greeted with not one, but two reasons for a migraine. First off, my seat in Mr. Klein's class is directly behind Lori, who probably wants to shoot venom at me this morning after her breakup with Austin. The second problem is what Lori's holding in her perfectly manicured hand. The minute I quietly sit down, I see the *Sizzling Celebs* cover with a big picture of me at the *Off-Key* premiere. Next to the photo is a caption in big white letters:

WHY IS KAITLIN BURKE HIDING?
  WITH *FAMILY AFFAIR* ON HIATUS, SHOULDN'T TV'S GOLDEN GIRL BE OUT HAVING FUN? THE REAL REASON SHE'S MISSING FROM THE HOLLYWOOD SCENE ON PAGE TEN!

Immediately, I feel dizzy. HAS SOMEONE FOUND OUT WHAT I'M DOING?? When Liz arrives a few seconds after me, she can't miss the look on my face.

"What is it?" she mouths, and plops her books down on the table next to me. I motion to Lori. Liz spots the magazine cover right away and gives me a wink.

"Hey, Lori," Liz says cheerily.

Lori doesn't bother looking up. She keeps flipping through the magazine. "Yes, I'm fine, *no* Austin didn't dump me, I dumped him, okay?" she snaps. "End of story." Then she looks up and realizes it's Liz. "Oh. It's *you*. What do you want?"

"Actually, I was just wondering about the new issue of *Sizzling Celebs*," Liz says. Today she's wearing this funny lavender tee that says HUGS NOT DRUGS in big letters. It looks cute with the frayed denim skirt and gold sequined sandals she's got on. "Mine didn't come yet."

"Oh." Lori casually flips her hair to the side. Ever since I was banned from my walk-in closet to play Rachel, I'm obsessed with what everyone around me has on. Lori's black Dior cami and Blue Cult jeans are hot enough to make me drool. I, on the other hand, am stuck wearing a pale yellow V-neck tee from Discount World and a hand-me-down plaid skirt from Nadine, which itches immensely.

"I can't be bothered with subscriptions," Lori says off-handedly. "Our chauffeur picks it up for me the morning it hits newsstands. I like to be the first to know everything."

I roll my eyes at Liz, but she ignores me. "That's cool. So what's the story on Kaitlin Burke?" Liz points to the cover.

Lori snorts. "She's, like, totally destroying her career." I dig my nails into my horrible synthetic skirt to keep from screaming.

"How?" Liz asks, leaning in closer for the answer.

"*Sizzling Celebs* says she's totally trying to destroy Sky Mackenzie and Trevor Wainright's relationship," Lori explains. "Apparently she hasn't gotten Trevor away from Sky, so she's become a complete recluse. She hasn't been going to parties or anything."

I stifle a groan. But I'm also kind of fascinated. It's weird to watch malicious rumors get spread about me right in front of my face.

"Wow," Liz says, acting all amused.

"Yep, Kaitlin Burke is losing her mind," Lori concludes. "The story even says that Kaitlin is thinking of quitting acting because she can't compete with Sky for roles. Sky is up for the same movie as Kaitlin."

I can feel my heart beating out of my chest. SKY! She's ruining my life even when she's not in it! Wait till I get hold of Laney.

"I hope they kill Kaitlin's character off *Family Affair*," Lori adds. "She's not half as talented as Sky."

That does it.

"You can't believe everything you read!" I blurt out.

Lori turns and looks at me in disdain. "No one asked *you*," she hisses. Liz looks at me like I'm nuts. Lori starts to say something else, but she's interrupted by Mr. Klein.

"Rachel? Mrs. Pearson would like to see you in her office

pronto," he says, hanging up the classroom phone on the wall. "The rest of you turn to chapter seven of your *History Today* textbook."

Lori looks at me smugly, like she knows I'm in big trouble.

When I reach Principal P's office, she's standing in the doorway. "Rachel, you have a phone call. It's your mother," she whispers loudly and winks. "You can take it in my office." Principal P quickly ushers me in the room and shuts the door behind us. I look at her questioningly and pick up the phone.

"Hello, this is Rachel," I say, since I still don't know who I'm talking to.

"KAITLIN? IT'S LANEY. WHAT TOOK YOU SO LONG? I HAVE REESE ON HOLD." This is an old Laney trick to make people jump, and I know better than to believe her.

"Oh hi, Laney," I say. Principal P hovers nearby, pretending to sort through her mail. "Sorry. I was in class two buildings away. What's up?"

"WE HAVE A SERIOUS CRISIS ON OUR HANDS!" Laney yells. I hear cars whizzing by in the background. She must be driving again. I hope she's using the hands-free headset I bought her. "I HAVE YOUR MOTHER AND NADINE ON THE LINE TOO."

"I know, I saw the *Sizzling Celebs* cover," I say.

"*Sizzling Celebs* cover? What *Sizzling Celebs* cover?" My mother cries. "Ours didn't come in the mail yet!"

"CALM DOWN, MEG," Laney orders. "IT'S JUST MORE TABLOID RUBBISH. I HAVE A CALL IN TO THEIR

EDITOR-IN-CHIEF ABOUT THEIR SOURCES. I'M THREATENING TO SUE!"

"Good!" Mom barks.

"Laney? Could you talk quieter? You're yelling in my ear," Nadine complains.

"Kaitlin, I called this phone conference to talk about the Sizzling Sixteen list," Laney says, lowering her voice without acknowledging Nadine. "*Total Teen* told me that Sky's mother won't allow her to be on the list if you're featured before Sky in the issue. Well, I turned around and told them that you are the bigger star and if you're not placed first then YOU DON'T APPEAR AT ALL!" Uh-oh.

"Kaitlin has to come first. What if it sways Hutch Adams's decision?" Mom's voice hits an anxious high note. "He could pick Sky because Kate-Kate isn't ranked high enough."

The thought makes my head throb even harder. "We've got to do something!" I blurt. I'm surprised at how upset I am about this.

HOLLYWOOD SECRET NUMBER THIRTEEN: Celebrities actually care about being on magazines' "It" lists. They may go on *Oprah* and make fun of being in *People's* "Sexiest Men" issue for the third year in a row, but that's just a front. I guarantee you they called their publicists when that list was being created and told them to make sure they're on it. These lists are an easy way to stay on the public's good side. The magazines run a super flattering photo of you and write a puff piece about how you're more popular than the President and kinder than the Pope.

"Not to worry. I did some research," Nadine soothes. "Based on *Total Teen*'s criteria for the Sizzling Sixteen list, Kates should appear first. She's had three more film roles than Sky, and on *FA* this year, Sam's storyline has been juicier."

"GOOD, NADINE," Laney yells, and feverishly honks her horn in celebration. "WE'LL SHOW THEM!"

"Have we heard anything from Hutch's people yet?" Nadine voices what I'm thinking.

"I have a call in to Kaitie-Kat's agent to find out," Mom says. "He told me we should hear something by the end of next week either way."

I think I may throw up. I look at Principal P and smile. She won't take her eyes off me.

"KAITLIN, I HAVE TO GO BACK TO REESE. WE JUST WANTED YOU TO KNOW WHAT'S GOING ON IN CASE ANYBODY ASKS YOU ABOUT THE LIST," Laney shouts. The phone goes dead.

Who's going to ask me about the list at school?

Principal P looks at me hopefully. "Was that about *Family Affair?*" I just stand there staring at the phone in my hand.

"That was Laney and my mom and my assistant." I walk around her desk. Principal P stands in my path to the door.

"I was hoping it was Paige with some scoop about next season." She plays with her hands.

I want to laugh, but don't. To be honest, it's kind of nice that Principal P is such a big fan. I don't seem to have many these days — in or out of school. "Principal Pearson, the show just ended," I say sweetly. "Even we won't know what's going to happen for a few months."

"I can't wait that long," she groans. "I was on the *Family Affair* message boards last night looking for answers. Does Paige survive the crash? Who is the father of Krystal's baby? Are they going to do a DNA test?" She looks at me hopefully. "You must know *something*."

I shrug. "I really don't. The writers are on vacation now just like I am." Principal P frowns. "But I'm sure Paige will survive. Melli just signed another two-year contract with the show." Principal P sighs in relief.

The warning bell rings for fourth period. "I'll tell you what." I inch around her and grab the door. "I'll have lunch with you next week and you can ask me all the *Family Affair* questions you want."

"Would you?" She claps her hands excitedly. "Let's make it Monday then."

"Deal." I smile and start walking out the door.

"Oh, and Rachel," Principal calls discreetly. I turn around. "If you talk to your *friend* this weekend, tell her they should really do a DNA test." She winks.

I wink back, turn, and run down the hallway towards bio. And that's when it happens. I run face-first into Austin's well-defined chest.

"WHOA. Are you fleeing stormtroopers or something?" Austin laughs, grabbing me with his strong hands to steady my balance. I feel my palms start to sweat. Why am I so nervous? I'm never this anxious around cute guys — and I've kissed plenty of them for *FA*.

I laugh nervously. "How are you doing?" I stare at the dirty linoleum floor tiles.

"I know what this is about," Austin says, watching my reaction. He drops his arms. "You heard about me and Lori."

"You and Lori? What about you and Lori?" I question, playing dumb.

"Look." Austin is staring right at me with his bright turquoise eyes. "You had nothing to do with our breakup Friday night. We were about to break up anyway. I was sick of seeing the way she walked all over people, including me. What she did to you Friday night was the last straw. I explained that you and I are just friends."

Friends. "Of course." I try to hide my disappointment. What's wrong with me?

"AUSTIN, LET'S GO!" Rob Murray calls from down the hall. "Coach K is going to let us practice for the game during gym!"

"One second!" Austin yells back. "I've got to go," he says apologetically. "Are you still free to study after school?"

I think for a second. No, Laney has me taping *The Ellen Degeneres Show*. "Uh, I have a doctor's appointment," I say apologetically. "I completely forgot."

"What about tonight?" Austin asks. "Lacrosse practice ends at six, so we could meet at my house at six-thirty." He grabs my notebook and green ballpoint pen out of my hands and scribbles down his address.

"COME ON!" Rob yells again.

"I better go." He starts backing away, grinning.

"See you tonight," I reply, clutching the page he's just written on.

My *Ellen* taping goes well. The morning talk shows are so much fun to appear on, because they're a relaxed atmosphere and the questions aren't prying. Ellen doesn't bring up Sky once! I knew I liked her. I'm still on a live audience high when Rodney drops me off at Austin's at 6:30.

"I don't know why I'm nervous," I tell Nadine on the car ride over.

"Maybe it's because this is the first time you've liked a guy who seems to like you for you, not for what your career can do for him," she offers.

"You think I like him?" I scoff. "I don't. We're just friends. And I can't like him, it's too complicated."

"Yeah, but that's how life works," Rodney mumbles from the front seat, where he's sipping a Jamba Juice smoothie. "You fall for someone when you least expect it." I wonder for a moment whether he's speaking from experience.

"But I'm living a lie," I protest. Ever since Friday night, when Austin and I had such a good time chatting, I've been hearing this nagging voice in the back of my head: *What's going to happen if he finds out the truth?*

"Well, it's too late to worry about that now, isn't it?" The sedan pulls up to Austin's sweet-looking colonial home. The house looks spacious, but not crazy big like Lori's or, well, mine. But what's so great about it, as I stare at the well-worn bricks, ivy climbing up the front porch, and the kids' bikes scattered on the super-green lawn, is how homey it feels.

"We'll pick you up at eight-thirty," Nadine says, checking her watch. "You've got a phone interview with *Access* on the East Coast to do at eight-forty-five."

I nod, give my Old Navy jeans and black velour zip-up hoodie a final once-over, making sure I'm in Rachel mode after *The Ellen Degeneres Show* (it was so nice to dress up in a Nicole Miller multicolored satin slip dress for an appearance), and open the car door. Rodney zooms away by the time I've reached the doorbell. Seconds later, Austin's mom opens the battered white screen door.

"You must be Rachel," she greets me warmly. Mrs. Meyers is wearing an apron that says #1 MOM over her khakis and red polo shirt. She wipes her hands on the apron and holds one out to me. "It's nice to meet you. Excuse my greasy palms. I'm making cookies."

Wow, a mom who bakes. "It's nice to meet you too," I say shyly. "I'm here to study with Austin." She has his sandy blond hair, only hers is tied back in a wispy ponytail.

"Hey!" Austin appears in the doorway. He's rubbing a towel over his wet head. "I just got back from lacrosse a little while ago. I had to shower."

I nod, trying not to blush as I notice his toned abs through his damp white t-shirt.

His mom shakes her head. "Austin, you never sit still. You two yell down if you're hungry." She disappears into the kitchen.

"Thanks. It was nice meeting you," I call after her.

"We can study in my room," Austin tells me, leading the way up the worn carpeted stairs. "Let me just introduce you to my sister first." He knocks on the first door at the top of the stairs.

"Come in!" a voice yells.

Austin opens the door and peeks inside. A young girl, around the age of eleven, looks up from the book she's reading on her stuffed-animal-strewn bed and smiles. Her mouth is full of braces. "Hey," she murmurs shyly. With short dark brown hair, she doesn't look anything like Austin, except for her similarly striking turquoise eyes.

"Hi," I reply nervously, as if I'm being studied. "I'm your brother's friend Rachel."

"We're going to be studying in my room, Hayley," Austin says. "Come down if you need any help with your homework." She nods and gives us another metal smile. Austin shuts the door.

"Your sister is so cute," I muse. "I wish my brother was always that quiet."

"I thought you were an only child," Austin comments as we walk to the end of the hallway.

"Yeah, well, I am," I correct myself quickly. "I meant my *cousin*, Matty. He's *like* my brother, we spend so much time together. He's always following me around and wanting me to help him with stuff and he's never happy no matter how much I do so . . ."

"Wow, come up for air!" Austin laughs, opening the door to his bedroom. "I've never heard you talk so much."

His room looks exactly how I'd pictured it, with lacrosse posters on the wall and sports equipment everywhere. There's also dirty clothing on the floor, much like my own room at home, before Anita's had a chance to clean it.

I feel my cheeks flush. "I have a bad habit of babbling," I admit sheepishly. "I've got to work on that."

Austin pulls a second chair up to his narrow old oak desk. I walk over and put my messenger bag down. That's when I see the picture hanging above the desk. It's from one of those fan magazines, and it's of . . . me. I'm wearing an ivory midriff-baring peasant top and jeans, and my hair is wind blown. It was for my *Allure* cover.

Austin catches me staring and now it's his turn to become beet red. "My sister gave me the picture," he explains. "She loves *Family Affair*. I just think, um, Kaitlin Burke is hot."

I don't know what to say. This is surreal. Austin thinks the real me is *hot*. Hearing Austin's confession makes my legs buckle. Sure, fans, interviewers, and magazines have complimented me before, but this is the first time I've ever really believed it. I think I have to sit down.

Austin sighs. "I don't know why I can't lie to you," he complains when I quietly drop into the beat-up wooden chair next to him. "Okay the truth is, I *do* watch *Family Affair*. My sister got me hooked. Can you believe it? The captain of the lacrosse team hooked on a soap opera!" He shakes his damp head. "If the guys on the team found out, they'd never let me live it down."

The thought hits me like a lightning bolt. If Austin were just another open-mouthed fan asking for my autograph, would I have noticed him when I finished signing his scrap of paper? How many other cute guys have I passed up because I didn't take the time to stop and really pay attention? But then again, even if I did notice a hot guy, how would I know if he was really interested in me, or my celebrity?

That's the cool part about being Rachel. I know, however odd it may seem, that Austin is truly interested in what I, or rather Rachel, has to say. For once, "Kaitlin's" face isn't getting in the way.

"You better help me do a good job on my history project or I'll blackmail you," I joke.

"You're funny," Austin says. "I haven't met a lot of girls like you before."

"Is that a good thing or a bad thing?" I ask.

"Both," he teases. "You're really laid back, which is awesome. So many of the girls I know are hung up on money and what designer they're wearing or what car they're going to buy when they get their license." He rolls his eyes. "You don't seem hung up on that stuff at all."

I smile. If he only knew.

We get to work after that, but I have a hard time concentrating. Sitting so close to Austin, with the smell of his freshly shampooed hair in my face, it's tough to focus. I hope he'll give me these Boston Tea Party notes to go home with because I can't remember a thing he's saying. I fare slightly better when it comes to math.

"So just remember that the sine rule for a triangle is ABC," I repeat.

He groans. "Just explain to me when I'm ever going to need to know the radius of a circle and the angles of a triangle."

I shrug. "I guess if you wanted to go into physics or be an astronaut . . ."

"I have no clue *what* I want to be, but I don't think it's either of those." He shrugs his sculpted shoulders. "What about you?"

"Do I want to be an astronaut?" I ask. "Only if I can visit places like Tatooine."

"No," he chuckles. "What do you want to *do*? Do you ever think about the future?"

What can I say? Austin, I already have a career. I'm an actress. Not only that, but I'm Kaitlin Burke. I'm sorry I didn't tell you before, but I promised I wouldn't tell a soul, and then I met you and you're funny and cute. . . .

"I . . . ," I begin. There's a knock on the door.

"Sorry to interrupt, kids," Mrs Meyers pokes her head in, "but Rachel, your Aunt Nadine is downstairs. She says it's time to go." I glance at the clock. It's 8:45. Have we been here over two hours already?

"I have to go," I apologize.

Austin nods. "What are you doing Saturday afternoon?" His mom smiles at me and walks away carrying a pile of clean laundry.

Is he asking me out? "This Saturday?" I ask meekly.

"Yeah." Austin grins. "The day that usually comes after Friday."

I smirk back.

"I know this great pizza place. A Slice of Heaven," he says. "We can study there and eat lunch."

Yikes. What if Antonio recognizes me?

"I hate pizza!" I blurt out.

"You hate pizza?" Austin widens his eyes in surprise. "Um, okay. We'll go for Chinese then."

"It's a date," I say. "I mean, it's a plan."

I say goodbye to Austin's mom on the way out and quickly sprint down the walkway to the black sedan. I open the back door.

"You're late!" Nadine exclaims. "I had to pretend to be your aunt!"

Rodney chuckles. "Are you hungry?" he asks me. "We got burgers at Carl's Jr. Don't tell your mom."

I gratefully take one out of the bag. "Sorry," I apologize. "I lost track of time."

"It went well then?" Nadine asks.

"Yes," I say somewhat giddily. "He asked me out."

"On a date?" Rodney prods.

"Well, not a date, but he wants me to study with him Saturday over lunch." Rodney whistles.

"Wait, Saturday?" Nadine panics. "You've got that *TV Tome* photo shoot with the *FA* cast. We have to be there at noon."

Sigh.

Having a double life is much harder than I imagined.

Monday 3/29
NOTES TO SELF:
ALWAYS check calendar before saying "yes."
Finish xtra credit paper 4 Mr. K. Due in 2 weeks!
Apologize to A — and RESCHEDULE "DATE"!!!

THIRTEEN: *The Beauty Buffet*

You know how the Oscars are the biggest night of the year in Hollywood? Well, at Clark Hall, the key event is the spring fling.

Don't get me wrong, I'm excited for the dance too, especially because it's my first one ever. But Clark Hall students are *insane* about it. Unlike the prom, which is organized by the school's alumni, the spring fling is completely run by the students — which makes it the best event of the school year. The student committee in charge has a say in everything from the papier-mâché decorations to the mini hot dog appetizers to the coveted party theme. That's the part the whole school votes on, and like the Oscars, there's some mega-campaigning to ensure the best theme wins.

Every group gets wrapped up in the campaign frenzy — except, it seems, Liz. ("We'd rather run the dance committee afterwards than waste time campaigning for a theme," Liz shudders.) Me, I'm taking my vote very seriously: this is the only high school dance I'll ever attend. That's why I'm so torn over my decision.

> PRINCESSLEIA25: Quick! Have 2 vote at the end of class. Who R U voting 4?
>
> POWERGRL28: K, I'm in math!!!
>
> PRINCESSLEIA25: Sorry. I'm so confused!
>
> POWERGRL28: Fine, but this has got 2 B quick.
>
> PRINCESSLEIA25: Tell me what is "History's Finest"?
>
> POWERGRL28: Sponsored by the Shakespearian Club and Mathletes. Mr. K's fave.
>
> PRINCESSLEIA25: Is that Y he handed out fliers dressed as Abe Lincoln?
>
> POWERGRL28: Yep. So lame. They want everyone 2 go as famous peeps from history.
>
> PRINCESSLEIA25: Beth is voting 4 them. She wants 2 B Pocahontas.
>
> POWERGRL28: U still voting for "Monster Mash?"
>
> PRINCESSLEIA25: Maybe.
>
> POWERGRL28: Liar! U so are! All bc A dressed up as Darth Vader and handed U that card that said "Vote 4 the Monster Mash or we'll squash U."
>
> PRINCESSLEIA25: Not true. A gave everyone fliers. The whole team dressed up! I think dressing up as a ghoul or a villain is cool.
>
> POWERGRL28: Cooler than being a celeb? That's the "Night of a Thousand Stars" theme.
>
> PRINCESSLEIA25: I live that life already, remember? No thx.

POWERGRL28: They're getting my vote. I'd rather dress as Angelina Jolie than Jabba the Hutt.

PRINCESSLEIA25: :(

POWERGRL28: U just don't want to vote for them bc it's Lori and Jessie's idea.

PRINCESSLEIA25: NO, I think it was wrong to sway the male vote by dressing up as Britney and J.Lo to hand out free lemonade.

POWERGRL28: Get over it. They're going to win so start planning your costume. Drool = votes.

After a week of campaign craziness, we voted for our favorite theme last Friday. Now we're all sitting in Mr. Klein's class waiting for Principal Pearson to come over the PA system and announce the winner. I swear, things are super intense in here. Everyone is sitting quietly and it's not because we're paying attention to Mr. Klein's lecture on the Native American agriculture system.

"Attention Clark Hall students, this is your principal, Mrs. Pearson," we hear over the loudspeaker. Jessie squeals.

"I know how hard you all worked last week," Mrs. P says, "and it pleases me to see how much you care about your school. . . ."

"Just tell us who won," Rob Murray groans.

". . . so I'm happy to announce that we have a winner. With nearly four hundred votes, the winner is 'A Night of a Thousand Stars.'"

Lori jumps up and down screaming. Jessie actually breaks down in tears. The other queen bees sitting around me knock over their chairs and clamor to hug each other. But all is not well in Mr. Klein's third period social studies. A dark cloud has formed over the other half of the class.

"The race was fixed!" Rob yells, and slams his textbook shut. Mr. Klein and the Mathletes in attendance look devastated.

"Now that we have a theme for the dance, we should talk about creating a committee," Mr. Klein finally calls over the commotion. The class grows quiet.

"You all did a tremendous job on your campaigns." Mr. Klein looks straight at the members of the Shakespearian Club. "That's why I'm hoping you'll do an equally good job of planning the dance."

Mr. Klein looks over at Lori. She's talking animatedly to Jessie about costumes. "Lori, I assume you'll want to help chair the committee?"

Lori stops chatting with Jessie and stares at Mr. Klein. "Me?" she responds blankly. "Why me?"

Mr. Klein looks flustered. "Well, you girls were the ones who picked this idea, weren't you?"

"Yeah, but we don't actually have *time* to put a whole dance together." Her friends sitting beside her nod in agreement. "We just wanted our theme to *win*. Now that it's happened, we have to concentrate on more important stuff — like our costumes."

"Do any of you girls plan on working on the committee?" He asks wearily. None of the girls around Lori raise their hands. He sighs. "Does anyone in this class want to work on the committee?"

Liz's hand shoots up. "I want to run it," she volunteers confidently.

"Doesn't she always?" Jessie whispers loudly. Liz gives her the evil eye.

"That's wonderful, Liz," he says happily. "Anyone here willing to join her?" Beth and Allison raise their hands. I keep mine down. I don't know if I can stretch myself any thinner than I already am. I have to miss school Thursday and Friday as it is so that Laney and I can do a forty-eight-hour trip to New York for the morning news shows and *Live with Regis and Kelly*.

Liz turns around and widens her long-lashed brown eyes at me. "It will be fun," she mouths.

Oh . . . fine. I slowly raise my hand.

Mr. Klein looks at me sternly. "Will you have time to do this and your other work, Rachel?" I know he means my next paper, which is due at the end of the week.

"Not a problem, Mr. Klein." I look at Austin and smile. He winks at me. I'm glad he was cool with me canceling last Saturday. I'm really going to need his help now.

"The committee will meet tomorrow morning before first period," Mr. Klein announces. "Please come with ideas, including what charity you think the proceeds should go to. With the dance just two weeks away, we really have to move."

While I'm writing myself a reminder on my Sidekick, I hear Lori and her friends discussing their costumes.

"So Lori, are you going to go as Jessica Simpson?" A chirpy redheaded girl pips.

"Nah, I'm over her," Lori scoffs. "Maybe I'll go as Kaitlin Burke from *Family Affair*."

What I wouldn't give to reveal myself right now and see the shocked look on her smug know-it-all face. . . .

"Cool," Jessie gushes. "Who should I be?"

"You can go as Sky Mackenzie," Lori says. "Then I can spend all night pretending to be jealous of you!" The others giggle.

Sigh. Does Sky's wrath have to follow me everywhere?

When the bell rings a few minutes later, I meet Beth, Allison, and Liz to walk over to the cafeteria for lunch.

"Can you believe Lori didn't want to work on the committee?" Beth shakes her head. "I, like, totally need time to work on my tan!" she mimics.

Allison laughs. "Her loss is our gain. I have to admit I love this theme."

Liz nods in agreement. "I know it's a lot of work, but it'll be fun to work on this together, especially since it's Rachel's first Clark Hall function." While I appreciate the idea, I think Liz forgets how much I have going on at the moment.

"You're going to love it!" Beth claps her hands. "We throw the best parties."

Liz looks at me slyly. "Who are you going to go as, Rachel?"

"I haven't thought about it yet." Zip it, Liz.

"Have you thought about a date?" Beth asks coyly. "Austin Meyers is back on the market." I feel my cheeks get red.

"You guys have been spending a lot of time together," Allison seconds.

"At the library," I say dismissively. "Studying. Remember?" There's no way Austin likes "Rachel," I know it. He even said we're just friends.

"All I'm saying is that a dance is a magical place to make a connection," Allison teases.

"I know who I'm going with," Liz offers. We all stop and look at her.

"Who?" I ask. She hasn't mentioned anybody before.

"Josh Hawkin. He's in my Saturday morning kickboxing class, and he's *so* cute."

"Does he know you like him?" Beth wonders.

"I don't know for sure," Liz admits. "But he did ask me to go to Rotten Tomatoes after class for lunch. And he paid. That means something, right?" We all nod. I can't believe Liz didn't tell me about this. I guess I have been pretty busy.

"We're going out again this Friday night. I think I'm going to ask him then." Liz has a far-off look in her eye.

"I wish I had your confidence," Allison says wistfully. "I could never ask a guy to go with me."

"What about one of the hip-hop guys in the dance company?" I ask.

"They're questionable." Allison grins. "Unlike the guys in Liz's kickboxing class."

"I'm sorry I haven't told you guys about him." Liz looks right at me.

"It's okay. We've all been busy," I say, feeling a little sad. "I'm really happy for you."

"That's great," Beth moans, running a hand through her tight black curls. "Lizzie has someone, Rachel will wind up with Austin." I start to protest, but she cuts me off. "Ali and I will be alone."

"You could ask Rob Murray," Allison suggests. "You guys seemed to hit it off at Lori's party."

Beth ignores her and looks around the crowded patio for a place to sit. Lori's gang has claimed their place at the shady table. Some drama students carrying scripts for *Bye Bye Birdie* are getting up. "I see one!" Beth yells, hiking up her low-rise Levi's jeans. She runs to put her books down.

"Enough about dates," Allison retorts. "Let's talk about how we're going to raise money for charity." She sits down at the table. "Mr. Klein said we needed to make over a thousand dollars for Child of Hope charity, and the only way we're going to do that is if we sell a ton of tickets."

I nod, trying to look knowing. Whenever I volunteer at a charity event, all the details are taken care of. Like last week's Celebrity Cares Carnival. All I did was show up and man the water-gun booth. How they raised the money for tickets or transported the games to carnival chair Samuel L. Jackson's mammoth backyard, I have no idea.

"What we need," Beth says after we've bought lunch and brought it back to the table, "is a celebrity host."

"What do you mean?" Liz asks, and takes an enormous bite of her club sandwich.

"Well, the way we make money is to sell tickets to the dance, right?" Beth explains. "If we have a celebrity host the event, then more people are likely to buy tickets."

"If only we could think of a celebrity willing to come to a cheesy high school dance." Allison frowns.

We sit there in silence for a few minutes. I could think of a bunch of stars that would do it for the publicity, but how would I explain to Beth and Allison why I know them? Or explain to whatever star I ask why I'm not actually going to the dance myself, since I'll be going as Rachel going as . . . oh, forget it.

Beth and Allison stare at Liz. "Please don't ask me," she groans.

I reach for my Vitamin Water and take a swig.

"Come on, Liz," Allison coaxes. "Can't you ask Kaitlin Burke?"

The water in my mouth sprays onto the table.

"Oh my God!" Allison exclaims. "Are you okay?"

"I'm fine," I whisper hoarsely. I guess I forgot that Allison and Beth know Liz is friends with me.

"I can't ask her that." Liz glances at me sideways. "That would be trading on our friendship."

"Friends ask friends for favors," Beth pleads.

"Can't we think of somebody else?" Liz says. "Kaitlin is

getting ready to film a movie and she's swamped with *Family Affair* stuff."

"Don't you mean she's busy cat-fighting with her costars?" Allison mumbles.

"Be nice," Liz cautions.

"Well, if you feel uncomfortable asking her, then maybe you can have your dad get us someone else," Beth suggests. I look from Beth to Liz.

"I don't know what's worse," Liz groans. "Asking Kaitlin or asking my dad to find me a host. When we got White Bandits to play the Winter Carnival last year, it took me three months of begging. He never lets me forget it either. No, we've got to get someone on our own this time." Liz shrugs apologetically, adjusting the pink- and silver-beaded necklace that dangles over her lavender crewneck sweater.

"Kaitlin's just so perfect for this," Beth coos. Liz purses her lips.

"Maybe there's a way to get her without you asking," Beth suggests. "My uncle's golf partner is Tom Pullman, the producer of *Family Affair*," she explains. "Maybe he could ask her for us." Oh God.

"I don't know," Liz says nervously. "I don't want Kaitlin to think I put her up to this. Maybe we should think of someone else."

"Yeah," I second a bit too loudly. Everyone looks at me. The problem is I can't come up with anyone else myself.

"She won't think you had anything to do with this," Allison assures her. "Beth, ask your uncle to try to get her." She turns to Liz. "Unless you want to call her yourself. . . ."

Liz shakes her head. "No, but . . ."

"Then it's settled," Beth declares. "I'll ask my uncle to ask Tom Pullman to ask her." She spears a forkful of Caesar salad and munches happily.

Liz and I look at our plates. I am so screwed. How am I going to explain this to Tom? He doesn't even know I'm at school. I've got to call Laney. I'm about to excuse myself when I hear the theme music to *The O.C.* It's Liz's cell phone ring tone.

"Who would be calling me during school?" Liz wonders. "Hello?" She jumps. "Sorry *Dad*. We don't usually keep our phones on during the day. Uh-huh. Well, you can ask her yourself if you want. Hold on." Liz hands me her phone. "It's my dad. He says you left your, uh, iPod at my house."

I take the phone from Liz. What the . . . "Hello?"

"IT'S ME." I recognize Laney's voice right away. "RODNEY IS PICKING YOU UP TO TAKE YOU TO THE BEAUTY BUFFET IN TWENTY MINUTES."

I quickly walk away from the table. I don't want anyone to hear Laney screaming. "Twenty minutes? I thought I was going at five," I whisper.

"NO, CHANGE OF PLANS. *ACCESS HOLLYWOOD* IS THERE NOW SO YOU NEED TO GO. I ALREADY TOLD PRINCIPAL PEARSON." I hear glasses clinking in the background and the low roar of a busy restaurant. "HOLD ON. HI, NICOLE! HOW ARE THE KIDS?"

"Has anyone heard from Hutch Adams?" I mumble. "Has he breathed in Sky's aura?"

"I don't know," Laney says more quietly. "I'm sure we'll hear something soon. NOW GO MEET RODNEY. WE'LL TALK LATER." She hangs up.

I walk back to the table. Maybe they didn't hear Laney yell. . . .

"Was Liz's dad yelling at you?" Beth asks, her round face creased with concern.

"No, not at all," I say quickly.

"My dad can be hard of hearing sometimes," Liz explains. "He doesn't realize he's yelling." We both giggle nervously.

"I have to go," I announce to the table. "I forgot I have a doctor's appointment this afternoon. My Uncle Rodney is waiting downstairs to pick me up." I look Liz in the eye. She nods knowingly.

"But we were just going to discuss decorations," Allison protests. "I can't meet later. I have dance practice at three."

"I'll think of some ideas and call you tonight," I promise, hurriedly gathering my things. Then I run — as usual — to find Rodney.

HOLLYWOOD SECRET NUMBER FOURTEEN: Celebrity events like the Beauty Buffet rock, but they come at a price. The companies who sponsor the event will give manicures, pedis, facials, Mystic Tanning, a massage, and a bulging bag of products. But in exchange for the loot, you become a walking advertisement for the brands. More than once I've opened *Us Weekly* and seen my name and picture next to a product I supposedly love ("Kaitlin Burke never leaves home without her Trendwatch messenger bag!"). Want free concealer? Then be prepared for the company to say you endorse their product, even though you got it for free, used it once, and maybe didn't even like it.

Today's gift suite is no different, in a private room at the Beverly Hills Hilton, a favorite of jet-setting models and Hollywood royalty. The Buffet looks like an upscale flea market with its rows of booths and services. A Buffet representative greets me at the door and shows me to each table, brightly colored with teal silk cloths. There, an eager publicist is waiting to tell us why a new non-sticky hair gel is the most innovative hair care product on the market. (I grab some for Paul.) I listen patiently at each booth and say things like, "Isn't that amazing!" or "That smells fantastic!" but only take something if I really like it (unlike certain celebs who clean house and then re-gift the stuff at Christmas).

In between booths, I catch up with industry pals that I haven't seen since the last big freebie event rolled into town (ahem, it was only three weeks ago). Some stars go to every single one, like Shana Ellison. I haven't run into others, like my pal Gina Jefferson, in months. We get pedicures together at the makeshift station located in an adjoining suite so that we can talk more about the WB pilot she just shot.

When I leave the Buffet, Rodney lugs my loot home —

including my favorite gift, an all-expenses-paid weekend at a new spa in Palm Springs — and drops me back off at school. It's 3:15, which means I'm fifteen minutes late to meet Austin to study.

When I get to the library, I spot Austin's shaggy blond head near the biography section and hurry over.

"I know you're probably mad at me," I begin before he even looks up, "but I have a good excuse. I was kidnapped by the Emperor." I'm hoping he'll get a kick out of the *Star Wars* reference.

"Don't lie to me." He looks at me hard. "I know where you were."

I feel my knees start to buckle. "You, you do?" I stutter.

"Yeah, picking out something to wear for the Spring Fling. I hear they're running low on Princess Leia buns at the Costume Factory." He grins. He's already dressed for lacrosse practice in his oversized red Clark Hall gym t-shirt and gray sweat shorts.

I exhale slowly. "You caught me," I laugh nervously. "I was afraid someone else would buy it first."

He clears his throat. "Do you have a date yet?" he asks, his turquoise eyes fixed on my face.

Suddenly my palms feel clammy. I shake my head no.

"I was wondering if maybe you'd want to go with me?" He looks away, staring at the overflowing card catalog station topped with a faded sign that says READING IS FUNDAMENTAL. "Together we could rule the galaxy, or at least the dance," he adds with a gorgeous mega-watt smile. He sounds almost shy.

I'm speechless. Is Austin really asking me? I thought he said we were just friends. I'm so confused. I want to go with him, but will that only complicate things further? If I get the Hutch Adams role, I'll be out of Clark before I know it. Is it really fair of me to start something now? What would Austin think if he knew who I really was?

My awkward silence is even more obvious in the quiet of the library. The only noise between us is the hushed whir of the central air conditioning duct above our heads.

The conflicted feelings must show on my face because Austin sighs. "Is this about Lori? We're over."

I shake my head again. This is weird. I've never felt this awkward with a boy before. But I know one thing: I want to go with him to the dance. Mrs. Blumberger, the librarian, walks through the nearby stack and stares at us menacingly. Even in hushed tones she can somehow hear us. When she's out of earshot, I look up at Austin.

"I was just thinking about who we'd go as," I say quietly.

"Is that a yes?" His voice sounds deeper than usual. I bite my lip and nod again.

"Well, you can forget about going as Anakin and Padmé." Austin grins. "They're not celebrities, just characters." I roll my eyes at his know-it-all tone.

"What if I go as someone completely off-the-wall and out of character?" he suggests.

"Like who?" I'm curious to hear what he'll come up with.

"This is going to sound lame, but the guys on the team think I look like Ryan from *Family Affair*." Austin looks even cuter when he's sheepish. "I've been thinking that I could go as the guy who plays him. What do you think? His name is Trevor Something."

"Wainright," I offer. This isn't happening to me. I'm afraid to even ask the obvious next question. "Would that mean I'd be going as Kaitlin Burke?"

"Yeah." Austin looks expectantly at me. "Supposedly they're into each other in real life. At least that's what my sister tells me. She loves those magazines." I guess I look nervous because then he adds, "You could pull it off, I'm sure."

"I bet I could." I try not to crack a smile. If he only knew. "Okay, why not? I'll do it."

"Cool," Austin says. He reaches over and gives my hand a quick squeeze. I instantly turn scarlet when he doesn't let go right away.

I can't look him in the eye right now. Part of me wants to faint at the idea of him touching me. The other part of me wants to throw up at my constant lies. I wish so much that I could tell him the truth. Nadine would say I'm being impulsive, but I feel like Austin knows me. Isn't Rachel Rogers who I really am inside? Rachel is Kaitlin with the glamour and hype stripped away — parts of me that have wanted to escape for a while now. Rachel *is* Kaitlin. And Austin likes *her*.

Austin stares at me, as if he knows I have more to say. I open my mouth, imagining the words, when I hear it go off in my bag. My Sidekick is vibrating.

I already know who it is. Nadine is waiting outside with Rodney to take me to the airport for my forty-eight-hour New York trip with Laney. "I have to go," I say regretfully.

The mood is broken. "We didn't even study." He pulls his hand away slowly.

"I know, I'm sorry. Something came up unexpectedly with my mum. I'll give you a call tomorrow night to talk about our costumes. I'm going to be out tomorrow and Friday for a wedding."

Austin nods. "Have a good time," he says. "I'm going to stick around here and get some homework done before practice. Maybe we can get together for a movie or something when you get back."

I stuff my books in my black mesh messenger bag. "Sounds good," I respond quickly. Then I turn and dash out of the library, trying to wrap my head around what just happened. I, Kaitlin Burke, am going to Clark Hall's spring formal as Rachel Rogers dressed as Kaitlin Burke, while my date, who is infinitely cuter than Trevor Wainright, is dressing up as Trevor because his friends say he looks like him.

It's official. My life is now more complicated than anything the *FA* writers could cook up.

Wednesday 4/14

NOTES TO SELF:

April 22nd. Date of Spring Fling with Austin. :)

Have Nadine find a "Kaitlin costume" to wear 2 the dance. Should look good, but not 2 real.

Have Paul find a bad blond wig. . . .

Make sure Laney booked us massages at the W after Letterman taping.

Call Seth about Hutch Adams. No — don't call. I'm 2 afraid to find out what H thinks of me versus Sky!

fourteen: *Denim Blues*

Yay! There's Saturday morning construction on the freeway again! It will take us an hour to get downtown for today's shoot.

Maybe I'm just hopped up on the Red Bull I downed in an act of desperation, but I'm loving the traffic situation this morning. It gives me a chance to fill Rodney and Nadine in on what happened at Clark Hall with Austin right before I left for New York. I've just flown the red-eye, and instead of getting some well-needed sleep or studying for my French exam, after forty-eight hours of schmoozing with Laney, I'm headed to an *FA* photo shoot for *TV Tome*'s "Fall TV Preview" issue. Yes, I know it's April, but now is the only time the whole cast will be in L.A. during hiatus.

"Wait, let me get this straight." Nadine pulls out her bible to double-check today's shooting schedule. "You're going to the dance as Rachel masquerading as Kaitlin and Austin is going as Trevor?"

"Yeah," I confirm slowly. "But you haven't even heard the best part — the Fling committee wants *me* to host the dance."

"I'm confused. Who do they want to host — the real you or the fake you?" Rodney mumbles as he sips his Ice Blended.

"The real me." I tell them about the girls' enlisting Tom Pullman's help. "For a split second I thought about going as both," I continue, "but Mom almost had a heart attack when I mentioned it. She quickly called Tom to thank him for a great season, and when he brought up the dance, she sweetly told him we had a previous family engagement. He was really disappointed."

"What did Laney say about all this?" Nadine questions.

"Laney," Rodney groans.

"I know." I rub my forehead. I still have a dull headache just remembering *that* conversation on the plane. "Laney freaked out that Mom turned down the offer. To quote her exactly, 'KAITLIN, CHARITY EVENTS MAKE YOU LOOK GOOD. HOW COULD YOU SAY NO?'" I yell, mimicking Laney.

"She wanted you to go to the dance as yourself and as the fake Kaitlin?" Nadine asks incredulously.

"I said no to a school charity thing. Well, not exactly, but she also didn't want the tabloids finding out. She begged Mom to find a way for me to make an appearance."

"That's crazy," Nadine says. "How would you have pulled it off?"

"I know." I rake my fingers through my dry hair. My tresses are taking a beating from that skull cap I wear. "But now I'm in an even bigger mess. Tom told Mom he'd find someone to take my place, so Laney's upset. And Liz told me that Beth and Allison think Kaitlin Burke is a diva because she, or should I say I, wouldn't host."

Rodney laughs. "You have gotten yourself into some mess, Kates."

Paul and Shelly say the same thing when I tell them what happened an hour later. They're doing my hair and makeup for the *TV Tome* shoot. Now Rodney, Nadine, Paul, Shelly, and I are all squished into a tiny dressing room at Boom! Studios trying to get me ready and discussing my latest dilemma.

"It sounds like you'll have to transfer to a new school," Shelly jokes.

"It's not funny," I protest. Nadine is biting her short nails again. She's not laughing.

"It's a sign, Kaitlin." She hands me a pair of ripped-at-the-knee hip-hugger jeans to try on. *TV Tome* wants everyone to wear their own denim and white t-shirts for the shoot. The matching clothes are supposed to make us look like one big happy family (don't laugh!).

"Nadine," I moan. I walk behind a curtained area in the dressing room to change.

"You wanted the school experience and you got it," she says matter-of-factly. "Now it's time to leave before you blow your cover. You need to concentrate on more important things, like snagging the Hutch Adams flick you're drooling over."

"The script is to die for," I admit, thinking of how I devoured the manuscript while I was in New York. The character has a ton of action scenes and is a master at karate. I have to remember to e-mail Liz about joining her kickboxing class. I need some muscle tone if I want to play someone as killer as Hutch Adams's movie heroine.

I slip on a fitted bright white V-neck tee that stops right above my belly button, and walk around the curtain. Shelly nods her approval and begins applying my makeup. "But I don't want to miss the dance," I add, thinking of Austin. I get goose bumps whenever I replay in my mind the moment he asked me — which I've been doing often.

"School dances." Paul shudders. "How exciting do you think a gymnasium full of boys in *rented* tuxedos is when you've already been to the Oscars?"

"The Oscar parties are fun, but attending the actual ceremony is a bit . . . dull," I say gingerly. Paul covers his mouth in horror. He's dying to sit in the audience for the Oscars, even if the ceremony is four plus hours long.

I'm not sure if Paul realizes HOLLYWOOD SECRET NUMBER FIFTEEN. When you watch an awards show from the comfort of your couch, you don't sit perfectly still in an uncomfortable floor-length gown and smile for four hours straight, do you? No, you wear your sweats, get up for bathroom breaks, and make popcorn during the Best Film Editing award. Well, thankfully, celebs don't have to stay in their seats the whole time either. Event coordinators for the Academy Awards and the Golden Globes hire seat fillers — volunteers who will literally fill your seat so that the auditorium looks full the entire taping. That way, we can run to the bathroom, or better yet, drool over Colin Farrell at the bar (which is what I did last year).

When Paul and Shelly have given me iron-straight hair and a fresh-scrubbed face that looks like I'm wearing no makeup even though I'm wearing a ton, Nadine and I walk into Studio #2, where we're shooting. The stereo is cranking out Usher tunes as a waitress from Boom! walks over to take Nadine's and my drink order. I notice the *TV Tome* photographer and his assistant are setting up their cameras and adjustable lights in front of a taupe silk backdrop that is hanging from the ceiling. Two rows of old wooden boxes of various heights are neatly arranged in front of the drape. I guess that's what we'll be standing on. I look around. Over by the breakfast table, which is loaded with fresh raspberry crepes (Sky's breakfast of choice), fruit platters, and Noah's Bagels, a young girl with braces is talking a mile a minute to an older woman in a black apron who is arranging the silverware. I don't see anyone else from *FA* here yet, so I plop down on one of the white leather couches and pull out my French notebook. Mrs. Desmond is giving us a quiz on Monday. As soon as I turn to the page of travel questions I need to memorize (*"Est-ce que vous pouvez me montrer où je suis sur la carte?"* which means "Can you show me on the map where I am?"), my Sidekick begins to vibrate.

POWERGRL82: Where R U?

PRINCESSLEIA25: Photo shoot. Y?

POWERGRL82: Beth called emergency mtg because "U" said no.

PRINCESSLEIA25: Mom wouldn't let me. Too risky.

POWERGRL82: She's right.

PRINCESSLEIA25: What time is the mtg?

POWERGRL82: 11.

PRINCESSLEIA25: Can't make it. The shoot is just starting.

POWERGRL82: I'll cover.

PRINCESSLEIA25: Thx. Remind me 2 talk 2 U about kickboxing. I need 2 join.

POWERGRL82: Maybe U'll learn how 2 kick Sky's bootie. Josh can give us private lessons:)

PRINCESSLEIA25: Aww . . . Josh. U R not off the hook about him. I want deets!

POWERGRL82: Uh huh. Talk to U later!

"Hey, K," A familiar voice coos. I look up. Sky is clinging to Trevor's arm as if she might fall over if she lets go. "We haven't seen you since my party." Sky's wearing Daisy Duke–style denim cutoffs, no bra, and a cropped white tee that says HIS in rhinestones. Her long black hair hangs straight down her back. Trevor's baggy white tee says HERS. Poor Trev.

I quickly close my notebook so that Sky can't read it. "Hey, Skylar, Trev." I grin. "Nice, uh, shirts."

"Sky ordered them." Trevor frowns. "Do you think I look

like a girl in this?" He points to the rhinestones across his chest.

"No, sweetie!" Sky gasps. "You look cute." She looks at me smugly. "And it shows the world that we're truly a couple." She looks thinner than ever, if that's possible. I can almost count her ribs through her tight t-shirt.

I raise an eyebrow. "So she finally wore you down, huh, Trev?" He turns beet red.

"Trev asked *me* out," Sky protests indignantly. "Not the other way around."

"Whatever you say, Sky." I smile sweetly.

"OH MY GOD! IT'S SAM, SARA, AND RYAN!" someone shrieks. The three of us turn around, alarmed. The girl I saw over by the breakfast spread is sprinting towards us clutching a *Family Affair Family Tree* scrapbook that was published last year. (It's a fictitious photo album with "handwritten" notes from Paige about our family's stormy history.) The girl stops at the edge of the couch I'm sitting on. She's wearing a pink shirt with the words FAMILY FANATIC painted across her chest. "I LOVE YOU GUYS!" she shrills, showing her mouth full of metal. She looks around the same age as Austin's sister. If she were older, I'd be a little nervous about her eagerness. But she's a kid, so I know she's harmless. I motion to Rodney to back away.

"You don't have to shout," Sky snaps. "We're not deaf." The girl looks stricken.

"What's your name, sweetie?" I ask, shooting daggers at Sky.

"Marlena, as in *Days of Our Lives*," she says. Sky snickers, but Marlena doesn't notice. "That's my mom's favorite soap, but mine is *Family Affair*. And you're my favorite, Sam." She points to me.

"Thank you." I nod to the scrapbook she's hugging to her chest. "Did you want us to sign that for you?"

"Yes, please." She sits down on the couch next to me. She opens the scrapbook to Sam's and Sara's "diary." "Sign it right here," she says, pointing to my picture. "And write 'to my best friend in the whole world, Marlena.'"

I smile and pull my purple Sharpie out of my large black messenger bag. "You got it," I say.

"I'm not writing that," Sky scoffs. "I don't even know you. I'll just sign my name. So will Trevor."

"Sky, she's a kid," I whisper hotly. "Can't you make her happy?" Sky turns her head away in disgust. Trev looks at me sheepishly and shrugs his shoulders.

"OOOH! Is that a Sidekick?" Marlena reaches over me and digs into my bag. The green bedazzled machine is sticking out.

"Um, please don't touch that," I say as nicely as I can. I reach over to take it out of her hands.

"I read in *Celeb Insider* that you're never without this thing!" Marlena exclaims in awe as she rotates the Sidekick in her hand. "Hey, do you have Hilary Duff's phone number in here? Could I have it please? I promise I won't use it."

Sky snorts.

I pry the Sidekick from her sweaty hand. "No, I don't know Hilary very well," I tell her, and drop it into a zippered section of the bag. Marlena watches me, her mouth drooping around her braces in disappointment. I hand her back the scrapbook. "Here you go. It was nice meeting you, Marlena."

She frowns. "Could I see your Sidekick again? Maybe I could just have one green gem off it. I read you glued them on yourself."

"You did it yourself?" Sky spits. "What, you couldn't afford to send it over to Swarovski?"

"Marlena!" The woman in the black apron hisses, hurrying over to us. She grabs Marlena by the wrist and yanks her off the couch. "Leave the cast alone. I told you to wait till after the shoot to ask for autographs."

"But Aunt Lil, the whole cast is here now!" Marlena whines, pointing to the sea of white tees and denim that has filled the room.

"I'm so sorry," the woman says to the three of us, wringing her hands.

"Are you supposed to be here?" Sky snaps. "Who are *you*?"

"A Boom! waitress," the woman explains sheepishly. "They said it was okay if I brought my niece in here to watch."

"I think you'll have to leave now." Sky motions to her beefy bodyguard to escort them out.

"Sky!" I protest. I turn to the pair apologetically. "I'm sorry. We're just getting ready to shoot now. Why don't you guys take a seat on the couch and watch. I'm sure everyone will sign Marlena's book afterwards."

"Thank you," Lil says gratefully.

Nadine walks over. "Kates, they want you to do a lighting check," she says, ignoring Sky. "Trevor, they want you too. You're doing a pose together."

"Gee, that's going to be awkward with that shirt you have on," I tease Trev. He looks at Sky nervously.

"I'll just have a word with the photographer, sweetie," Sky says through gritted teeth.

Nadine rolls her eyes and leads us away from Lil and Marlena, with Sky following close behind.

The shoot itself takes less than an hour. Sky would only agree to the shoot if it was that quick. It's fine by me. Maybe I can still catch the meeting. Or finish studying. First, I hug Melli goodbye and whisper to her about Marlena. She walks over to the couch with me to meet her.

"Marlena, this is my TV mom," I say, putting a hand on Melli's shoulder. "I thought you might want her autograph." Marlena squeals with delight and jumps off the couch to hug us both. Melli laughs.

"Got everything?" Nadine appears at my side.

I pick up my nylon bag and sling it over my shoulder. "Yep," I say, patting it.

"Bye, Marlena." I smile. She's busy chatting with Melli. "Oh yeah, bye, Sam!" she says, distracted.

Melli shakes her strawberry blond head, and I walk away.

It's not until we're halfway home that I remember I was supposed to e-mail Laney about the shoot. She had to skip it because she had a press conference in Santa Monica. ("I can't trust Russell alone with reporters," she said.) I reach inside the bag and feel around for my Sidekick. When I can't find it, I pull my bag onto my lap and start pulling things out of it. My Gucci sunglasses, my French notebook, my other pair of jeans.

But it's not there.

"Is something wrong?" Nadine asks.

I start unzipping the inside compartments. "Yeah, I can't find my Sidekick," I say, trying not to panic. "I know I had it with me."

"It's got to be there," Nadine soothes.

I lift the bag over my head and frantically shake it to see if anything falls out. It's not inside. "Nadine, I think we have a problem."

FIFTeen: *Hallway Meltdown*

Dread. Gloom. Panic.

That's the pervading theme at my house, which resembles a scene out of *King Kong*, with everyone screaming at each other over the whereabouts of my missing Sidekick. And for once, I'm in total agreement with my whole team.

If my Sidekick wasn't swept away with the trash (which is doubtful) and was in fact stolen, then I'm FINISHED. DONE FOR. Or as we say in French class, *danger de mort*.

I've looked everywhere for my Sidekick, including Boom! Nadine, Rodney, and I retraced our steps at the studio, turning the place upside down. But we found nothing.

Liz kept e-mailing my Sidekick, hoping someone would answer. She sent notes like,

> PRINCESSLEIA25: If U turn this Sidekick over 2 the police, U'll get a $$$ reward (or if I find U first, a total butt-kicking!).

Laney called the editors at *TV Tome* and did what she does best — threatened to sue. She was worried that my Sidekick notes would turn up on the Web, which happened to a famously hard-partying socialite. Hackers were able to read her e-mails and download her phonebook, which had digits for all her fabulous celeb friends. The story was all over the news.

Nadine thinks that kid Marlena swiped my Sidekick. I did leave my bag on the couch next to her at the shoot. She says Marlena was probably a fake fan instructed by Aunt Lil to swipe my Sidekick so that they could sell it to the tabs for a small fortune. Laney was so crazed by the mere suggestion of this that she called Boom! and demanded to speak to Lil. Turns out she quit after my photo shoot Saturday afternoon and the phone number the studio has for her is *out of service.*

"SHE'S PROBABLY NOT EVEN HER AUNT!" Laney had shrieked at the poor Boom! receptionist who took her call. After Laney threatened to have the operator's job if she didn't find Lil's address, the girl broke down in tears. Nadine felt so bad for the girl, she suggested we arrange for the Boom! receptionist to be my own personal guest on the *FA* set this fall. Laney, however, thinks the girl is in on the Sidekick conspiracy.

I can't say I blame her. All I can think about is who could be reading my Sidekick right now. Is it the photographer's assistant? Marlena? The bathroom attendant at Boom! who scowled at me when I smiled at her?

I wanted to question Sky. She saw me using my Sidekick Saturday morning. She's the perfect suspect, if you ask me.

"But if it was Sky, you would have read about it in the *New York Post* by now," Laney says dismissively. "She never would let it sit idly in her hot little hands. She would have used it to get the Hutch Adams part over you."

I guess. . . .

Mom won't voice it out loud, but I think she's afraid my missing Sidekick will cost me the Hutch Adams role. While Dad's response is to be rational ("Your Sidekick is not in sinister hands") and Matt's is to laugh about it ("I can't believe you left your Sidekick *on the couch*"), Mom is in a state of panic.

"Are you sure it's not somewhere in your room?" she asks for the fortieth time as she ransacks my bedroom, which Anita has just finished cleaning, and pulls clothes out of my closet. She hasn't changed out of the black PB&J Couture suit she's been wearing since yesterday, which is very unlike her.

"Mom, I told you. I had it with me at the shoot!" A pair of white Pumas fly past my head.

"You wouldn't have left it in your bag and walked away." She's frowning, which she usually tries to avoid because it encourages wrinkles. "Maybe you threw it away by accident."

"Let's *pray* she threw it away," Nadine mumbles. She's clutching her bible. She hasn't put it down since the Sidekick incident happened, paranoid that someone will get my other source of information. She even took it to bed last night and slept with it under her sensible Discount World pillow. That couldn't have been comfortable.

My phone rings and I pick it up. It's Laney. "Put me on speaker phone," she orders cheerfully.

"I have some good news," Laney announces to all of us. "Sky's demands at the *TV Tome* shoot will be on *Celeb Insider* today."

"You mean about her only agreeing to shoot for an hour?" Nadine asks. "How'd they find out about that?"

"I might have called over there and slipped," Laney coos. "They'll be so busy looking into Sky's antics that no one will pay attention to Kaitlin for a few days. That should buy us some time till we figure out where her Sidekick is."

HOLLYWOOD SECRET NUMBER SIXTEEN: Sometimes publicists, yes publicists, will play as dirty as their clients. They'll plant items in the press themselves if it will help their desperate situation. It's not just PR folks who use this trick either — celebrities, magazine editors, photographers, anyone out to get revenge can dial a gossip hound's digits and cause some serious image damage.

"People know you're my publicist," I panic. "Won't they be suspicious?"

"I didn't call them myself," Laney responds dismissively. "My assistant called. And she called from our mail carrier's cell phone and used a fake name." I bite my lip. I hope Laney's right.

"You should get to school, Kates," Nadine points out. "Your mom will help me search your room again."

"Actually, I have a deep tissue massage at ten," Mom protests.

"The more people looking, the better," Nadine adds, ignoring her. "We'll also call your cell if we find it," she tells me.

"Or if you hear from Hutch Adams," I remind her. I actually called him on Saturday after the Sidekick fiasco, as Laney had suggested, to see if his nieces liked the autographs I sent over. He was in the editing booth at Wagman finishing up the sound on his latest film, *Die Harder*. He was a bit distracted, but I could have sworn he said, "They're looking forward to spending time with you." But maybe I imagined it. My mind obviously isn't all there right now.

Rodney and I drive all the way to Clark Hall in silence. All I can think about is my Sidekick in the wrong hands. My whole life is in that thing — my friends' phone numbers, my homework assignments for Clark Hall, and some seriously incriminating e-mails about my double life. If someone finds it, I'm more than *danger de mort* — I'll drop from the Hollywood food chain completely. And I'm starting to realize that as hectic as my life is, I really don't want that to happen. And I *really* don't want Sky to win the Hutch Adams role either.

After Rodney drops me off, I drag my huge feet across campus to my locker. I was so bummed out this morning, I didn't realize I put on a pink ten-percent cotton turtleneck sweater with my favorite Chloe jeans. I hope Liz doesn't notice. Especially since she's standing in front of my locker wearing the same exact pair. She, however, isn't wearing a polyester sweater. Instead, she's wearing a funky strapless navy-and-red-striped top. She sees me and frowns.

"I know I'm wearing my own jeans," I spill before she even opens her mouth. Liz purses her ruby red lip-glossed lips, but doesn't answer. "What?" I demand anxiously. "Is it my Sidekick?"

"No, but you're not going to like this either," Liz says slowly. Before she can clarify, Beth and Allison arrive. Beth is clutching a clipboard that says SPRING FLING.

"Did Liz tell you?" Allison asks breathlessly.

"Tell me what?" I look from a frowning Liz to a smiling Beth and Allison.

"We found a replacement for Kaitlin Burke!" Beth exclaims.

I breathe a sigh of relief. That's one less thing to worry about. "Great. Who'd you get?"

Beth and Allison look at each other and giggle. "Sky Mackenzie," they chorus in unison.

"YOU GOT SKY MACKENZIE?" I shriek, forgetting my British accent. People walking down the hall turn and stare.

"Hey . . ." Allison points at me. "Your accent . . ."

"That sounded pretty good," Liz interjects quickly, pounding me on the back. "You're learning an American accent already."

"You don't like Sky?" Beth asks me.

"It's not that . . . ," I begin, trying to pull myself together.

"She's even a better get than Kaitlin Burke," Allison

interrupts, tossing her long brown hair. "Sky isn't all over *Hollywood Insider* like Kaitlin is." She glances at Liz out of the corner of her eye. Liz glares at her.

"She seems very nice," Beth adds. "We're going to talk again tonight. Sky wants to know all about Clark Hall and how she can help us. With the dance on Friday, we don't have much time to plan."

Sky is calling Beth? That's weird. She usually makes her publicist handle all her menial calls. Beth must be mistaken. But before Beth and Allison can nominate Sky for Actress of the Year, the first bell rings.

"We've got to go, but remember, we're starting to decorate the gym after school today," Allison reminds us. She reaches down and massages her calf, visible below her hot pink pleated skirt. "I spent two hours in dance class last night to make up for missing this afternoon." The two of them leave Liz and me standing there.

"I shouldn't have volunteered for this committee," Liz apologizes. "If I had known they wanted a celebrity host . . ."

"It's okay," I assure her, shaking. But the truth is, it's not. Nothing's okay and I can't hold it in any longer. My eyes start to well up with tears. Leave it to Sky to ruin everything. Again.

"It's going to be okay, Kates," Liz promises, hugging me.

"It's so unfair," I bawl, not caring about the people in the hallway who turn and stare curiously. I keep my voice low, though. "My Sidekick is probably being examined by someone at *In Touch*, Hutch Adams still hasn't said he wants me in his movie, and to top it all off, now I can't go to the dance with Austin."

"First off, your cover is *not* blown," Liz reminds me softly. "Secondly, we don't know where your Sidekick is. For all we know, it could be at a landfill by now." I sniffle. "You said Laney's been calling some of the gossip reporters, and no one's said anything, right?" I nod. "So why would you have to skip the dance?"

I give her a you-should-know-better look. "Sky is not going to suspect anything," Liz whispers confidently. "Why would she? I go to school here, not Kaitlin. This is just a crazy coincidence." I sniffle again. Liz reaches into her oversized, slouchy denim handbag and pulls out a pack of tissues.

"Thanks." I blow my nose with an unladylike snort, then grab another tissue to wipe away my tears. I'm trying not to smudge my eyeliner and mascara, but then I remember that "Rachel" doesn't wear makeup. Get your head glued on straight, Kaitlin!

From all the crying, my right contact lens seems to be out of whack. I look in my locker mirror and try to shift the lens back in place, but instead it pops out of my eye.

"Liz, I lost a lens!" I hiss. I drop to the ground to look for it. Liz quickly drops her bag and begins searching too. The two of us run our fingers along the red-specked floor.

"Lose something?" Out of the corner of my eye I look up. Oh geez, it's Austin. He looks adorable in boat shoes, knock-off Burberry shorts, and a royal blue Polo shirt.

"Hey, Austin." I try to sound casual and quickly put my head back down. "I, uh, lost a contact."

"But don't you wear glasses?" he queries, looking confused.

Oops. "I have a trial pair of contacts to try," I cover quickly. "It doesn't seem like it's going to work out, though."

"Do you need help looking?" he offers.

"No, we've got it covered," Liz says hastily. Austin kneels down anyway.

"It couldn't have gone far," he reasons. His hands slide across the ground. Liz looks at me. I know what she's thinking. If he notices that the contact lens is brown, or worse yet, sees my one green eye. . . .

"Found it!" Liz yells. She holds out her palm. I grab the lens and stuff it back in my eye, dirt and all.

"Gross." Austin laughs, looking shocked. "Aren't you supposed to use cleaner or something?"

"I don't have it with me," I admit. "And I can't walk around with one lens, so . . ."

"We should go, Rach," Liz says. "We're late for first period."

"Me too," Austin agrees. "My mom got stuck in traffic, so I'm late for Mrs. D." He holds up a note. "I'm hoping she'll accept this. My mom wrote it in French."

"If that doesn't work, I don't know what will." I gather my books off the floor. I stuff my tortoise-shell glasses in the pile, hoping Austin won't notice.

"I'll see you guys in Mr. Klein's room. I have to book it over to North Hall for geometry." Liz dashes off, leaving Austin and me alone.

"Ready to go?" he asks.

I nod, my eye twitching from the dirty lens. With everything happening, maybe I should tell him I can't go on Friday. "About Friday night," I begin.

"Oh yeah," Austin says, running a hand through his gelled hair. "I tried calling you all weekend to talk about the details, but you weren't home." I think of Nadine carrying around the "emergency" phone line we set up for Clark calls. I'm sure she ignored the rings because of the Sidekick drama.

"Yeah, I got back from the wedding later than I planned," I explain, relieved that I remembered my excuse. "But about the dance . . ."

"Yeah, so do you want me to rent us a ride or something? I don't think I can get away with driving my Mom's car with just a learner's permit." He laughs.

"No, that's okay." What am I thinking? I can't cancel! If the rest of my life is going down the toilet, then at least I can enjoy one last night of happiness . . . that is, if my Sidekick notes don't get reprinted in *US Weekly* before then.

"Why don't we meet at the dance?" I suggest, sidestepping the dilemma of Austin showing up at my McMansion. "I don't want Beth and Allison to walk in alone. They're going solo."

"Yeah, you're right." He looks deep in thought. "I'll meet you there. But I hope we recognize each other."

"What do you mean?" I ask confused.

"You'll be dressed as Kaitlin!" he laughs. "I can't wait to see how you pull it off."

"Me too," I respond truthfully.

sixteen:
Night of a Thousand Stars

"Aren't you glad you didn't cancel on Austin?" Liz asks me as we hoist a huge A NIGHT OF A THOUSAND STARS banner onto a wall of the gymnasium.

It's Friday morning, and Allison, Beth, Liz, and I are putting the finishing touches on the gym. The room has been off-limits to everyone but the committee and volunteers all week. We even put black construction paper on the gym door windows so that nobody, including snoopsters Lori and Jessie, can see the room before tonight.

"Nah, this dance thing seems overrated," I joke. "Maybe I won't show up." We both laugh.

By Thursday, when no mention of my Sidekick had turned up in the gossips, Laney, Nadine, my parents, and I started to relax a bit. I guess I *did* accidentally throw it out.

"A trash compacter probably ground it to pieces by now, taking all your incriminating e-mails with it," Laney said gleefully. She celebrated by ordering me a Sidekick II covered in Swarovski crystals. ("Sarah Michelle has one just like it!" she boasted. Sky would approve.) Mom was so happy she offered to help me find something Kaitlin-appropriate to wear to the dance. I guess Sky hosting the dance is just a regrettable coincidence. Laney still came up with a worst-case scenario excuse to use if I get caught ("You're doing top-secret research for a *Marie Claire* cover story. They wanted you to try living a normal life," Laney concocted. "I'm sure I could convince their editor to cover for you.") I really don't think I'm going to be exposed though. Tonight I'll be concentrating on dancing with Austin in the middle of the basketball court under a sea of streamers to the strains of "Wonderland" by John Mayer. (Cue the eye roll from Paul.)

And tomorrow ... well, tomorrow, after Hutch Adams gets back from Vienna, where he's vacationing with his third wife, Seth swears he's calling with his decision. The word is that Sky and I are the top two contenders. It makes me want to throw up. "When you get the part," Laney said confidently, "you have to sit down with me and your parents and Nadine and figure out how this 'Rachel' will exit school without anyone noticing."

I'm hoping if things go well enough, maybe, just *maybe*, I can find a way to tell Austin tonight who I really am. I'm dying to talk this over with Liz, but if Laney or Nadine overhears me even hypothetically telling Austin who I am, I won't live to see nightfall.

I have a feeling everything about tonight is going to be perfect. The gym looks amazing. On one end of the room is the stage, which will hold the DJ and Sky. (She's sticking around for the first hour to announce some tunes and gush about how happy she is to be there.) In another corner, we created a faux outdoor seating area that resembles The Ivy restaurant. That's where we have all the food, which is pretty much chicken fingers, corn dogs, and pizza — the kind of food I always wish I could get at the real Ivy.

The best part about the gym transformation, though, is the murals. The Anime Club put its talent to good use by painting a different backdrop for each wall: there's the Hollywood sign, Grauman's Chinese Theatre, a street on a studio backlot, and the fourth — my idea, thank you very much — is a picture of a group of paparazzi snapping photos. The school photographer will be set up in that corner to take pictures of each couple. Everyone who takes a picture will get a memento photo sleeve that says, I WAS STALKED AT CLARK HALL'S "A NIGHT OF A THOUSAND STARS."

Cool, huh? It's amazing to think that decorations made from papier-mâché, Elmer's glue, and glitter could feel more exciting than any blitzed out Hollywood affair I'm normally on the VIP list for.

"Rachel, I have to hand it to you," Allison says, stepping back to admire the starry banner Liz and I just hung. "For someone new to the States, you really know your Hollywood culture. That paparazzi wall is a riot!"

"Thanks." I grin. "We have camera stalkers in the U.K. too, you know. Just ask Prince Wills."

Beth pulls the four of us in for a group hug. "I'm so proud

of us," she exclaims. "Even Mr. Klein can't say a bad thing about the awesome job we've done."

"And you know he'd try to come up with something if he could," Liz points out.

"The biggest props go to Bethie for pulling off the celebrity host." Allison claps. "*Especially* after Kaitlin Burke said no."

Just a few more hours of this, and hopefully I won't have to hear how awful I am for a while. At least not in person.

"Let's not start that again," Liz warns.

"Do you know Sky called me again last night?" Beth relates, awestruck. "She told me that she might stay longer than an hour. She may even bring Trevor Wainright!"

Allison sighs. "I love him."

"Sky's so cool," Beth gushes, shaking her curly head in amazement.

"Um, let's not forget she's getting something out of this too," Liz grumbles. "She's bringing a magazine reporter with her. She's doing this for publicity, guys." Aww, thanks, Lizzie.

"She promised her publicist that she'd do that," Beth retorts defensively. "Sky *wants* to do this. She told me that the Spring Fling came up at the perfect moment. She was calling Tom Pullman to ask him how she could get involved with some charity work for the show...."

That's hard to believe.

"...And he said, 'It just so happens that I have an opportunity for you that Kaitlin just turned down,'" Beth continues.

Aha! She'd never pass up something like that!

"She seems very nice," Beth adds. Liz snorts. "The only thing that was odd was when she screamed at her mom for interrupting our phone call. I mean, my mom walks in on my private calls all the time."

Now that sounds more like the girl I know.

"Did she say she knew me?" Liz asks. "We don't get along that well."

"She said she vaguely remembered meeting you," Beth says dismissively.

Sky *definitely* would remember Liz. She's met her a dozen times!

"What time are we meeting at your house, Liz?" Allison interrupts.

"I was thinking right after school, so that we have time to get ready before Josh arrives," Liz says gleefully. Liz is going as Angelina Jolie. Her date, Josh from kickboxing, is going as Brad Pitt. Beth is going as Halle Berry. And Allison is going as Lindsay Lohan — from classic red hair days.

"Did you tell Rob you'd save him a dance?" Allison ribs Beth.

Beth turns as red as the streamers dangling high above her head. "Yeah," she squeaks. "What time are you meeting Austin, Rach?"

"I told him seven-thirty in front of The Ivy." Now it's my turn to blush. I'm saved by the bell before anybody can say anything else.

"My house! Three-thirty!" Liz yells as she races out of the gym. I watch the others leave, and hang back to call Nadine. At this point, Mrs. Desmond knows I'm never on time, so what's another late mark?

"Hey," Nadine answers the phone. "Everything okay?"

"I think so." I fill her in on what Beth said about Sky. "Don't you think it's odd that Sky's this excited about a high school dance?"

"It is strange," Nadine agrees absentmindedly. I can hear her jotting notes in her bible. "But I think you're over-reacting."

I feel my palms begin to sweat again. "I don't think so. I think this proves she snagged my Sidekick." I say, getting hyper.

Nadine pauses. "She could have taken your Sidekick. But if she had, she would have leaked it to the press by now to snag the Hutch role. She's always so quick to call the tabloids. Why would she sit on something this juicy?"

"I don't know." Now I'm getting *really* nervous.

"You're just anxious about seeing Austin tonight," Nadine soothes. "But I tell you what. If it makes you feel better, I'll call your mom and Laney and tell them about Sky. I'll call you back if we think there's a problem. Just get through your classes and go over to Liz's to get ready."

"Okay," I say, trying to be calm. Nadine's right. I'm sure I'm just looking for a problem. But I can't help feeling jumpy when Nadine texts my Sidekick II.

Friday 4/16 6 PM

FUTUREPREZ: Spoke to Laney. The only call she got about U is 1 from *Celeb Insider* asking 2 do a piece on U being up 4 the Hutch role.

PRINCESSLEIA25: U swear?

FUTUREPREZ: Yes. But your mom, Laney, and I aren't taking chances.

PRINCESSLEIA25: R U worried?

FUTUREPREZ: No. Just prepared. Rod and I r coming w/U to make sure nothing goes wrong..

PRINCESSLEIA25: How?

FUTUREPREZ: U'll see. Just give Liz a heads-up.

"Rachel, who are you texting?" Allison asks as she paints her nails bubble gum pink.

"Oh, just my Mom." I quickly drop my Sidekick II in my bag.

"Well, stop texting her and go get ready!" Beth exclaims, waving her mascara wand. "We've got to leave in an hour!"

At 6:55 PM, Angelina, Halle, Lindsay, and I, the fake Kaitlin Burke, are finally ready. All that's left to do is meet Liz's date, Josh, who is being dropped off at her house at seven. I've never seen Liz look so nervous. She keeps playing with her hair extensions and double-checking her fake tattoos to make sure they haven't smudged.

"Liz, you've outdone us all," I say in awe, admiring her strapless black leather gown and laced-up strappy heels. I peer over the upstairs landing and see a guy below holding a pink corsage box. He's pacing the marble tile floor. "He's here," I whisper. Liz pushes the hair from her extension behind her ear and takes the lead down the entrance hall's ten-foot-wide pink marble staircase.

"Hey," Josh murmurs, clearing his throat at the sight of Liz looking so bootylicious. For his Brad Pitt look, Josh is wearing beat-up jeans, a stained gray tee over his muscular upper body, and is sporting bluish bruises on his arms and face.

"Wow, who did your makeup?" Beth asks him. "Those bruises look awesome."

"They're real," Liz explains proudly. "Josh won our kick-boxing championship on Wednesday night." Josh blushes slightly, the pink hue matching his strawberry blond hair.

"Hi, girls, Josh," Mr. Mendes greets us, walking by the staircase as he throws on his coat. "Have a good time." He's wearing a leather jacket, and black shades cover his bald head, even though it's nighttime. Mr. Mendes gives me a little wink. I wink back. He's the only other person outside my camp who knows my secret. Laney thought my lawyer was a good person to inform, in case of emergency.

"Wait, Dad — aren't you driving us?" Liz asks.

"Actually, I have a better idea." He grins and opens the front door. We look outside. In the large circular driveway is a deluxe black Hummer limo. Standing in front of it, wearing a tux, is none other than Rodney. He's not used to dressing so formally and looks uncomfortable with the top button of his shirt done up.

"Rod!" Backup has arrived.

"Good evening, ladies." Rodney cuts me off before I can put my foot in my mouth. "I'm Rodney. I'm going to be your driver for the evening." He tilts his hat forward and bows.

Allison laughs. "This is so cool. I bet no one else is arriving in a limo tonight."

"Other than Sky," Beth reminds her.

"Have fun, ladies." Mr. Mendes winks at me and Liz again. "And Josh, make sure you get my daughter home on time tonight."

"Yes, s-sir, Mr. Mendes," Josh stutters. Mr. Mendes gives Liz a peck on the check and jumps into his red Jag. He's probably off to have dinner with Gavin Rossdale and Gwen Stefani.

When Rodney opens the back door to the limo, I can't believe my eyes. Out pops Nadine wearing a crisply tailored cream-colored pant suit. She has a digital camera dangling from her neck. She strides over to Liz, never once looking in my direction.

"You must be Liz." She shakes her hand firmly. "I'm Nadine. Your dad asked me to take professional pictures of you as a memento of the evening."

I have to hand it to Nadine. She's sneaky enough to run for office.

"Wow," Beth exclaims. She looks at her watch. "We don't really have much time though. . . ."

"Actually, I'm going to be riding along with you," Nadine informs us. "I can hang out with Rodney here and take pictures of you and your dates afterwards too." Liz looks shyly at Josh.

"Yeah, no date here," Allison announces wryly, pointing at herself.

"You've got me." Beth links arms with Allison.

"Rach, she can take a picture of you and Austin," Allison offers.

"Aww, you guys are going to look so cute together," Beth teases. "I can't believe how much you look like Kaitlin Burke." She stands back to admire my vintage green silk Oriental dress by So Chic. It's Sam's from a dinner party episode. I wore the dress home one night after a late shoot and forgot to bring it back. I don't think anyone even realizes it's missing.

HOLLYWOOD SECRET NUMBER SEVENTEEN: Costume designers make several copies of a crucial outfit. If it's something the actor has to wear all the time, they can't risk it getting damaged during filming, so they buy more than one. When you go to Planet Hollywood and see Superman's cape, just remember, there are several more just like it sitting in a studio warehouse. On *FA*, we have about ten copies of Sam's cheerleading uniform.

The hardest part about my Kaitlin costume was the wig. I had to put a cheap pale blond synthetic wig over my own blond hair. I locked myself in Liz's bathroom to do it and crammed my short brown bob under Liz's sink.

"Thanks, Bethie. You look better than Halle yourself." Beth smiles at me. She's got her hair pinned back smoothly and is wearing a gorgeous taupe bridesmaid's dress that she wore to her sister's wedding. The crushed satin gown looks a lot like something I saw Halle wear to the SAG Awards last year. Allison looks good too in a pin-straight long red wig and a skin-tight black mini-dress that shows off her dancer's legs.

Josh takes Liz's hand and helps her climb into the limo, then turns around and helps Beth and Allison. As they each giggle and disappear into the dark cabin, I can't help but feel a little guilty. Beth and Allison have been so nice to me. Well, the fake me. I wonder what they're going to think when Rachel leaves Clark.

"Rach, or should I say, Kaitlin, are you coming?" Allison asks, sticking her head out of the shiny stretch. I take Josh's hand and climb inside. At least I won't forget my name tonight. I sit down, and the green sequined clutch resting on my lap begins to vibrate. I pull out my cell phone and look at the screen. It's Laney.

"Hi, *Mum*," I answer.

"FEEL BETTER ABOUT TONIGHT?" Laney shouts. I hear cheering in the background and the sound of cameras going off. She must be at a movie premiere.

"Yes, *Mum*." I look at Liz and Nadine. "You should see the limo and photographer Liz's dad got us. They're amazing."

"NADINE'S IDEA. NOT THAT YOU HAVE ANY-THING TO WORRY ABOUT. THE ONLY CALL I'VE GOT-TEN TODAY IS FROM *CELEB INSIDER*. THEY WANTED TO DO A PUFF PIECE."

"Good." I breathe a sigh of relief.

"BUT REMEMBER — SHOULD ANYTHING GO WRONG, GIVE REPORTERS THE *MARIE CLAIRE* STORY."

"Nothing's going to go wrong," I reassure her.

"FIRST SIGN OF TROUBLE AND RODNEY AND NADINE ARE UNDER ORDER TO WHISK YOU OUT OF THERE," Laney warns me anyway.

"Deal," I agree.

"I WON'T START WITH YOU NOW, BUT YOU KNOW THIS IS A SIGN YOU SHOULD START WRAPPING THE SCHOOL THING UP."

Across from me, Beth and Allison are giggling as Nadine takes a picture of them wearing each other's wigs.

"I know," I say sadly.

"YOU SHOULD START PREPPING FOR THE HUTCHIE FILM. I'M SURE YOU'RE GOING TO GET IT."

Next, Nadine takes a picture of the three girls together, all wearing opposite wigs. God, I hope they don't ask me to take off mine. "We'll talk about wrapping it up this weekend, okay?" I agree, watching them.

"OKAY. HAVE FUN," Laney orders. I hear muffled voices in the background yelling the word "Julia." "HOLD ON. GUYS, WRAP IT UP," I hear Laney bark. "JULIA HAS TO GET INSIDE . . . KAITLIN, I HAVE TO GO."

"Okay. But did you just tell me to have fun?"

She chuckles. "WHY NOT? I DON'T HAVE ANYTHING ELSE SCHEDULED FOR YOU TONIGHT."

"Thanks, *Mom*." I sigh. "I'll talk to you tomorrow." I hang up just as we pull up to Clark's stone wall gates. Rodney drives the limo across campus and parks in the packed gymnasium parking lot. As we begin to exit the Hummer, I notice through the covered gym windows red and blue lights from the DJ booth pulsing to the faraway sounds of the Black Eyed Peas.

"If you don't mind, I'd like to escort you all inside," Rodney announces. "I promised your father I would," he adds, looking at me.

"Thanks, Rodney," Liz says, holding Josh's hand. "Will you be here to pick us up after?"

"Yep. In the same spot," he tells her as we walk towards the door. "Your father said to take you anywhere you want to go."

"Maybe we can get something to eat afterwards," Liz suggests, looking at Josh.

"Yeah, if Rach plans on joining us," Beth teases. "We may not be able to pull her away from Austin."

"Ha, ha." I poke her in the ribs.

"Hey, what is that van from *Celeb Insider* doing here?" Allison asks as we get closer to the gym's double doors. A white van with electrical wires poking out of the door and winding into the school is backed up to the gym steps.

"Oh, that must be for Sky," Beth comments absently. "She told me she may have some press here to cover her participation."

"That would explain why *Hollywood Nation* is here too," Allison adds, pointing to another van located a few parking spots away.

"I thought you said it was just a magazine reporter," Liz exclaims.

"What's the difference?" Beth shrugs.

I look at Nadine and Liz. Nadine looks from me to Rodney.

Nadine never gets ruffled, but now she looks a little nervous. She walks in front of us and blocks the doorway. "Why don't we get a few more pictures of you guys before you go inside?" She motions to Rodney. "Rodney could you get my assistant *Laney* on the phone?" He quickly pulls his cell out of his tuxedo pants pocket and begins dialing.

"We can take more pictures later," Beth says, pushing ahead of Nadine and opening the door before I can stop her. "I'm dying to see how the gym looks filled with people." She grabs my hand and Liz's free one. "Come on, you guys."

Beth pulls Liz, Josh, and me through the open double doors before Nadine can stop her. I look around the crowded dance floor nervously. I see Tom Cruises, Paris Hiltons, and a lone Johnny Depp, but nothing out of the ordinary. As Beth pulls me along, I turn around and look for Nadine. She's standing in the doorway talking animatedly on the phone. I must look nervous because when Nadine looks up and sees me, she smiles weakly and motions to Rodney, who appears to be tracking me at a distance.

"Are you okay?" Liz frees her right arm from Beth's grasp. "I'm sure everything is fine." I nod. "We'll be by the photo booth if you need us." She squeezes my bare arm and walks off with Josh and Allison.

"I want to introduce you to Sky," Beth squeals, tugging me along.

"Actually, I have to go meet Austin," I tell her, and free my arm. "I'll meet her later."

"It will just take a minute," Beth insists, looking around the packed gym. But before she can grab my arm again, Rob Murray walks up dressed as Will Smith. He smiles at Beth shyly. That distracts her.

"I'll be right back with Austin," I apologize, hurrying off. I peer over people's bobbing heads and see The Ivy across the room. I try to hurry through the dance floor, but it takes forever. Every few feet, I see someone I know and wind up chatting about costumes. (I have to keep from laughing when people ask, "You're dressed as who?")

When I finally make it over to The Ivy, I see Austin standing alone in front of the crowded café. He looks cuter than Trevor ever could, I think as I take in his seersucker pants (a bad Trevor trademark), white Lacoste shirt (I don't think Trevor knows what Lacoste is), and black aviator shades. Austin sees me and breaks into a wide grin. My stomach drops to the floor. And that's when I realize — despite everything going on at the moment, all I care about is reaching him and telling him how much I like him. Could it be that Austin feels the same way? He strides towards me, never breaking eye contact, and I feel my cheeks burn hotly. I'm a few feet away when someone grabs my shoulder.

"I found Sky," Beth exclaims excitedly as Rob bounces to the Mariah Carey tune behind her. "She really wants to meet you." Before I can protest, Beth yells, "Sky over here!"

"What do you mean she really wants to meet me?" I demand, whirling Beth around so fast that her pearls whip her in the face. She and Rob look at me surprised. "She's been asking me all kinds of questions about Clark Hall," Beth says. "She wanted to know all about you guys — especially you, Rach."

Sky wanted to talk about someone other than herself?

"Is that so?" I try to remain calm. "Why is that?" I turn my head to the left and see Sky strutting straight towards us with two bodyguards at her side and a *Hollywood Nation* crew following close behind her. She's causing such a commotion a crowd has formed around her, including Lori and Jessie, who are dressed as Mary-Kate and Ashley Olsen. I turn around desperately and search the crowd for Rodney. I see him barreling towards Sky. Two more bodyguards appear and start pushing him back. Oh man, this isn't good.

"She loves English people," Beth explains. "She asked me all about your accent, what you looked like, and how good of friends we were. She said she couldn't wait to meet you." I think I might faint. I reach out and grab Rob's arm for support.

"Are you okay, Rachel?" Rob asks.

Oh my God . . . *She knows.*

Sky took my Sidekick. That's why the gossip vans are here.

I've got to get over to Rodney. I look towards the DJ and see Nadine totally uncomposed, screaming at her cell phone. When she sees me, she starts frantically waving me over. She must know too.

"Hey, Kaitlin," Austin jokes as he walks up behind me. "You look great. I bet even Sky Mackenzie is fooled."

"Thanks," I say distractedly, looking for a break in the crowd to get to Nadine. I've got to move fast. I grab Austin's arm and start pulling him away. I'll take him with me and try to explain everything. "You look good too. Let's get out of here."

"Hey, Sky!" Beth calls. To Austin's surprise, I duck my head into his chest. He wraps his arms around my waist. If it were any other time, I would melt, but now I'm too freaked out to enjoy the moment. Maybe she won't see me. She'll just walk by with her camera crew, going on about that risqué fast food chain commercial she just shot wearing nothing but a string bikini. (What does a bikini have to do with eating a hamburger?)

"Cute costume," Sky says, stopping in front of Austin and me. She's wearing a fiery red mini-dress and looks like she's ready for war. I stare at the ground. "I feel like I've seen it somewhere before . . . Hmm . . . maybe *FA*'s wardrobe department?"

She *definitely* knows. There's no longer any question.

"Austin, I'm sorry, I have to go. Come with me," I say quickly, pulling myself away.

"Wait, we just got here." He reaches for my hand.

But Sky grabs it first. "Where you off to, K? Got someplace to be, Kaitlin?" she taunts. Liz, Allison, and Josh are pushing through the crowd, but they're still several feet away. I see Rodney yelling at two beefy guys aggressively holding him back. I look desperately at Liz. She knows I want to scream.

"Sky, her name's really Rachel," Beth corrects her as Rob looks on.

"She's not Rachel, Bethie," Sky sneers. "She's Kaitlin Burke."

"You mean she's *playing* Kaitlin Burke," Allison laughs, oblivious to the tension seething in the room. "It's a great costume, right?" Sky laughs shrilly.

"Sky, this is wrong," Liz yells as she pushes her way closer.

"Sky, don't," I plead as Austin whispers in my ear, "What's her problem?" I yank my wrist away from Austin and try to make a run for it, but I trip and fall over my three-inch Nine West heels. Austin reaches out to help me up, but one of Sky's other two bodyguards holds him back while another pulls me up and roughly locks me in his arms.

"Hey," Austin protests gruffly. But Sky cuts him off and eyes me smugly.

"Ladies and gentleman, I have an announcement to make," she says into a wireless microphone that a crew member from *Hollywood Nation* hands her.

"Liz, I've got to get to Nadine," I shout as I fight to pull away from Sky's man handler. She can't reach me but she starts desperately pushing towards me. "Let me through," she shouts. But Sky has thought this through. The camera crews, four bodyguards . . . she left nothing to chance. The DJ cuts the Mariah tune that's playing and everyone on the dance floor turns to see what the commotion is about.

"Let her GO," Austin shouts at the beefy bald guy I'm struggling to get away from.

Sky covers the microphone. "You probably want to turn

your cameras on now," she tells the *Nation* crew. Then she smiles at me coldly as she uncovers the mic. "I'm not the only *FA* star in attendance here tonight," she announces calmly.

"DON'T!" I beg, and scramble to grab her mic. "I can explain!" But my voice is drowned out by the commotion around me.

". . . My *Family Affair* costar is also here!" she shouts. "Clark Hall, give it up for the real Kaitlin Burke!" The crowd starts to cheer, not realizing what's going on.

"You've got it wrong!" Austin calls out to Sky. "Rachel's *dressed up* as Kaitlin."

"There is no Rachel, cutie," Sky says coolly. With my free arm, I take a swing at Sky, like the kind Liz taught me from her kickboxing class, but she's too quick. She pulls the wig right off my head, then grabs my glasses. Allison gasps. My heart is pounding out of my chest and I feel like I'm going to pass out as the *Nation* crew shines a bright light on me. The crowd standing around Sky starts murmuring at once. Liz breaks through the mob and tries to grab me, but a bodyguard sees her and pushes her back.

"You've got to be kidding me," Lori scoffs, and nudges Jessie. "*She's* Kaitlin Burke?"

Jessie shrugs. "I thought she was a nerd."

"What the . . ." Austin looks beyond confused.

"Oh my God, you're the real Kaitlin." Beth claps her hand over her mouth.

"Cool," Rob Murray whispers.

"I've been working on a story for *Marie Claire*," I say desperately, blinking in the bright light and looking from Austin to Allison to Beth. But my voice is drowned out by Sky.

"You've been duped," she announces to the now quiet crowd. "Rachel is not Rachel at all, she's Kaitlin Burke. She's been pretending to be someone she's not — wearing colored contacts, a wig, dopey glasses, using a bogus accent — she's been lying to you for months."

"You stole my Sidekick! That's why you're here!" I scream angrily, pushing to get away. "Rodney, do something!" I yell. Rod is bumping the men around him, trying to get to me.

Sky bats her eyes at me, then addresses the *Hollywood Nation* camera. "Do you see what I'm talking about, America? My *Family Affair* sister, Kaitlin Burke, is desperately crying out for help." She chokes on a fake sob. "She wants out of her contract, out of movie-making. She wants a normal life. I knew I had to help her and expose her for who she really is. She doesn't care about any of you," Sky adds, addressing my new friends. "She's just using you to hide from the world."

"You LIAR!" I yell desperately, then break down in tears as flashbulbs start popping all around me. Austin's face is numb. I want to reach him and explain, but he pushes past Lori and Jessie, disappearing into the crowd. Sky steps back and watches all of this with a sly grin plastered on her face.

"Kaitlin, why did you go undercover?" someone shouts, shoving a microphone in my face.

"Kaitlin, is it true you hate Hollywood?"

"Kaitlin, why the disguise?"

Tears are streaming down my face as I look at Beth and Allison's hollowed expressions. People are shouting, but I can't make out what they're saying anymore. That's when I see Liz with Rodney. Sky's bodyguard lets go of me immediately and Rodney tries to shield me. Nadine appears on my other side to block the crowd.

"We've got her," I hear Rodney say into his phone. The next thing I know, they've pulled me from the crowd, out the door, and into the waiting limo. I sob hysterically the whole way.

seventeen: *Facing the Press*

WHY IS HOTTER-THAN-HOT ACTRESS KAITLIN BURKE LIVING A DOUBLE LIFE? WE'VE GOT THE ANSWER FROM HER COSTAR SKY MACKENZIE — AND THE FOOTAGE FROM HER HIGH SCHOOL DANCE — TONIGHT AT 7, ONLY ON HOLLY-WOOD NATION!

I flip to channel seven.

HAS ONE OF HOLLYWOOD'S MOST LOVED STARLETS DE-CIDED TO RETIRE AT THE TENDER AGE OF 16? SUZY WALKER INTERVIEWS KAITLIN BURKE'S BEST FRIEND AND COSTAR, SKY MACKENZIE, TO FIND OUT.

Sky's face flashes across the TV screen. She's being interviewed by *Celebrity Insider* reporter Suzy Walker.

"I've been worried about K for a long time," Sky says to Suzy, her big brown eyes shining with tears. "That's why I had to help her go free and expose what she was doing. Only someone truly unhappy with her life would create a façade like that."

"Why do you think she's so unhappy?" Suzy tilts her head to one side to show that she's listening seriously.

Sky wells up with tears. "She doesn't want to act anymore. She's just doing it to please her family. . . ."

WATCH THE REST OF THIS EXCLUSIVE INTERVIEW, ALONG WITH THE REACTION FROM KAITLIN'S HIGH SCHOOL. . . .

The next thing I see is Lori and Jessie standing in front of South Hall at Clark.

"Kaitlin is welcome back at Clark Hall anytime," Lori gushes. She's wearing a homemade "Family Fanatic" tight tee.

"We're big fans," Jessie seconds. They both maddeningly wave to the camera as it pans to a group of angry-looking parents standing next to them.

"Kate Bubble lied to our children and passed herself off as someone she's not just to fulfill some whim of hers. It's absurd!" seethes a harried-looking woman wearing a wrinkled linen suit.

YOU'LL FIND THE WHOLE STORY HERE, ONLY ON CELEBRITY INSIDER!

I turn off the TV and chuck the remote at my bedroom door. It lands with a *thud* on the floor.

"What was that?" I hear Nadine ask. She's been sitting

outside my door for an hour. "Kates, you can't hide in there forever."

"Yes, I can," I reply stubbornly. "I have everything I need right here." Bags of Cheetos and cans of Sprite and M&M's litter my unmade bed. It's Sunday morning and I haven't gotten out of my sweats since I tearfully slipped them on Friday night.

"You're going to run out of snacks eventually," Nadine says coolly.

I ignore Nadine and my phone, which is ringing again.

"DON'T ANSWER IT!" I hear my mother yell through the door. "LANEY SAID NOT TO ANSWER IT!"

The phone hasn't stopped ringing since Friday night, when Rodney walked me to my front door, as I still cried like a baby. A white-faced, shell-shocked Mom and Dad were waiting for me.

"I told you this was a bad idea . . . ," Mom begins.

I ignore her and march past all of them into the kitchen, where Anita is making a midnight snack for herself. I grab some of her loot, run upstairs, and lock my door.

I turn on the radio to drown out Nadine's and Mom's pleas.

ROB SEABRIGHT HERE AND THIS IS MY CELEBRITY RANT FOR SUNDAY! AFTER KAITLIN BURKE'S STARTLING DECLARATION THAT SHE'S THROUGH WITH ACTING, HOLLYWOOD IS HOT ON THE RUMOR THAT THE TEEN TITAN WILL BE WRITTEN OUT OF FAMILY AFFAIR NEXT SEASON. THE BUZZ IS THAT SKY

I turn off the radio and let out an ear-piercing scream.

"Kaitlin! I demand you open this door immediately." It's Mom again.

"I'm never coming out of my room again!" I yell at the door. "My career is ruined, Austin thinks I'm a fake, and Rob Seabright says Hutch is hiring Sky! And all I ever wanted was a couple months off to be normal." I throw myself back on my bed and dissolve in tears.

"Who's Rob Seabright?" I hear my mom ask Nadine.

"Kates, don't cry," Nadine whispers.

I just sob harder, ignoring the sound of my doorknob jiggling. Next thing I know, the door is wide open.

"Hey," Matt says calmly. He walks into the room carrying a pizza box.

"How'd you do that?" I demand, sitting up quickly and wiping my face with my food-stained t-shirt.

"Give us a minute," Matt tells Mom and Nadine, who are peering in the doorway at me. Matt shuts the door again and locks it. He holds up Mom's Amex. "Works every time." He grins. "I've busted into Dad's office with this too."

"Go away." I throw my head down on my pillow. "You got what you wanted. My career is over. Call Tom. Maybe he'll give you my job."

Matt sits down on the edge of my bed. "I don't want your job, Kates. I just want to bring you some sustenance."

He holds out the box. A SLICE OF HEAVEN is stamped on the top. In the corner is a hand-written note. "We still love you," it says, and it's signed by Antonio. I lift the box lid. The aroma of peppers, broccoli, and cheese fills the air. I look at Matt skeptically.

"Why are you being so nice to me?" I ask him, and grab a slice.

He shrugs. "Believe it or not, I feel bad for you." He pulls out a slice for himself.

I roll my eyes.

"I'm serious," he insists, then chuckles. "Besides, if you don't clear the family name, no one will ever hire me!"

That makes me laugh. "There's the brother I know and love." For a few minutes, we both quietly chow down on the hot pizza.

"Your career is going to survive this," Matt says suddenly. "Everybody gets bad press. Look at Britney Spears."

I shake my head sadly and tell Matt about HOLLYWOOD SECRET NUMBER EIGHTEEN: In this town, you're loved one minute and yesterday's news the next. That's especially true when you're a young star. I mean, look at that *Home Alone* kid. He was hot one minute and now he can barely find work. You go through one awkward stage or make one bad movie and the town forgets about you. There's always someone younger, prettier, and more talented ready to take your place. At a much smaller salary, I might add.

Matt looks at me and smiles. "But you're forgetting something," he says. "You also said Hollywood is a town where anyone can revive their career if they want it bad enough. You can fix this, Kates. You just have to come clean about why you pulled the stunt in the first place."

Downstairs, I hear the doorbell ring.

"Probably more press coming to tell me what a horrible person I am," I sigh.

"KAITLIN BURKE, COME DOWNSTAIRS THIS INSTANT." Laney's voice is unmistakable as it blares over the house intercom system. Matt and I look at each other, instinctively terrified.

"DO YOU HEAR ME, KAITLIN? I DON'T CLIMB STAIRS IN JIMMY CHOOS, BUT I WILL MAKE RODNEY GO BREAK THAT DOOR DOWN IF YOU DON'T COME TO THE DINING ROOM AT ONCE."

"Come on." Matt pulls my arm. "I don't want to tick her off. She just signed me." Rodney, Nadine, Mom, and Dad are sitting at the twenty-five-foot-long dining room table waiting for us. Laney paces back and forth in front of them, wearing a very responsible-looking black Versace pant suit.

"Oh, honey, you're out of your room!" Mom gives me a hug, the feel of her baby blue PB&J Couture jacket warming my cheek. Then she whispers in my ear, "You couldn't have combed your hair for company?"

Some things never change. I pull away and eye Laney suspiciously. "Don't say it."

"Well, I'm going to say it anyway," she retorts sharply. "You've made quite a mess here."

"She knows that, Laney." Nadine leaps to my defense.

"I've been on the phone all weekend," Laney continues. "I didn't even try to use the *Marie Claire* coverup. This is too big of a problem to use that now. I had to call all the gossip shows and threaten to never grant them another interview again if they keep airing this story. Then I had to call Liz's dad and start legal action against Sky's bodyguards for restraining you, Liz, and Rodney. Then I called Principal Pearson and asked her to speak on your behalf."

"What did she say?" I ask glumly.

"She said not to come to school on Monday," Laney tells me. "Like we were going to let you. You'll finish out the term with your tutor."

I'm not surprised.

"But she is doing interviews to explain why she accepted your plan and thought it was a good idea. She also wanted me to tell you that this incident will in no way affect her love of *Family Affair*." Laney rolls her black eyes.

"Well, I hope she'll still watch if I'm no longer on it," I mumble.

"Tom called this morning," Mom interjects. "He's worried about you, Kates. No one said anything about firing you."

"Have we heard from Hutch Adams?" I ask anxiously.

Mom looks at Laney and shakes her head no. "We're still trying to get ahold of him," she confirms sadly. My eyes start to well up again.

"I won't tolerate crying, Kaitlin." Laney slams her hands down on the table. "Hutch is probably waiting for some answers. Everyone is. Your fans, the students at Clark Hall. They want to know why you'd do such a crazy thing."

"But you said I couldn't tell anybody!" I protest. "You said it would destroy my career."

"That was *before* this happened," Laney says. "Now that it's out there, you have to explain yourself. Tell the world what you told us the night you strong-armed us into letting you go to Clark Hall. Tell them that you wanted to see what it was like to be a normal teen — as boring as that might be." She cracks a small scarlet-lipped smile. "And tell them what that conniving brat Sky Mackenzie has been up to."

"Finally," Nadine groans.

"That kid has it coming to her," Rodney seconds.

"I don't know," Mom frets. "Should we really knock her? I mean, it might make Kaitlin look worse."

"I don't think so," Dad muses. "If anything, it will show that Kate-Kate has the stamina and the speed to cruise through career bumps and keep going."

I look at Laney. "I thought you said not to bash Sky."

"You're not going to hurl insults at her," she explains. "You're just going to tell exactly what happened. If you don't say something, someone else will anyway. Don't you think people are going to begin to wonder how she knew about your alter ego?"

"Yeah, Kates, she doesn't have an alibi for that one," Matt points out. "We've got her cornered."

I plop down in the velvet-cushioned seat next to Matt and sit quietly for a moment. "I don't want to lose my career," I say finally.

Hearing those words out loud surprises me. All this time I was running away from my harried life. But now that I'm in danger of losing it, I desperately want it back.

"Then don't," Laney snaps. "Fix this."

"But there's got to be a middle ground," I protest, getting mad. "I can't be the only actress who wants to work and have a private life too. What star doesn't need vacations once in a while? I just decided to take mine at, well, school."

"Keep going," Nadine encourages me, pressing her bible to her chest eagerly.

"And going in disguise was the only way I could attend school like a normal student. I wasn't trying to hurt anybody. What Sky did was cruel. Why would she expose her 'best friend'?" I make air quotes with my fingers. "I am NOT losing the Hutch Adams role to her!"

"Get that engine to full throttle, Katie-kins," Dad says with a pumped fist. Whatever that means.

"How do I fix this?" I ask Laney.

"By getting even," she answers. She throws a folder down on the table. OPERATION KAITLIN is written across the front in Nadine's perfect penmanship. "You're going on national television and you're going to tell everyone what you just told us."

Nadine grabs the folder and opens it up for me to see. She slides a paper in front of me. It's an itinerary typed up by

Nadine. "We thought Jaime Robins would be the best person to do an interview with."

I nod. Jaime hosts one of the most popular weekly news shows. She's grilled everyone from Madonna to the Pope.

"She wants to hear my story?" I question.

"Everyone wants to hear it," Laney exclaims.

"Okay." I take a deep breath. "Let's do this."

The minute I'd given Laney the okay, she called Jaime, who jumped at the chance to come *today* so that she can run my interview tomorrow during prime time.

"Remember," Laney warned as she and Nadine finished my practice interview. "Don't use four words when three will do. Don't ramble on when one sentence is all that's needed. Keep a smile planted on your face — not that tears won't go a long way if you need to cry — and look directly at Jaime the *entire* time. Knock your knees or play with your hair and you appear nervous. Look away and the audience will think you're lying. Got it?"

"Got it," I answer firmly.

Two hours later, Jaime's three-member crew is setting up cameras and lighting in our spacious living room. Mom thought it was the best place to sit, since our periwinkle floral couches have their backs to floor-length windows that face the lush gardens in our backyard. Throughout the room, Anita arranged ceramic vases overflowing with lavender and roses (my favorites) that our gardener cut, the largest bunch sitting in front of me on the plush leather ottoman coffee table.

"You look great," whispers Paul, who'd rushed over with Shelly the minute Mom called. He gives my coiffed hair a final once-over. Even Mom agreed with Laney that a simple, classic chignon would make the best impression today.

"Knock 'em dead, sweetie," Shelly seconds, and gives me a final dab of nude lip-gloss. Laney, who has orchestrated my every move today, wanted my makeup to look fresh and clean. ("Not overdone like you have something to hide," she'd explained.)

I exhale slowly and smooth out the front of my fitted Stella McCartney khaki blazer that Laney called in for the occasion. Paired with matching wide-leg trousers and low-heeled pink Manolos, Laney says I look the picture of grace. "And innocence," she adds, approvingly.

I'm ready for this.

"Kates?" Nadine gently touches my arm. "You have a phone call."

"Nadine, you know I don't want to talk to anyone," I say nervously.

"It's Liz," she clarifies and hands me the phone. "She's on the 'okay' list, right?" Nadine smiles and walks away.

"Hey, Lizzie," I whisper.

"Hey," she answers softly. "How are you holding up?"

I quickly fill her in on my meeting with Laney and my family. I tell her about the Jaime interview too.

"I know all about it," Liz says once I'm finished.

"You do?"

"Yeah, Jaime just left my house," she tells me. "Laney asked me to go to bat for you, not that she needed to."

"You were interviewed?" I ask incredulously.

"Yep," Liz affirms. "I told Jaime what an amazing friend you are and how stretched you've been this past year. I told her how you've always wanted to go to a real school and how much you cared about Clark Hall and the friends you made there and even volunteered to be on the boring dance committee."

"I don't know what to say." I feel so lucky to have Liz. "Unfortunately, I think you're the only friend I have left at that place. Well, you and Principal P."

"Don't forget us," someone says softly.

"Who said that?" I ask, freaked out.

"It's Beth."

"And Allison."

I pause, nonplussed. "But, I figured . . ."

"We were mad at first — especially at Liz," Allison explains.

"That's for sure," I hear Liz mutter.

"But we also felt really bad about what happened with Sky," Beth adds. "What she did was *so* wrong. We had to defend you!"

Wow. "I'm so sorry I lied." My voice cracks. "I hope you believe me when I say that I truly care about our friendship."

"It's okay, Kaitlin," Allison assures me. "Liz told us the whole story." She pauses. "God, it feels weird not to call you Rachel!" Everyone laughs.

"Rachel, Kaitlin," Beth concludes, "the point is, whoever you are, we really like you." Beth might never believe it, but that genuine, unguarded statement is one of the nicest compliments I've ever received.

Laney motions to me from across the room and taps her platinum watch. The camera crew is ready to take some supplemental shots. They want footage of me sitting at the breakfast table reading *Variety*, me walking in the garden with Matt, me practicing my lines. Moments that make me appear more real to the viewer.

"I really like you guys, too," I tell them, motioning to Laney that I'm wrapping up.

"I just hope you'll forgive me as well," Allison says quietly.

"What for?" I watch a cameraman move a light closer to the deep green velour chair Jaime will be sitting on across from me.

"For those Kaitlin remarks I made," she explains.

"You didn't know it was me," I tell her. "And besides, I had it coming. I just hope we can still be friends."

"We *are* friends," Beth assures me. "You can't get rid of us that easily!"

"But if you want to lavish us with gifts — or get me a date with Trevor Wainright — that's okay too," Allison jokes.

"Deal," I laugh. I bite my lip. "Have any of you spoken to Austin?" I have to ask.

"No," Liz answers reluctantly. "He won't take any of our calls."

I respond to Laney's frantic emotions to let her know I'm

hanging up. "One problem at a time, right?" I try to sound positive.

"That's right," Beth replies firmly.

"Good luck, Kates," Liz says. "Call us afterwards."

I hang up the phone and make my way over to the cameraman who is taking the background footage. Fifteen minutes later, we walk back into the living room to do the main interview. Mom, Dad, Matt, Laney, Rodney, and Nadine are busy talking animatedly to Jaime. For a moment, I feel warm and fuzzy inside just looking at them all. As crazy as my entourage makes me feel sometimes, I know they have my back when it really counts.

"It's a pleasure to meet you, Kaitlin," Jaime says huskily in her trademark southern drawl. Jaime looks even better in person than she does on TV (isn't that always true?). Her usual prim newscaster attire has been replaced with jeans and a coral sweater set, and her long light brown hair is neatly tied in a loose ponytail.

"It's a pleasure to meet you." I shake her hand and smile warmly. "Thank you for coming."

"Well, thank you for bringing your story to me first," she answers. "Are you ready?" Someone from Jaime's crew wires me with a mic, and I nod my head. Jaime smiles and takes a seat on the green chair across from the couch I'm sitting on.

"If at any time you want to stop, or you need to take a sip of mineral water, just say so," Jaime tells me. "Okay then, let's get started." She cues the cameraman standing behind her and he begins to record.

Jaime throws me some slow balls at first. She asks about my years on *FA*, my movie career, and my family life. As we talk, I block out everyone standing around me and focus on Jaime's questions and the answers I rehearsed with Laney.

"If you were so happy, then why pretend to be someone else?" Jaime finally asks the million-dollar question.

I take a deep breath and exhale slowly. Then I start to describe my fascination with a normal life. "I guess everyone wants what they don't have," I begin slowly. "I have a career people would kill for, but I wanted to see what it would be like to be a regular teen."

Jaime nods. "So you hatched a plan to go to high school in disguise."

I tell Jaime how burnt out I was and how obsessed I was with meeting people who didn't care if my movie opened at number one at the box office. "When your face is on the front of a Cheerios box, it's hard to do that without being followed everywhere you go. I knew if I wanted to see what high school was like, I had to do it without the press knowing. That's when my friend Liz and I came up with the disguise."

"Didn't you think people would be upset if they found out?" Jaime asks. I reflect for a moment, taking a sip of my water to help my dry throat. I stare at the reflection in the gold mirror behind Jaime of the waterfall that cascades into our kidney-shaped swimming pool in the middle of the garden.

"It was a perfect plan, until I actually walked through Clark Hall's doors," I reply. "I never meant to hurt a soul. But from the minute I walked into my first class, I slowly realized my fantasy was just that. High school isn't a fairy tale. Really, it's no different from Hollywood. I thought hanging out with regular teens would mean no more backstabbing or bickering. But I learned high school has those problems too." I look over at Nadine and Laney. They're beaming at each other. A rare sight for sure.

"How so?" Jaime prods, fingering the emerald pendant dangling from her neck. It's a good question, and I turn it over in my mind for a few moments.

"You can't hide from your problems." I shrug my shoulders, admitting that I don't really have the answer. I settle deeper into the striped throw pillows on the couch. "Girls will be girls, no matter where they are. We hate someone else just because she's different from us." I think of Lori. "I've realized that there are always going to be people who are jealous of you and make you feel badly — whether you're in high school, Hollywood, or someplace else."

"So was it worth it then — to put your career on the line for a few months of anonymity?" Jaime asks.

I look at Mom and Dad, who are studying me closely. Matt is leaning forward in his chair, hands on the knees of his pre-ripped jeans. Nadine is practically chewing off her fingernails. Meanwhile, Laney looks as cool as a cucumber. "Yes and no," I answer slowly. "Clark Hall was a vacation for me. I met some amazing friends and got to make real high school memories." I pause. "But going to Clark didn't help me escape my problems. It only created more of them.

"Instead of embracing who I really am — a teen actress who loves her job despite the occasional drama and lack of vacations — I dragged a whole school into my mess. I went into hiding. I should have faced those tabloid rumors about Sky and me, instead of lying about them." My voice rises with confidence. "And I should have demanded a little R and R instead of overextending myself and then complaining about it after the fact. I should have come clean to my fans a lot earlier." I breathe deeply and grin. "As I'm talking to you, I can feel the weight lifting from my shoulders."

"That's great, Kaitlin," Jaime says, a little distractedly. "But are you saying the rumors about you and Sky are true then?" She motions for her cameraman to come in closer for an emotional headshot.

I think of Sky's behavior this past year. "It's true that we don't always get along," I admit. It's nerve-racking to be so honest for the first time. "But you can't tell me you like everyone you work with either," I add. Jaime's hazel eyes sparkle with amusement. I choose my next words carefully. "That doesn't mean I'm not professional. I *love* working at *FA* and just because my life there has its challenges doesn't mean that I hate being there. I'm grateful every day for the chance to be on a hit show.

"Sky's done some things that have really upset me. We're not close, but that doesn't mean we throw tantrums, like you read in the gossips. It just means that we don't hang out outside work. And it means that I won't be sharing a dressing room with her anytime soon." We both laugh.

"I interviewed your friends earlier," Jaime tells me, leaning forward and smiling. "They had wonderful things to say about you. Even the ones you misled."

"I'm lucky, aren't I?" I give Jaime a cheeky grin.

"Your friend Liz in particular made a passionate argument against Sky," Jaime says. "She claims that Sky stole your Sidekick at a photo shoot, and that's how Sky found out about your double life."

"I don't know if Sky took my Sidekick," I reply. "I do wonder how she found out about my alter ego. Only the people closest to me knew, and they'd never betray me. But even if Sky did deliberately try to hurt me, it won't keep me from returning to *FA* this fall, if they'll have me."

I pause for a moment and exhale deeply, then look straight into the camera's dark lens. "If I have one regret about this whole experience, it's that my double life hurt people more than I could have imagined." Austin's stunned face looms in my mind. "You know who you are. I just wish there were some way I could tell you how sorry I am."

Jaime smiles at me. "What will you take away from this experience?"

"Going to Clark made me realize how much I need my friends outside the business. It's great to talk about something other than the industry for a change. But it also reminded me how deeply I love my career," I add, thinking of the Hutch Adams role I still desperately want, even though

I probably won't get it. "I would really miss acting if I weren't doing it. And I hope I'll be doing it for a very long time."

Jaime motions to the cameraman to stop taping. She pulls off her mic. "Perfect final line, Kaitlin," Jaime says, standing up and shaking my hand. "I didn't have to press you to answer the hard questions either."

"That interview was better than therapy!" I laugh. "Thank you." I pull off my mic and grin at Laney, Nadine, Rodney, my parents, and Matt. Nadine starts to applaud, and they all join in. Rodney puts his fingers in his mouth and gives a loud whistle. My smile is wide enough to split my face.

I know it's been a while, but watch out world — Kaitlin Burke is back.

eighteen: *No Place Like Home*

After the Jaime Robins interview airs, our phone starts ringing off the hook. This time it's for a happy reason — people are calling to congratulate me.

And to ask for an interview, of course.

Over the next two weeks, I'll hit the talk show circuit to tell my whole scandalous tale again. I speak to the weeklies and the newspapers. With Zara's help, I do a first-person story for *Teen People*. Even Liz, Beth, and Allison get in on the frenzy. They're being interviewed by all the glossies. Beth and Allison love having Paul and Shelly make them camera-ready. Beth's even found herself a new part-time job because of it — modeling. *Hollywood Teen* called her and said she'd be perfect for a fashion story they're shooting next month.

The fickle press has become my best friend again. One minute they were roasting me, the next they're calling me "the most breathtakingly real teen in Hollywood." (Thank you,

Entertainment Weekly.) Sky's worries about my split personality were forgotten. Instead, *she's* been busy sidestepping questions from the media about how she came to know about Rachel Rogers in the first place. So far, she's hasn't answered that burning question.

But far more important than the press's applause is the support I'm getting from my friends and costars. Melli sent me flowers and a note that said, "I couldn't be more proud if you were my own daughter." Principal P sent me a bouquet of daisies with a note signed, "Your number one Family Fanatic."

Tom Pullman calls me the morning after Jaime's interview airs and says I should have called him sooner. "I would have told you that you always have a job at *FA*, no matter what happens," he chides.

As I hang up the phone, it rings again in my hand.

"Hello?" I answer, confused.

"Kaitlin, doll, fabulously entertaining interview," a voice coos in a smooth-as-velvet tone.

It takes me a second, but then I realize who it is: Hutch Adams. I'm at a loss for words. "Hello," I manage to get out.

"I haven't phoned your people back because I was scouting locations," Hutch continues. "My nieces have told me about your nasty little internal drama. Fascinating stuff."

I listen breathlessly for what is coming next. Is he calling to say I didn't get the part? Better luck next time? The only sound I can hear is my heart thumping loudly.

"The range of emotions you expressed in the Robins interview is better than any audition you could have done with my casters. Great job, Miss Burke."

"Thank you Mr. Adams." I'm dumbstruck at the compliment. But is it a consolation prize? "If I may, I'd like to make a case for myself in your lead role. I really hope you will still consider me. I know you wouldn't be disappointed. I would work . . ."

"Save your breath," Hutch laughs. "I'm calling to tell you you're hired. Warts and all." I put a hand over my mouth to keep from screaming and start jumping up and down on my bed, something I haven't done since I was ten. The *thuds* must have reached Mom, Dad, Nadine, and Matt downstairs, because within minutes they're at my side, Rodney barreling through the door first. I can see on their faces that they're all wondering what's going on. I mouth "Hutch" with a big smile on my face.

"You got the job?" Matt whispers, incredulous. I shake my head vigorously, and Mom begins to weep. Dad gives me a big thumbs-up sign. Nadine quickly dials Laney, whom I can hear screaming through the cell phone.

"Don't forget to ask him about a role for me," Matt urges, clutching my shoulder.

I listen to Hutch for a few more minutes, tuning out the chaos around me. If I'm hearing him right, not only do I have the lead in *The Untitled Hutch Adams Project*, but he also wants to turn my school escapade into a movie!

"You can help me write the screenplay," he suggests as my family jumps up and down around me.

"I'll definitely think about it," I say giddily. "Thank you, Mr. Adams. Thank you so much. You won't be disappointed."

"I'm sure I won't, Kaitlin," Hutch agrees. "Your agent will be beeping in any minute now to have you sign the papers that I've already sent over. We'll talk again soon." With that, he hangs up, and I scream at the top of my lungs.

"I GOT THE PART!"

"*We* did it!" Mom shouts excitedly.

"Katie-Kat," Dad interrupts. "Did he mention hiring me as a producer?"

"Or me for a role?" Matt adds, pulling himself up on my bed so he can jump as well. "I didn't hear you say my name."

Nadine groans.

I just smile. My family might give me a hard time, but I know they care about me. When things get tough, which I'm sure they will again down the road, my family has my back.

With six weeks till I have to report for pre-production on *The Untitled Hutch Adams Project*, I've set out to clean up the rest of the mess I started. I start by paying my "favorite" *FA* costar a little visit.

Turns out, Sky isn't in the mood to kiss and make up.

"She's not home," states the matronly housekeeper when Rodney, Liz, and I appear in their double-size black-and-white ceramic doorway.

"Funny, isn't that her Escalade in the driveway?" I ask sweetly.

"That's her father's car," the housekeeper answers, wiping her hands nervously on a white apron emblazoned with Sky's face.

"Gee, Kates, I thought that's the car Sky's mom drives her to work in every morning," Rodney retorts. "Isn't Sky's car candy-apple red?"

"Yes, Rodney, I believe it is," I reply, fiddling with the spaghetti straps on my sage green peasant top. "Sky told me she had the color custom blended so that it would be one-of-a-kind." Liz, Rodney, and I stare expectantly at the wide-hipped woman blocking our way.

The housekeeper looks desperate. "She's still not home. Please leave or I'll have to call the authorities."

"Speaking of authorities, Kates, didn't you have a talk with Tom Pullman this morning?" Liz prompts me.

"Why yes, Lizzie, thank you for reminding me," I say with a sly smile. "Tom said my job was completely secure. He also told me how terribly upset he was about the lies that appeared in the press. To keep that kind of thing from happening again, Tom's implementing a new set rule: If anyone at *FA* makes false statements to the press, they'll be fired."

"You don't say." Liz's voice echoes in the long hallway. "Did Tom ask you if you knew who was talking about you to the press?" Rodney chuckles as the housekeeper chokes and starts coughing wildly. She tries to close the door on us, but Rodney puts his combat boot in her way.

"Yes, as a matter of fact, he did," I answer loudly. "I wasn't going to tell him, but maybe I should."

"I would call him right now, actually," Liz suggests coolly.

I pull out my cell phone and pretend to dial. Suddenly Sky appears in the doorway wearing a pink silk cropped pajama top and matching capri bottoms. She shoves the distressed housekeeper out of her way.

"What do you want?" she asks coldly.

"Oh, hi, Skylar." I smile sweetly. "I thought you weren't home."

"You can't prove anything." Sky looks calm, but I can see her chest rising and falling rapidly, and her crossed arms are shaking slightly.

I look at Rodney and Liz. They take a step back to give me space to do this alone.

"You don't scare me," Sky responds, eyes flicking back and forth. "You have no proof that I talked to anyone at the tabloids, and you certainly can't prove I took your Sidekick."

"That's not why I'm here." I tell Sky. "I don't care if you did take my Sidekick. And I don't care if you're the one who planted those stories in the press either." Sky looks confused.

"Actually, I just came over to thank you," I explain. "Whether you intended to or not, you did me a big favor by pulling those stunts. That tabloid garbage was making me feel like I had to choose between acting and having a life. But you know what? I've realized I don't have to choose, Sky. No matter what you say or do, you can't make me give up my career. I work too hard and I love it too much. I'm *not* going away anytime soon."

Sky's jaw drops, but she doesn't say a word.

"So you can pack your bags and head to Mexico this hiatus to do your miniseries," I continue. "*I'm* reporting to the Hutch Adams set to work on my next blockbuster movie."

"You got the part?" Sky screeches angrily.

"And when we go back to *FA* in August, you better be ready." I ignore her angry spluttering. "Because next time I get some bad press, I won't be afraid to speak up about where the rumors are coming from. As you might have noticed from the Jaime Robins special, Sky, I know how to give a good interview too." I spin on my funky banana heels from Fred Segal and walk down her steps. Rodney and Liz follow me.

"Enjoy your summer, Skylar," I call out as we stride away.

"That was awesome!" Rodney exclaims when the three of us pile back in the car. Liz squeezes me tightly.

"I can't believe you!" Liz applauds. "You really gave it to her."

"I did, didn't I?" I lean back into the seat, content. "Hopefully she'll be more careful about how she treats me from now on."

"So that's it then," Rodney says. "You've taken care of everything."

"Not everything," I tell them both. "We have one more stop to make, but this time, you two are staying in the car."

*   *   *

Twenty minutes later, we pull up in front of Austin's cozy redbrick house.

"Are you sure you want to do this?" Liz asks quietly.

I look at the front door. "I have to," I explain softly. "He won't take my phone calls."

"You can do it, Kates," Rodney booms encouragingly. I smile at them both, take a deep yoga breath, and open the car door. I slowly walk up the path, rehearsing what I'm going to say in my head. I ring the doorbell and look back at the car. The windows are tinted, but I know Rodney and Liz are pressed up against them, watching.

"Kaitlin Burke," Austin's sister Hayley murmurs in awe when she opens the screen door.

"Hi, Hayley." Suddenly I feel shy. I remain standing on the doorstep. "I was wondering if I could see your brother."

Her turquoise eyes are wide. "I'm not sure. He's still pretty upset," she whispers, fidgeting with a buckle on her jeans. "Personally I think he should be flattered that a celebrity wanted to hang out with him."

"Well, I, I . . . ," I stutter, embarrassed. Hayley's eyes are glued to me, as if she can't believe I'm really here.

"Hayley, did you borrow my white Lacoste shirt again?" I hear Austin yell. Hayley freezes as Austin appears in the doorway wearing baggy jeans and a white undershirt. His surprised face is every bit as handsome as I remembered.

My breath catches in my throat. "Hi," I mumble.

A smile flashes across his face, causing my heart to soar.

But within seconds it's gone. He stares at me and does a double take. Now he's serious.

"Oh, it's you," he says, flustered. He runs his fingers through his blond hair. "What are you doing here?"

"I came to see you." I look down at the brick steps, my heart pounding. Why is it that I can do a live interview beamed out to millions of viewers, but the sight of Austin still makes me jittery?

Austin turns to his sister. "Hayley, this will just take a minute."

Hayley smiles at me shyly. "Maybe we'll get to talk about *Family Affair* sometime," she suggests.

"I'd like that," I tell her.

Austin and I stare at each other silently while Hayley slowly walks away. Even though I can see he's mad at me, I can't tear my eyes away from him. What if it's the last time I see his face?

"What are you doing here?" he asks me again, kicking one of his bare feet against the floor.

"You wouldn't take any of my calls," I answer, my voice barely a whisper.

"That's because I wasn't sure who I'd be talking to." Something like anger flashes in his beautiful eyes, and my heart breaks all over again. "Who are you playing today, Rachel or Kaitlin?"

The words are like a slap in the face, even if I do deserve them. "I'm truly sorry." I hang my head.

"It's too late for that." Austin shrugs his broad shoulders. "You made me look like an idiot."

"I would never . . . ," I start to protest, trying to find the words that will make everything okay again. I just want to go back to that day at the library, when everything was perfect and all that mattered was finding a way to go to the dance with him. I should have told him the truth back then.

"I don't want to hear this," Austin interrupts me, putting his hand on the screen door. "You got to know me, but I don't know you. I never knew you."

"Yes, you did," I say urgently. "That was me you spent all that time with. I really do like *Star Wars* and math, and I stink at history. I'm the same person."

"I liked Rachel," Austin answers, running his hands through his hair again. "But she doesn't exist. And Kaitlin Burke is a movie star. You don't need to hang with a regular high school guy like me."

I interject quickly, "You're actually the coolest guy —"

"I'm sorry, Kaitlin," he says, cutting me off again. "I can't do this." He slowly pulls the front door closed, shutting me out of his life forever.

"Did you really expect him to forgive you?" Nadine asks as I recount the sad story to everyone over hot chocolate at the twelve-foot-long cherry wood kitchen table.

"I hoped so," I admit, stirring mini marshmallows in my R2-D2 mug.

"I'll try to talk to him, Kates," Liz suggests.

"Thanks, but we should leave him alone," I say glumly. "I have to accept the fact that I hurt Austin so badly that he'll never forgive me."

"I'm sure there's a cute boy in your new movie," Dad offers.

"I read in *Variety* this morning that they cast Drew Thomas as your costar," Mom swoons. "He's a big up-and-comer, Kaitlin."

"I don't think I'll be interested in opening my heart to anybody again for quite a while," I sigh. "Especially not Drew." I think of those horrendous few dates last year.

"You really had it bad for Austin, didn't you?" Nadine comments.

"I did," I whisper, staring into the rich brown depths of my cocoa.

"Well, I know one thing that will cheer you up," Dad says. "I spoke to Steve Mendes this morning. We're taking you and Liz to Cabo this weekend before you start shooting the Adams movie." Liz looks at me and grins.

"Are you serious?" I stare at them in surprise. Dad nods. "Thank you!" I exclaim, jumping up and giving him a hug. I run over to Mom and throw my arms around her as well.

"You really held your own in that Robins interview," Mom tells me. "We were so proud of you. I guess that downtime at school really helped."

"I can't believe Kaitlin's got you thinking of school as downtime." Matt shakes his head.

"Since the school thing is out of the question now, I guess we'll have to let you rev up the vacation plans." Dad puts his arm around my shoulders.

"As long as you work them around Laney's press schedule," Mom adds, dabbing a paper towel on the cream-colored PB&J Couture hoodie she splashed cocoa on.

I bite my lip and chuckle to myself, then walk over to the hulking stainless steel Viking stove to pour another cup of steaming hot chocolate. "Everything in my life is finally falling into place," I think aloud. "Hutch Adams, *FA*, Sky, Cabo. The only thing missing is a guy to share it with."

"Maybe not for long," Liz squeaks. I turn around. Rodney is leading Austin into my kitchen.

"What are you . . . ?" I'm so startled, I can't get a sentence out. I look into Austin's nervous face, searching for answers.

"I found him down by the front gate," Rodney explains.

"I was hoping we could talk," Austin says. His voice is so quiet I can barely hear him.

"I guess we should leave you two alone." Nadine motions to the rest of the group.

"I want to see what happens," Matt protests.

"Come on, Matty." Liz tugs him by the arm. "I'll let you wait with me in Kaitlin's room and you can look through her phone book."

"Okay," he agrees gleefully, and follows her out. Dad puts his arm around Mom's shoulder and leads her away. She keeps looking back, though, and smiling. The room grows quiet.

"How'd you know where I lived?" I ask Austin.

"Beth," he says. "My mom dropped me off at the gate, but I didn't know how to get inside. That big dude happened to be leaving, and he saw me and drove me up the driveway. Your house is huge," he adds, sounding awestruck.

My heart is racing.

Austin walks towards me. "Can I sit down?" He grabs a wrought-iron stool near the island.

"Sure." I blush. I grab the seat next to him and, without asking, pour him a cup of hot chocolate. My hands are shaking as I add marshmallows. We sit there, just looking at each other for a few minutes.

"I don't know what I'm doing here." Austin finally breaks the ice. He runs his hand through his shiny blond hair, the way he always does when he's thinking about something. "I just knew I had to come."

"I'm so sorry," I begin again.

"Let me say this before I change my mind," Austin interrupts firmly. He takes a deep breath. "After you left, I watched your Jaime Robins interview. Hayley TiVo'd it. You were really good."

"Thanks," I say shyly. "That apology I made was for you, you know."

"I was wondering about that." He looks into my eyes intently, then looks away. "I heard what you said about Clark Hall being your chance to experience a normal life. I thought about what you said on my doorstep too, about how all that time I spent with Rachel, I was really spending with you. And I realized I had to ask you one important question."

"Anything," I promise. I feel my cheeks burning, and take a swig of hot chocolate.

"I wanted to know," he says slowly, "if you actually liked me, or if it was part of your act."

I look into Austin's eyes. "I really like you," I answer honestly. Suddenly I feel dizzy. I swish the remaining chocolate in my mug. "You're different from the guys I know. The ones I'm around just want to talk about their dream of winning an Oscar."

Austin chuckles.

"At your house, you said that you didn't understand how a movie star could fall for a regular guy. But being a movie star is just my job. The real me, the girl you met, wants to have a life like everybody else."

He shakes his head, wide-eyed. "I'm still having a hard time getting past the fact that you're Kaitlin Burke," he admits.

"I'm the same girl you knew before," I say softly. "I just look different."

"That's for sure." He grins crookedly.

"Why don't we start over?" I slip off my stool and extend my hand. "Hi, I'm Kaitlin."

He stares at my hand for a moment, then slowly extends his to meet mine and shakes it. "Je m'appelle Austin," he responds.

I groan. "Please, don't start that."

"Okay," he laughs, "but this is weird."

"It's not," I promise. "Ask Liz. I'm really just like everybody else."

"No, that's not what I meant," he says, sliding off his stool and stepping closer to me. I swear I can feel the heat of his body. "What's weird is what I'm about to do."

"What's that?"

"I'm going to kiss Kaitlin Burke," he whispers. Then he cups my head in his hands and pulls me towards him.

The kiss is better than any kiss Sam ever got from Ryan on FA, and I know why. Because this kiss is real. And at this moment, when Austin's soft lips are pressed against mine, I discover a new secret. HOLLYWOOD SECRET NUMBER NINETEEN is short, but the most important one I've learned so far.

It's simply this: To be a happy and successful actor, you've got to have two lives — one in front of the camera, and one behind it. And I finally have both.

PSST . . . Don't think the end of this story means I've run out of secrets to tell you. Join me "On Location" for more drama, more backstabbing, and of course, more killer couture. . . .

secrets OF MY HOLLYWOOD LIFe:
on Location,
available now.

secrets of my
HOLLYWOOD LIFE
on location

a novel by Jen Calonita

It seems like the summer of dreams come true for Hollywood princess Kaitlin Burke: the media loves her (again), super-cute and funny Austin Meyers is finally her boyfriend, and she's starring in a movie by her all-time favorite director Hutch Adams. What could be sweeter? But life on set is not nearly as perfect as the designer make-up and couture costumes. And with a slimy ex-boyfriend and a scheming new studio executive on the scene, it's about to get a whole lot messier. . . .

Dying for more on-set passes to the celebrity "it" world?
Turn the page for an exclusive sneak peek. . . .

secrets of my hollywood life: on location

The sound is unmistakable as it rises in decibel, frightening the blue jay that is drinking from the Italian marble birdbath and causing our new landscaper, Joe, to drop his gardening hose. Only one thing could cause this much commotion on a beautiful, eighty-six-degree Saturday morning in Southern California — and it's not an earthquake.

"KAITLIN BURKE, YOU'RE BACK ON TOP OF THE HOLLYWOOD FOOD CHAIN WHERE YOU BELONG!" My publicist, Laney, loudly bursts through our living room French doors over to the pool area with my excited entourage in tow. Laney's pale blond hair, recently colored the exact shade she was born with, flies behind her as she strides ahead carrying a thick, glossy magazine.

It takes exactly two seconds for Austin and me to realize that we're being ambushed. He quickly jumps on the empty chaise next to me and tries to look like he's been busy worshiping the sun.

"What food chain? Were we supposed to have lunch

today?" I'm feeling disoriented from the marathon kissing session that Laney just interrupted. All I can remember right now is how good Austin's coconut-scented sunblock smelled when his face was nuzzled into my neck.

Laney must smell weakness because she stops in front of my chair and squints her dark-as-coal eyes at me. "What's wrong with you?" she asks suspiciously, pointing a ruby red manicured finger in my direction.

"Nothing," I lie, putting on my oversized black sunglasses to hide my guilty look that says, "I was making out with my boyfriend instead of memorizing lines."

My mom, dad, and younger brother are breathing down Laney's neck before my sunglasses are even pushed onto my nose. Matty pushes through the group and looks at the magazine in Laney's airbrush-tanned hands.

"That's what this is about? Another Kaitlin cover?" Matt rolls his emerald green eyes that match mine. "How exciting. NOT."

My best pal, Liz, would say Matty's being obnoxious because that's what thirteen-year-old boys do best, but I know the real reason he's been dissing me more than one spoiled socialite to another: Matty's itching to nail a part in the movie I just signed on to, which is currently known around town as *The Untitled Hutch Adams Project* (or as *Variety* dubbed it, "Hutch Adams's next surefire blockbuster").

"This is not just any cover. This is your *Fashionistas* cover!" Laney's smoky voice explains as she flashes the fashion magazine in Austin's and my face. On the front is a serious, or what some would call sexy, picture of me wearing a skimpy silver tank top, bikini bottoms, and Jimmy Choos. I'm sitting cross-legged with my bare arms wrapped around my chest. A ton of makeup (very unlike me) accents my face and my long honey-colored hair is wild, overblown with curls and piled high on my head, as only a high fashion magazine would request. Next to my picture in silver letters it says:

"My life was spiraling out of control and I knew I had to be daring if I wanted to fix it."
Kaitlin Burke: Confessions of the Comeback Kid

My mother-turned-business manager (who could pass as my twin after an hour in a makeup chair) squeals with delight as she pushes past my beefy bodyguard, Rodney, and my assistant, Nadine, to squeeze onto the chaise on the other side of me.

"You see, Katie-Kat? I knew this town would forget what happened!" Mom shakes her highlighted hair and gives me a light hug, trying not to wrinkle the cream-colored silk cami that she's paired with ripped Earl Jeans. (My mom has traded her PB & J Couture sweat suit obsession for jeans in every brand, color, and style.) "Oh, hi, Austin," Mom adds stiffly, glancing over my shoulder. "I didn't know you were here."

My boyfriend of exactly four weeks, two days, and fourteen hours (but who's counting?) blushes a violent shade of fuchsia while I try not to grin. For once, I have to agree with Mom — landing *Fashionistas*, the most coveted magazine cover of all, is a big deal. My TV show *Family Affair* may be a ratings cow and *Entertainment Nation* may have named me "Teen Most Likely to Win an Oscar Before She's 30," but six months ago, Laney couldn't have booked me *Fashionistas* even if she begged, borrowed, and stole enough Ebe bags for the whole staff.

Nadine pries the magazine from Laney's grip. "'The comeback kid,'" Nadine reads aloud as she plays with her short, strawberry red hair. "This is a comeback? Please, you were only on the outs for a month!"

Sometimes I think Nadine is wiser than Yoda. Nadine hates Hollywood, which is why she and Austin are the perfect people to give me a sometimes urgently needed reality check. Raised in Chicago, Nadine doesn't hide her plan to use the money she's earned with me to go to business school so she can become the first U.S. female prez. I'm dreading the day she finally makes good on that threat. After three years, I don't know what I'd do without her running my schedule and, well, my life.

Laney squints menacingly at Nadine. "Maybe you've forgotten what a hideous month the last one was." She rummages in her white leather tote for her cell phone, which hasn't stopped ringing since she set foot on the poolside bluestone.

"Congratulations," Austin says softly, his tropical ocean-blue eyes dancing as they gaze into mine. It feels like 1,000 volts of electricity are pulsing through my fingers. A few weeks of pool time at my house have lightened Austin's growing blond hair, which now falls over his eyes. His red surfer-style swim shorts show off his lacrosse-toned arms and tanned abs. "I think that cover is cause to celebrate." He flashes his even white teeth. "How about dinner tonight?"

"Dinner is a great idea," my dad booms, obviously listening in with his free ear. His other one is on the phone setting up his golf tee time for Rancho Park Golf Course. His golf tee and khakis, along with sunglasses perched atop his blond head, gave it away.

Mom nods eagerly. "Nadine, see if you can reserve a table for all of us at Koi."

Before I can protest, Nadine begins dialing the silver Motorola I re-gifted to her.

"Done," Nadine announces a few moments later, snapping the cell phone shut and writing the change to my schedule in her leather folder, which we dubbed "the Bible" because it has all my personal info inside. "Eight o'clock at Koi, party of six." She smoothes the faded jeans and pink breast cancer awareness tee we both got at a benefit last week. "I thought you might want to invite Liz."

I nod. Well, I guess if everyone is coming. . . .

"Perfect!" Mom jumps up from my lounge chair. "I'm off for a treatment at Face Place. Jessica and Ashlee's mom is meeting me there." Before she takes two steps in her Kate Spade pumps, Mom notices my unopened script and frowns. I've been carting it around in the large white and multicolored Louis Vuitton agenda she gave me when I won the part. It's lying on the ground, next to my chair, and may have absorbed a little pool water. "You might want to run through lines with Matty this afternoon, Katie-Kat," Mom says coolly, raising her right eyebrow at me. "You've got a table read on Wednesday."

"I'm ready, Mom," I assure her.

"I've got to go too." Laney snatches *Fashionistas* back from Matty, who is thumbing through it, probably looking for their occasional artsy topless model fashion spreads. "I have to meet Uma at Il Sole for lunch." She stuffs the issue in her bag and hurries back into the house. Like cattle, everyone else moves to follow.

Nadine spins around. "Kates, don't forget — four o'clock wardrobe fitting."

"Four," I repeat, fumbling for my relatively new Sidekick 3, which is covered in Swarovski crystals. Laney bought me the Sidekick 2 after Sky stole my original one, but when the newer model came out a month later, she promptly upgraded me again. ("You can't walk around with last year's version," she said dismissively when I claimed the 2 had more than enough gadgets for me to handle.)

When the French doors slam shut, it's so quiet you can hear the pool jets. Austin and I are finally alone again — well, if you don't count Joe, who is standing behind the rosebush with his pruning shears in hand and a bewildered look on his face. Good thing Laney left. I know she'd think Joe was spying on us for the tabloids.

"Where were we?" Austin creeps back onto the teak wood chaise and kisses me again. My stomach does a series of somersaults like it does every time Austin's lips are on mine. I can't help thinking how good it feels to be me for a change. Here's a guy who's not intimidated by my job, my family, or even my over-caffeinated publicist.

This leads me to the first of many new Hollywood secrets that I'm dying to divulge. HOLLYWOOD SECRET NUMBER ONE: When it comes to celebrity dating, many stars talk about the benefits of dating a fellow actor. They reason that only someone inside the biz could understand when you work such grueling hours or collect a paycheck for playing a spelunker in peril. Between you and me, that "celeb-only" dating speech is week-old baloney. The truth is, it's *tough* to date a fellow actor. There's too much competition over who's the bigger star and too much stress over spending six months apart when you ship off to shoot a movie in Bangladesh and he is on location in the West Indies. The real reason why actors so often date other actors? We've got nobody else to date! Stars mostly spend time with other stars (and reality show hangers-on). A famous actress is unlikely to find her next relationship while pumping gas at the local Mobil.

That is, unless . . . you spend a few months pretending to be someone you're not. That's how I met a real guy like Austin. Now I just hope he can handle living under a microscope.

I kiss Austin's chin, then reluctantly lean away so I can look him in the eye. "Can we talk?" I ask nervously.

"Now?" Austin laughs. I nod and pull my longish legs and gargantuan feet up into a ball so that I can put a little space between us. That's the only way I can get through this conversation without reaching over and kissing him again.

"These past few weeks have been amazing," I start slowly.

"I know." Austin draws an imaginary circle on my knee, giving me goose bumps.

"I think you're vying for Boyfriend of the Year." Just last weekend, Austin surprised me with my first trip to the circus and took me to Santa Monica Pier to try a corn dog. Since my film training sessions have been in the morning, and production meetings have been few, I've had my afternoons free to hang with Austin after he finishes lacrosse practice. Mom thought a few weeks off would leave me bored, but I'm cherishing every minute of freedom I have till filming officially begins. "I still can't believe they have go-cart racing in the Valley," I add out loud.

"Don't forget — you owe me a rematch, Burke," Austin teases. "I would have beat you if Larry the Liar and Sam the Slug hadn't set off flashes in my face."

"You remembered their names." I'm surprised he recalled my most persistent shutter hounds. "I'm impressed, Meyers." Austin's the only one who doesn't call me one of the million Kaitlin nicknames — Kates, K, Katie-Kat, Katie-Kins . . . take your pick — that everyone from my family to strangers on the street use. When Austin calls me "Burke," I feel like a completely different uncomplicated person that only he knows. It's exhilarating. I've started calling him by his last name too.

"But that's kind of what I wanted to talk to you about," I

reply. "My free time is going to be scarce once I start Hutch's movie. And our start date is only two weeks away." As if either of us needs reminding.

"You'll be busy, but I have a lot on my plate too." Austin sounds a tad defensive. "Final exams are coming up and we made the division lacrosse finals. I told you what a bruiser Coach Connors is. Practices are going to be twenty-four-seven. Plus I'm coaching peewee lacrosse when school ends. I'm going to be pretty tied up myself." Austin's hair falls over his eyes and I can't read his expression.

"I just thought we should have a State of the Union before both our lives get crazy," I say hurriedly. "Once I get on set, who knows what will happen. Call times get bumped, my work schedule will constantly change, and I'll have appearances to make. But I'm sure I'll be able to bring a guest to most of them," I add.

"I'm not going to lie — sometimes I think it's surreal that I'm dating the famous Kaitlin Burke," Austin confesses as his cheeks turn as red as his swim shorts. "I guess that's why I'm nervous about going to events with you. This celebrity world of yours is a bit overwhelming." He smiles sheepishly, revealing the dimple by his left cheek.

"Mingling with other celebrities is the same as hanging with me," I promise, and lay a hand on his wrist. "Most stars are quite normal."

"If you say so." He doesn't look convinced. "But as far as your nightmare datebook, I get the picture." He shrugs. "I knew this wasn't going to be cake when I showed up at your compound a few weeks ago and said we should give this a shot."

"You're right." I bat my green eyes at him, hoping I look cute in this harsh sunlight, hoping the image of me in this teal bikini is enough to make him remember his words a month from now when the only time we have to see each other is 3 AM for a very, very early breakfast.

"I told you, all I ask is that you be honest with me." Austin's voice is soft and quite serious. "The one thing I can't stand is being lied to." He wraps his arms around my knees and rests his chin on them. "As for the rest of the Hollywood protocol, you can teach me as we go along. Sound good, Professor Burke?"

"Works for me." I kiss him softly on the lips. "That means I can give you this present." I blindly reach under the lounge chair and search for the small box wrapped in shiny silver paper that I planted there early this morning. I pull away from Austin and put the box between us. Austin takes it and tears the wrapping curiously.

"A Sidekick?" he laughs.

"This way we can talk anytime we want without interruption," I explain as he opens the box. "I can e-mail you when I'm waiting to shoot a scene and you can text me before class. These babies are quick."

"Thanks." Austin blushes. "But I feel weird about you buying me something so expensive —"

"Don't," I interrupt. "It's one of the perks you're going to have to get used to. And believe me; this gift is purely selfish on my part, Meyers." I flash him a toothy grin.

"Whatever you say, Burke." Austin pulls me close and we begin to kiss again. The familiar scent of coconut is enough to make me forget all about Hutch Adams, my lines, or my wardrobe fitting . . . for the moment.

Later, when Austin's left and I've stopped questioning how I lucked out in getting the greatest boyfriend in the world, I whip out my Sidekick to send myself a few reminders.

SATURDAY 6/2
NOTE TO SELF:

Sunday schedule
6 AM — Capoeira martial arts session — HOME w/ Paulo
7:30 AM — stretching w/Cirque du Soleil gymnast
MEMORIZE LINES!!!

***Movie Start Date: Monday, June 18

SECRETS OF MY HOLLYWOOD LIFE:
ON LOCATION,
available now

RIPPED FROM NADINE'S "BIBLE":
SECRETS OF MY HOLLYWOOD LIFE author Jen Calonita's bio

Name: Jen Calonita

Nickname: Sadly, I have none (but don't call me Jenny—I won't answer)

First job: Gift-wrapping flowers (yes, flowers) at a local plant nursery

Worst job: Gift-wrapping flowers (yes, flowers) at a local plant nursery

Perfect date: Dinner at Poco Loco (my favorite Mexican jaunt) followed by a good movie, Raisinettes and a ton of movie trailers (I live for those!)

Favorite Place: The Magic Kingdom at night

Guilty pleasure: Rachel Ray's 30-Minute Meals show. I try all her recipes and usually fail miserably, probably because whenever I cook a recipe of hers it takes me at least 90 minutes to make it.

Best friend's first name: Uh-uh. You're not trapping me into naming one girlfriend! My friends will kill me if I just mention one of them.

Good luck charm: My son Tyler.

Tuesday night activity: If I'm home, it's watching Gilmore Girls and probably something I've TiVo'd (like Prison Break). But once a month, my girlfriends and I meet for dinner so we can gab, gossip and eat way too much dessert.

Last thing bought at the mall: Ballet flats in three different colors. They're my latest obsession.

Favorite movie(s): It's a Wonderful Life (anytime of the year), Pirates of the Caribbean, Legally Blonde and Never Been Kissed.

Biggest fashion blunder: Picture this: It's junior year of college and it's my first week interning at YM magazine. I'm wearing what I think is a killer sundress. I walk thirty blocks from the train to the office. Men smile at me the entire walk there. I think: This outfit rocks! One block from the office an older man stops me. "Miss," he says. "You might want to fix your skirt. It's tucked into your underwear." Needless to say, I never wore that dress again.

Item on your grocery list: Skinny Cow caramel ice cream cones. My freezer isn't complete without them!

French fry dip: Plain old ketchup (but if it's late at night and we're at the Apollo diner, there's nothing wrong with fries covered in gravy)

Astrological sign: Sagittarius

Favorite TV show: I love Gilmore Girls, How I Met Your Mother, Prison Break, Las Vegas, Grey's Anatomy, Ugly Betty and reruns of Friends

Lucky color: green (just like Kaitlin!)

Midnight snack: Pepperidge Farm Goldfish

Celebrity crush: Ben Affleck, Josh Duhamel and Orlando Bloom

Favorite book(s): Homecoming (by Cynthia Voight), anything and everything by Meg Cabot and The Nanny Diaries

"I ah-dored *Bass Ackwards and Belly Up*. It's about four BFFs who, for a juicy reason I won't divulge, decide to not go to college to pursue their dreams. It's one of those things most of us fantasize about but don't have the guts to do."

—**Lisi Harrison**, author of the #1 *New York Times* bestselling **CLIQUE** series

Also available in paperback!

Harper Waddle, Sophie Bushell, and Kate Foster are about to commit the ultimate suburban sin—bailing on college to pursue their dreams. Middlebury-bound Becca Winsberg is convinced her friends have gone insane...until they remind her she just might have a dream of her own. So what if their lives are bass ackwards and belly up? They'll always have each other.

BASS ACKWARDS AND BELLY UP ✦ AVAILABLE NOW

For readers of the #1 *New York Times* bestselling *Gossip Girl* and graduates of the #1 bestselling *Twilight* and *New Moon*

FOR THREE SEVENTEEN-YEAR-OLDS, DARK MYSTERY HAS ALWAYS LURKED AT THE CORNER OF THE EYES AND THE EDGE OF SLEEP.

Beautiful Morgan D'Amici wakes in her meager home, with blood under her fingernails. Paintings come alive under Ondine Mason's violet-eyed gaze. Haunted runaway Nix Saint-Michael sees halos of light around people about to die. At a secret summer rave in the woods, the three teenagers learn of their true origins and their uncertain, intertwined destinies. Riveting, unflinching, and beautiful, *Betwixt* is as complex and compelling as any ordinary reality.

B E T W I X T

a novel by Tara Bray Smith

COMING OCTOBER 2007

If you enjoyed SECRETS OF MY HOLLYWOOD LIFE,
you may also enjoy:

The gossip girl series created by Cecily von Ziegesar

the it girl series created by Cecily Von Ziegesar

THE A-LIST series by Zoey Dean

THE CLIQUE series by Lisi Harrison

and keep your eye out for a new juicy series about
four LA teenagers who start their own fashion label,

POSEUR by Rachel Maude,
coming in January 2008.